NOCTURNAL [

CW01660295

SWEET INFERNO

ELLIOTT ROSE

by Elliott Rose

Sweet Inferno

Published by: Cosmic Imprint Publishing

Cover Design: Maldo Designs

Copy Editor: Kerryn Hewson

2nd edition, July 2023

Paperback POD ISBN: 978-1-7385953-0-3

Ebook (EPub) ISBN: 978-0-473-66206-6

Ebook (Kindle) ISBN: 978-0-473-66207-3

Created with Vellum

For all the witchy women who have fire dancing in their veins.

CONTENTS

FIELD MAP &
Mountains
(Healing Wate
Dark fae
Fae Dominion
†portal/transference point
Demonic Realm
Soterian Realm
†portal/transference point
caution
Shifter Clans
Vampire Territories
Wolfs wolve

EXPLORATORY NOTES
A living Guide to the realms & places of exploration beyond the land of non-magic Beings
Nymph Palace
Sprites
Non-Magic
portal/transference point
(caution)
Elharean?
Yet too to explore
Ancestral Plane
Underworld Terraines
Mer Clans (Water fae?)

Living Legend

To accompany field notes
& expand upon as explorations allow
across the realms of the supernatural

Fae

+Notable for pointed ears
A fondness for material possessions
magics to conjure items of golds
and gemstone kind

witches

+powers of connection to 'source'
Magics of varying elementals
in addition to other gifts bestowed
& beings of self-healing abilities
+Powerful witches may PORTAL
to travel anywhere hence they desire

Vampires

+Strength & heightened senses
+Myst-mysting will transport
vampire/Vampiress to known location
(can be amplified by consumption of
blood for memory access)

wolf/wolven shifter
[Werewolf]

+Strength & heightened senses
Transfiguration between animal
form-that of regular being
Gifted with knowing/intelligence

CONTENT NOTES

Sweet Inferno is a paranormal romance novella that contains dark elements, blood, plenty of spice, explicit sex, discussions about sexual assault (alluded to, non-graphic), and torture (occurs off-page).

For more information please visit my website

This novella is Book One in the Nocturnal Hearts series.

playlist

I'm On Fire - Ilaria

Dream Girl Evil - Florence + The Machine

Firefly - Drax Project, AACACIA, Fetty Wap

Wolves - Selena Gomez, Marshmello

Whole Lotta Love - Beth Hart

Fire For You - Cannons

The Wolf - Live - Mumford & Sons

Wolf - Yeah Yeah Yeahs

No Good - KALEO

Howlin' For You - The Black Keys

CHAPTER 1

The world had forgotten its magic. Abandoned it to time. Turned away from the old ways.

Idalia's grandmother had often wrapped her hand in her own and reminded her to always be wary. To safeguard her secrets and her heart.

"There are those who would take your power and turn it to blackness, my little draga."

That was long ago. A shadow of a memory of a little girl once surrounded by the love of her grandmother. A brief flicker in time before she was left alone in this world.

Lia slipped through the dark castle corridors. Her bare feet padded along the flagstone floors with the glow of her fire magic swirling from her fingertips. The faint embers danced at her command, lighting her way forward in the midnight air. The cool of these small hours didn't worry Lia.

Her fire magic was like a furnace of warmth from within. Burning hot and passionate. A simple cotton wrap was all she needed to wear over her bare skin as she made her nightly rounds tending to the castle's lamps and hearths. The moonlight slid over her bronzed arms and legs through the barred windows high in the wall above her head.

Rounding the corner from her sleeping quarters in the depths of the lower castle, she could hear the kitchen maid slopping a sodden mop against the stone floor.

Damn the matron for picking on me yet again. I've scrubbed these floors every bloody night this week on my own until near dawn...

Lia heard the maid's thoughts as clearly in her own head as if she had been speaking them out loud. She had been a telepath her whole life, a rare thing indeed, but thanks to the warnings from her grandmother she had never allowed the others here in the House of Elharean to know of her unique gift.

It was not unusual to wield magic, in fact everyone had the ability lying dormant within them. Most regular people — non-magical folk — had forgotten over time or had intentionally shunned their gifts, closing their minds off to their true potential. Lia came from a long lineage of practicing witches, including her grandmother who had raised her in the ways after the disappearance of her parents. Presumed dead.

Rumours of battles and warring supernatural factions had long chased Lia through her dreams. The orphanage attached to the House of Elharean had taken her in as a young girl. Upon turning eighteen she had been assessed and transferred into the castle to begin service to the powerful Elharean dynasty. Who could be anything but grateful for a life being provided for. Given employment, food, shelter, and protection.

How many times had she quietly padded these castle halls, tending to the fires and lamps long after all the others had taken to their beds to ensure her master's rooms were filled with warmth. While Lia did not feel the cold, a chilled air swept through the ancient stone passages. Her youth and her talent for wielding fire had given her security in her service to the great house.

Her gift of telepathy might just have given her a slightly unfair advantage. Lia smiled as she swirled the embers hovering above the palm of her right hand. It was helpful to know the thoughts of another and simply position herself in the right places at the right times. Not that she would ever tell. That danger lurked ominously, wondering what might befall her if anyone found out. Safer to stay quiet on that front, living safely in her line of duty alongside the rest of the castle's servants.

With a stretch upwards she flicked her wrist and let loose a stream of embers into the lamp affixed to the wall above her head. Bringing her palm to her lips she blew gently and watched as each lamp along the corridor began to flame in turn.

The familiar path that wound along the passageways led

Lia into the castle's grand entrance hall. She paused behind the lavish tapestry hiding the way to the servants quarters listening with bated breath. All was quiet. The masters had retired to their upper chambers long before she made her nightly rounds.

It should be safe. Best to be cautious just in case someone was still awake and roaming the castle.

Lia knew the rooms were empty so she would not be seen, but especially while dressed in her wrap. Hardly the formal attire of the castle servants during the day, but at this late hour she never saw another soul and this was far more comfortable against the molten heat of her olive skin. Those heavy woollen skirts she had to wear during the day were intolerable.

She rarely saw the House of Elharean masters other than in fleeting moments with head bowed and making sure to back herself up against a wall to be out of sight. There were those who were hand selected to attend to the master's beck and call, far above her station. They were the chosen elite within their witch community.

Lia slid past the heavy weight of the gilded tapestry, stepping into the cavernous hall that lay before her. Raven black stone walls climbed impossibly high into vaulted ceilings. Polished marble stairs in onyx and gold ascended grandly to the castle's upper reaches. The vastness of the entrance hall took her breath away every time she passed through.

With another flick of her wrist the grand entrance hall fire strengthened its blaze. Lia glimpsed herself reflected in the mirror hung above the flickering golden light. Her long dark hair curled wildly around her shoulders and down her back. Almond eyes held the bright flames of her essence dancing within them. At this time of night she loved to see her magic express itself freely. She twisted in the flare of the firelight, watching her rounded curves become highlighted and accentuated. Her full breasts pressed against the join of her wrap. While diminutive in height, her ample figure made up for what she didn't possess in stature. A strength from her ancestors that those scrawny little kitchen maids didn't have.

She could pass for around her mid-twenties, however it was the choice of a witch as to how they desired to appear in age. Witches and other supernaturals aged slowly, many choosing to use their magic to maintain peak physical use of their gifts. Lia was still incredibly young for a witch, with many hundreds of years ahead of her, but in linear time she was in her thirty second year.

With a sigh she ran her fingers over her lips. It had been years since her last lover. The latest less than inspiring experience resulted in a stern resolve to shut away that part of herself. She was done with fumbling, boorish boys only interested in a quick fuck. Lia now chose to focus on simple gratitude for her life, even if it did have layers of sexual frustration attached. Stars, for it was far better to be celibate with a roof over her head and food in her belly than wind up destitute and on her own.

Most non-magical people had attached such short-sighted ideologies to marriage, chastity, purity, and such for women. Among supernatural beings there was an understanding that when you lived for hundreds if not thousands of years there was far more nuance to mate-hood, sex, and love. Lia had experienced enough fleeting moments with partners in bed in her short life to know what she did and didn't desire in a companion between her thighs and in her heart.

While some beings such as vampires and shifters were more likely to find their mate and be bonded for life there were others who chose not to make such a commitment to another being. Especially for witches, such as she, who were indebted to servitude within the House of Elharean.

Continuing on through grand room after grand room. Lia set them each with warm blazing fires to last through til morning. Her spells would last until well past dawn and keep the castle warm for her masters. It had taken her years to learn how to pace herself and not exhaust her magic too quickly each night. She always looked forward to collapsing into her small bed in the hour before dawn, exhausted after the rigours of wielding the flames.

Fire magic really took it out of her.

The castle library loomed up ahead. Always her final and favourite destination for the night. Lia loved to linger over the gilded book covers and spines pressed together in row upon row of black shelving that stretched high into the rafters. A treasure trove of knowledge and ancient witchcraft. The House of Elharean was proud of their long lineage and this library contained their secrets from millennia gone before. Goosebumps skittered across her skin in the presence of such power.

With a slow run of her tongue back and forth over her bottom lip Lia imagined what it would be like to reach out and touch the sacred texts. She pictured herself browsing the pages and taking whatever she would like back to her quarters to read at her leisure. What life would be like to have such an abundance of fine things?

Of course these books were forbidden for the servants. No one was to touch anything belonging to the masters. But nothing prevented her from simply reaching out and removing one of the richly gilded leather tombs. Only the knowledge that punishment, if discovered, would be swift and direct. Lia knew her masters did not tolerate any form of disrespect to their rules.

She knew her lowly place in the hierarchy of this world.

An absent minded swirl of embers glinted above her palm. She allowed herself an extra moment to wander the room. Gazing at the antiques, sumptuous oil paintings, and gilded fabrics adorning the stone walls. Opulence and grandeur oozed from every surface. With a final sigh Lia turned and moved towards the enormous fireplace and granite mantle that dwarfed her.

A sudden tingle of awareness pricked the back of her neck.

Spinning in place she flared the embers above her palm to throw a glow across the room. All stood still and exactly as it had been seconds before. Lia shook her head. Surely it must be the gnawing tiredness and anticipation of sliding into bed. Of course she was alone.

With an exhale she raised her palm to her lips, closed her eyes, and blew gently towards the fireplace. Feeling warmth spread outwards it to fill the hearth before her. The flames started to grow and flicker as their warmth radiated to occupy the few feet in front of where she stood. With her eyes still closed Lia rolled her neck. Her work finally complete. Her shoulders dropped back to release the tension of another long night practicing her craft. She stretched upwards, arched her back, and ran her fingers to lift her long hair from her shoulders.

A powerful hand from the darkness clamped around her mouth. Her eyes flew open. A predator lying in wait ready to pounce. Lia let out a muffled shriek as she wrestled against her captor's hold in vain. She was pinned with her back against a rock hard physique. Her wrists were both held tightly together. Panic rose in her chest as she realised she was trapped, immobile.

"Not one single move or your throat will be ripped out." A low growl rumbled against her ear. Sharp claws laced with the potential for death pressed into her wrists. Menacing intent accentuated by the adrenaline coursing through her veins.

"Now be a good little girl and we won't have to tear out that pretty throat of yours." Sharpened black talons sank further into Lia's wrists, stopping just short of piercing the skin with a frightening precision. A predator that knew exactly how far to push their prey. A highly calculated move practiced thousands of times.

"I've watched you..." He paused. A twitch flicked in his jaw. "...all night." He continued. "And it is clear you know every damned corner of this castle. You're going to take me to the Seal of Elharean."

The what? Lia's eyes widened. Amidst her terror she realised not only was her captor towering over her but they were asking about something she had never even heard of in her life. To make her situation even more stressful she was wiped of her fire magic unable to defend herself. And there was no voice in her head.

Something or someone was blocking her telepathy. *Shit. Shit. Shit.*

The hand covering her mouth squeezed tighter.

"Do you understand?"

Mind racing, Lia decided she would have been bleeding out on the stone floor already if this predator had actually wanted her dead. Time to play the smart game.

A feeble nod. She could feign compliance long enough to figure out a plan.

First step, get claws away from vital arteries.

"Don't try anything foolish, little girl."

Her skin flamed. For the briefest second lips brushed the shell of her ear. A scent of earth and wood smoke ... something strange and yet familiar flooded her senses.

Pressure released and she lurched forwards from a sudden shove to her back, catching herself quickly on the table in front of her. Fury reared its snarling head to replace her original sense of panic. How dare this intruder come here to her master's castle. How dare they step foot in the House of Elharean.

Massaging and flexing her wrists Lia turned to face her captor. A huge chest met her at eye level with powerful arms covered in inked markings, patterns she had never seen before. Her jaw clenched at the realisation she would have to tilt her head upwards to look into the face of who owned those filthy paws. With every effort to keep a look of disdain on her face, Lia crossed her arms and jutted her chin. Prepared to stare down a monster.

Not a monster.

A rugged man with sun kissed skin and shoulder length dark hair lightened to caramel at the ends from obvious time spent out in the elements. Cheekbones gave his face an elegance that contrasted against the wildness that clung to him. Her eyes swept over those lips that had brushed her ear, taking in the slight beard and scar that ran vertically through his left eyebrow. Finally, when her eyes met his for the first time she was startled by the forest green and amber piercing her with the intensity of a true hunter.

"Speak." He barked his order in a menacing whisper.

Jarred out of her study of the mountain of a man in front of her, Lia's fury came rushing back.

"I know nothing of this Seal you speak of. I am merely a servant to the great house."

"Hah. A great house? Such arrogance."

Lia stiffened at his dismissive tone. She was truly furious now and what little was left of her inner fire tingled hotly in her belly.

"You will take me to the Seal."

Raven claws glinted in the firelight. Sharp edges extending from powerful hands.

"I cannot possibly do so if I know nothing of that which you are seeking. For a rotten *thief* you really should have planned your crimes more carefully."

A smirk crossed the man's lips.

"A thief you say. I guess I must be so. If you say it, little girl."

With heckles rising, Lia tensed and balled her fists.

"Stop. Calling. Me. That."

"I could easily torture you to find the location, you know. But I'll give you one last chance. Take me to the Seal and then I'll be gone from here at once."

He stepped forward, putting her at an even more awkward angle to hold his glare. She was caged in with her back against the wall beside the fireplace.

The scent of earth and woodsmoke flooded her senses once more. Only now she recognised the sandalwood notes. *Grandmother used to burn sandalwood incense.* How was he preventing her from accessing his thoughts?

Rage intermingled with a new sensation moving through the air between them. He was so close she could feel the power radiating from his broad chest. Angry at being threatened and belittled by this thief, Lia quickly made up her mind. She decided to play the card she would usually reserve for times when she knew someone's thoughts. She would negotiate.

Only this time she would have to pray she guessed correctly as to what he would be prepared to negotiate for.

"Fine. I'll give you information on the Seal, but I have a proposal. A negotiation to put to you." The lies tumbled from between her lips. Her life depended on this plan.

Fuck.

CHAPTER 2

Fehrn waited impatiently for the diminutive woman standing before him to hand over the information he so desperately needed. His instinct told him she was hedging. Hiding something. Yet he couldn't help but stare at her full lips as she spoke.

His mission was dangerous and potentially deadly. Capture within the walls of the castle would mean certain torture and execution. The House of Elharean were power hungry dark witches. Notoriously merciless in their drive to gain control of both people and territories. Corrupted by an obsessive need for power.

Infiltrate the castle. Retrieve the Seal of Elharean. Gather intel on their latest movements to take back with him.

Being a spy in the elite guard was laced with danger that was nothing new after three hundred years.

As a shifter Fehrn had the power, heightened senses, and intellect of his wolf even while in human form. A fearsome skill set of animalistic instinct and predatory speed. All hidden beneath a human form.

Shifters became initiated into their ability to shift into their animalistic form as desired upon coming of age. The tattoos across his arms and body marked his journey of initiation. They also granted him full access to his powers. A connection to Source unlocked with every stroke of the sharp blade and drip of ink.

Hundreds of years of training held firm in the face of this unexpected interruption to his mission. He had intended to simply observe the girl from where he lurked in the shadows these past few weeks until she led him unknowingly to the Seal. But the longer he had tracked her the more his body had compelled him to strike and take her hostage. It wasn't part of the plan but his instincts were blazing and drawing him out of the shadows.

Logic, intellect, and duty to his mission threatened to dissolve like the first snowflakes of winter upon his tongue every second he spent in the presence of her scent. Her curvaceous form drew him like a moth clung to the flame she so effortlessly wielded. That expanse of soft bronzed flesh magnetised him. Night after night spent fixated on the roundness of her hips, the swell of her voluptuous bosom. How her body arched in the flickering firelight when she surveyed herself in the mirror.

Frustration stirred deep within. This girl was part of the

Elharean world. She was insignificant. She was aligned with the darkness. Simply collateral damage in a much bigger battle waged over centuries.

"The Seal you seek is not easily found. Either you gravely misjudge who you intend to steal from or you are truly as brutishly simple minded as you appear." Her scorn interrupted his thoughts.

Irritation stirred within his chest. Chased by hunger. To actually hear her voice after watching from afar for so long cracked open something unfamiliar.

His training taught him to tread only in certainties. Never to dally in the realm of the little-known. For that was fraught with unmitigated risk.

"Careful where you tread. I haven't decided whether to permit you to keep breathing." He warned.

"The Seal is housed in my masters guarded chambers." The witch continued dismissively. "There is a fortress deep within these walls protecting it. So unless you have an army waiting outside you won't be leaving here tonight with the Seal." She narrowed her eyes in his direction, goading him in a way that had resulted in many a dark entity losing their life at his hands.

"You had better watch your tongue lest it becomes ripped from your mouth." Fehrn lowered his voice to a hush as he leaned in.

Irked by her stalling. Drawn down undeniably to her scent. Eyes locked on her neck. He watched a hasty swallow betray her fiery tone. Physical tells were his instinctive speciality.

"My proposal is this, *thief*. I'll get you the damned Seal from my master's guarded chambers." Another swallow. "The guards allow me in there during the day as part of my duties." Her eyes flicked to his lips then back up again. "If you let me keep my life I shall meet you tomorrow night to deliver the Seal." A twitch in her jaw.

"And why should I trust you?" He cocked his head to one side.

"I have powerful magic, you know." Her fingers flexed.

He did in fact know. After studying the witch every night for the past weeks. The lie by omission had slipped out easily. To let her think he had only watched her tonight. Fehrn could sense her powerful gifts radiating from her smooth skin. Although he was yet to see evidence to suggest she had ever fully tapped into her potential. Hardly surprising considering her alliance with the House of Elharean and their taste for harvesting the powers of anyone within their clutches.

"So confident are we? So sure of yourself? And what do you know of the definition of power? You possess mere childish sparks."

Pink flushed her cheeks.

"I know you are a shifter."

His wolf briefly rose to the forefront of his consciousness as if on command at her words. His eyes flecked gold with the momentary shift.

"...or werewolf, as some would call your kind. You can change into your wolven form as you desire. Many of the myths about you have been distorted by non-magical folk to incite fear."

He felt the corner of his lips smirk dangerously at the edges. The witch boldly continued.

"I know of other supernaturals such as vampires and fae creatures. Us witches outnumber other supernatural beings and most people in this world don't even realise they have some kind of dormant magical power waiting to be awakened within them."

"And do you know why that is? Do you know why there are so many who are lost and unaware?"

He pressed closer to her using his height to further his advantage.

"You're standing in the very grounds that have a vested interest in it staying that way."

A glow of embers rose above her fingers. The pink in her cheeks deepened and spread down her neck. His eyes traced the creep of blush with hungry intent. The curve of her breasts quivered under his stare.

"Now I know you are not only a *thief* but a liar too." She narrowed her eyes. He caught the subtle shift in her shoulders. The straightening of her spine. An attempt to draw herself up to her full height in the shadow of his giant frame. He found himself enjoying her refusal to submit to their physical mismatch.

"Trust that in this, I would never lie. You are caught in

their twisted trap just as all those who live their lives blissfully unaware of their power."

A snort. The insult drawing another rise of haughty disdain to her beautiful face.

"I bet you haven't tapped the mere surface of your potential, little girl. I bet using your gift leaves you weakened and exhausted."

A brief crease between her eyebrows. Lips pursed. He had watched her disappear to the servants quarters each night. The way her feet dragged over the flagstones. Fehrn knew well the physical cues of the bone weary after battle. The witch may as well have fought a horde of demons each night from the palpable exhaustion in the way she carried herself in the pre-dawn hours.

"The House of Elharean wield their power by draining the life force of all those in servitude to their supposed legacy. You, the other servants, the villages surrounding this castle for miles where they are so revered. All supporting this very place with their blood as though it were gold." He pressed on. A sharp exhale of frustration left her lips.

"My masters have been nothing but kind. They saved me from a life of ruin. I owe them everything."

Her eyes flashed obsidian under his stare.

How her fierce passion stirred him. His wolf paced back and forth. Impatient to make his mark. To explore that intoxicating heat. Finally to be up close had aroused him like no other in three hundred years.

"You're so blinded by their twisted cruel world. One day

you'll see the truth. If only you knew what you were capable of. Sadly, I bet you'll never know, choosing to stay trapped inside your pathetic cage." His words rasped out. Low and intent on stoking that spirit radiating from her aura.

"I'm expected to trust in the word of a common, dirty *thief*?" She spat, her fists clenched by her sides.

"Ahhhh..." Fehrn breathed. His arm raised above her head leaning against the wall. The reaction he desired. His lips curled upwards as he stared down at her. His bulk caged her in. That sense of something unfamiliar pooled lower in his stomach.

"Of course. You have only the word of a *thief* ...yet you expect me to trust in you. A little girl who works for the darkest hearts of all." The tanned skin of his forearm reflected the crackling fire. His wolf wore a mask of menace that promised to burn her with just one touch.

"These castle walls are running with the blood of innocents and yet you dare to defend those monsters as your so called benevolent masters."

He clicked his tongue and dragged his claws across the stone above her head in mockery of her. Fehrn caught a glimpse of the faintest jump in her throat at the grinding sound. Good. She should be scared of him. He knew he only provoked her rage but he couldn't help himself

"It seems we're at an impasse *thief*. Either you get it over with and kill me now... or agree to my bargain." She lifted her chin and fixed a steely glare in his direction.

Heat rushed low in his stomach at the sight of her fierceness. Her intensity was breathtaking. Her beauty gut wrenching.

"And how do I know you won't simply kill me after I deliver the Seal and you get what you want? What guarantee do I have as I risk my safety, my entire life, simply to please your demands?"

Fehrn watched the line of her throat as she swallowed hard. Embers began to glow brighter around her fists. A new layer mingled with her scent. Fear. But not of him. This was connected to something else. Here she was prepared to fight. Despite their physical mismatch. A fierce dragon lying inside the body of a witch.

"So it's a guarantee you're after?" His mouth quirked. The sound of her heart hammering in her chest drew his eyes to drift lower. The swell of her breasts rising and falling as though running. *Another tell.*

A new scent washed through his awareness. Fehrn's wolf howled inside.

Arousal.

"You can't possibly expect me to go through with this without something in return. Surely even for a dirty *thief* you can get it through your thick skull that this is a negotiation."

His body stiffened, a predator ready to strike.

"Or are you truly as dim witted as it seems—"

Fehrn lunged forward, his mouth crashing against hers. A taste of molten honey burst through his senses. His lips caressed slowly, passion spreading through his extremities. How many nights in the past weeks had he stared at her full mouth wondering what she would taste like. How she would feel beneath him.

With a pause he drew back. His instinct barely contained. The wolf inside urged him to pounce on his beautiful prey. Sucking in a sharp breath he hovered over her lips. The silent question lingered. He gave her the opportunity to respond. *Fuck.* He knew she was feeling the passion between them but forcing a kiss from a stranger had never been his style.

He ran his tongue across his bottom lip. Fiery warmth spread from where their mouths had touched. A molten stroke of pleasure now burned into his mind forever.

Her eyes widened. The bravado from mere moments before evaporated from the way she held her body. Tension drained from her shoulders and she softened beneath him.

Almond shaped pools enveloped him. His eyes searched hers. There were bare millimetres between their mouths and yet he waited as agonising seconds passed. Tentative fingers reached for his chest and curled into his shirt. Sultry warmth radiated from soft palms. Her body shifted beneath him and she brought her lips to meet his. The simmering something burst into flame, expanding between them. She melted beneath his kiss, a soft moan let loose from her throat in response. His tongue pressed between her lips asking for more of that addictive essence.

Her hands pulled him down closer as their bodies moulded together. Intertwining. Searching. Exploring. He drowned in a sea of golden tendrils with flames that reached out and licked at his core.

One hand cradled the back of her head, fingers twining through her long dark curls. The other slid to her breast skimming lightly over the fine cotton. He felt her nipple harden beneath his caress. No other sensation compared to how her skin radiated a tingling heat. He was consumed by the addictive feeling of her power seeping into him, melting the safeguards he had long placed around his heart.

He teased the bud of her nipple between his fingers. Her soft moans against his mouth came louder and more frequent. Reaching for the tie at the join of the material he tugged down, her hard nipples exposed against the cool night air.

Fehrn ran his lips along the side of her neck, mesmerised by the heat radiating through beneath his kiss. She pressed up against him, aching for his touch as he was aching for hers. As he bent lower still to run his tongue over the mounds of both breasts he could hear the thundering of her heartbeat. A tell if there ever was one. Smiling to himself he cupped one nipple to his mouth and sucked down on that searingly hot flesh. Like a brand held against him the sensation sent a pulse of blood to his rock hard shaft pressed up against her hip. Her back arched in response.

"Ohhh... yes, please, that feels so good. Don't stop." She let out a breathless cry.

"Let me hear what your pleasure is, my *little dragon.*" He circled her nipple with his tongue.

"It's ... it's ... too much, but not enough." Her body undulated and pressed towards his mouth, lifting those dusky nipples higher in silent pleading for more of him.

His senses were consumed. Undone by this goddess made flesh in front of him. He could think of nothing that he would rather do than worship at her feet. Her fingers twisted in his hair. Breasts pushed together in a vision of womanly power.

Every trail of her fingers drew lines of flame that led straight to his chest. His heart thudded harder with each new inch of her flesh pressed against his. The sound of her breath, shallow and panting, set his wolf on the hunt for more. To seek pleasure in those curves. That softness. The flawless contrast to his raw muscle. In this witch lay a fierce feminine power wrapped in divine rounded curves. His gaze devoured every one.

Fehrn reached around and lifted her off the ground, flexing his fingers against her luscious thighs. He spun them both until she was seated on the edge of a table. Her mouth opened in silent protest as his lips left her breasts, and he slanted his mouth over hers once more. Tongues tangling, possessively taking hold of what his instinct was loudly claiming to be his. *Only his.*

His hands slid below the hem of the cotton draped across her legs, slowly exploring up and over her inner thighs. Her soft flesh quivered beneath his touch as he paused. Fehrn's heart felt like it might break through his chest from hammering so hard. Her thighs widened in response, allowing him to sink closer into her incandescence. He swiftly yanked her to the very edge of the table. Her breath caught in a gasp, at the force in his movement. His wolf riding him hard, crying out to taste her.

"What are you..." Her voice came out as a hoarse croak. She seemed entranced by what he was planning for her next. His cock now throbbing to burst forth. It took all of his resolve to continue focusing his attention on her needs and her needs alone. His own could wait. He kissed once more down the front of her throat to lick across those breasts that would now forever appear in his dreams.

"Tomorrow night." A rough growl saw goosebumps fleck across her skin under his breath. "You will deliver the Seal to me." A flick of his tongue across the tight bud. A gasp of pleasure.

"Ohhhh..."

Rumbling came from deep within his chest.

"Midnight. The walled garden. You will meet me at the gazebo." Another devilish flick of his tongue as his hand pinched at her other nipple. "Nod if you understand."

Eyes closed, she nodded. "Yes... I mean... I will... I mean."

He dropped to his knees and stared up at his little dragon queen. She opened her eyes to reveal flames of lust dancing in their almond shaped pools. Passion scorched the air from where she stared down at him. He was her subject kneeling before her, taking in her curves, her breasts, those erect nipples. Firm hands moved higher now towards her core. He bunched the cotton at her waist, exposing her sex glistening wet in the flickering light.

"Look at you, *little dragon.* You're dripping. So fucking wet and beautiful."

He kept his eyes locked on hers as he planted an open mouthed kiss on the inside of her thigh. His hand stroked over her core. A slide of his thumb finding that tight nub of her clitoris. Her head dropped back as her hands gripped at the table edge to steady herself.

Fuck, what a vision. He lost himself in the driving need to bring the pleasure he craved to give her. When his mouth closed over her she bucked uncontrollably and gripped at his head.

"Oh Spirits... that feels so good."

If her lips tasted like molten honey, this was like tasting the nectar of the fire gods. Searing along his tongue as he licked her up and down. She writhed beneath his powerful strokes. Unravelling as he sucked, kissed, and flicked at her core. She arched her back with soft moans in reply.

Fehrn worked his tongue faster. Her gasps spurred him on.

"I'm so close."

Her head fell back. Eyes and mouth only half open. Lips full and wet. The length of her throat exposed. Her thighs trembled against his head.

"Come for me, *little dragon.*" He breathed against her pussy, then immediately sucked in ever increasing pressure against her clit. His strong hands gripping and kneading at her thighs to hold her against his mouth.

His goddess practically burst into flame as she cried out,

waves of pleasure rippling outwards. Her back arched. One hand gripped his head, the other stretched out behind her.

The most erotic sight of his long life. He just about lost control at the sight of her. Fehrn gently massaged her with his tongue as she came down from her orgasm. Long languid strokes matched the waves as they rippled through her shaking body.

He sat back on his heels to take one last look at her magnificence. His eyes swept across every stunning inch of flesh. Gently he pulled the hem of her cotton wrap back into place around her legs and up to cover her breasts. He stooped and placed a kiss against her forehead as he extended a claw and dragged it leisurely across her chest.

His goddess sat open mouthed. Panting. The mounds of her breasts damp with a sheen of sweat. His cock jerked painfully against his trousers.

"So... you have your bargain with a *thief*. Until tomorrow night, *little dragon."*

Then he vanished into the inky night.

CHAPTER 3

"Idalia! Watch where them embers are going or matron will stuff your head on a spike!"

The piercing shriek of Alzar the kitchen maid cut through the haze clouding Lia's thoughts. Her attention rocketed back to the present. She looked down at her hands to see swirling embers had begun scattering themselves wild and unruly across the kitchen floor. She dragged her focus back to the task at hand and charged the stove with her magic.

This was the tedium of her days within the castle. Lighting and maintaining fires throughout every day and night.

Lia watched the glow of the kitchen stove begin to burn brighter and her thoughts drifted to the night before. Heat coiled low between her legs. Memories of powerful hands gripping her thighs. Unimaginable pleasure rippling through her body. His growling whispers against her core.

Fuck. Fuck. Fuck. She needed to get a grip on herself. A potentially, maybe, almost certainly deadly thief was expecting her to find some unknown magical Seal and hand it over to him this coming night. Surely once he realised she had lied to him he would make good on his promise of tearing her throat out.

"My proposal is this, thief. I'll get you the damned Seal from my master's guarded chambers." Liar. *"The guards allow me in there during the day as part of my servants duties around the castle."* More lies. *"If you let me keep my life I shall meet you tomorrow night to deliver the Seal."* Shit.

Her fury flared at being in such a dangerous position. Yet that flame inside her now intermingled with a deeper desire for more of the pleasure he gave her. A complete stranger had managed to make her blood boil while simultaneously giving her the greatest orgasm of her short life.

She clenched her thighs together as another aching wave washed over her as she remembered his touch. *His tongue.*

"I—da—lia!" The elongated screech from Alzar ricocheted through the air. "Get moving or matron will have us both on spikes!"

Hoisting up her heavy wool skirts Lia disappeared out of the kitchen. Her footsteps echoed off the stone floor as she moved along the narrow passage towards the castle's courtyard.

Surely there must be some faint memory? Some dim

recollection from the stories her grandmother told. The whisper of a myth long forgotten that mentioned this Seal. Lia grasped to clutch at something, anything she might remember as she moved through the passageway. Were there tales of powerful ancient artefacts that might be connected to this Seal?

She hefted a shoulder against the heavy wooden door that led outside. The glare of midday sun blinded her after the dark passages of the servants quarters. Hand raised to shield her eyes, it took three blinks before she adjusted to the brightness. The scent of damp earth rising through her nostrils.

Nothing. No memories. She came up blank. Frustration rasped from her throat in a loud exhale.

It was now or never to find out if this supposed Seal of Elharean existed and she knew exactly who to ask. If she rushed through her duties this afternoon she could squeeze in just enough time to make it to the stables.

She grabbed a fistful of heavy wool in each hand and side-stepped the mud puddles. The last thing she needed was to explain having a hem inch deep in filth to the matron. She had so much to do, every day on repeat. Yet this matter couldn't wait. The unknowing around this Seal gnawed at her. There was only one person in the castle she felt comfortable enough to turn to.

Whether they chose to assist or not might pose a different kind of hurdle to navigate entirely.

There weren't exactly any friendships formed between

the castle servants. All had been in servitude their entire lives. Only those who died or were dismissed had ever moved on. A life sentence. Rather than friendships, it was more a series of uneasy alliances with every witch looking out for themselves.

Lia had one such ally. The stable-master. Lia had never been told her real name, despite their years of alliance. All the servants knew was that the stable-master had been the longest serving of all. The only one still alive that was. Secret bets had been placed on her true age, but they could only speculate she was many hundreds of years old.

Clanging metal pulsed rhythmically as Lia scuttled across the dirt of the courtyard towards the long stable building. At least she wouldn't have to look far to find her target. Gruff grunts could be heard in time with the metallic collisions. The stable-master's snow white hair pulled back in a messy bun had mostly escaped with the exertion of straightening out horse shoes. Her muscular yet wiry arms looked as much like leather as the saddles, stirrups, and harnesses adorning the walls.

"You get yourself lost between tending to them fires?" Her gruff greeting came without looking up from her work. Never one for unnecessary pleasantries or formalities here in the stables.

"No, but I do so love the warm welcome I receive every time I see your beaming smile." Lia knew the old woman had what could be almost deemed a soft spot for her. She paused her assault on the metal, huffed out a breath, and swiped grimy sweat from her face with what might have been a barely perceptible flicker of a smile in the corners of her crinkled eyes.

"I've come to seek an answer, but I cannot tell you why I am enquiring."

"Oh, so just simple conversation then today is it?"

"Well, I could stay here and ask you about your day if you like?" Lia twirled the leather of a nearby bridle between her fingers, grinning coyly.

"Hurry it up, yer lump of coal. I've got stables to muck and carriages for the masters that need preparing."

"Are the masters leaving the castle today?" Dropping the leather abruptly, Lia's interest was suddenly peaked. The House of Elharean were notoriously private and rarely travelled on short notice.

Nosy little witch.

"They'll be making their way to some other grand castle somewhere no doubt." The servants were never given much information about their masters movements. Only those in the highest ranks were privy to such details.

"You seem awfully interested in that fact, coal-face."

Lia smirked at the usual round of creative fire themed pet names tossed her way by the stable-master.

"Ooooh, I'm certain you have used that one a hundred times or more now. You'll honestly have to start getting more imaginative."

"Get to the point, you filthy hearth brush."

"What do you know of the Seal of Elharean?" The stable-master flinched on hearing the words. Her raised arm froze in place mid-strike. White lines formed across her knuckles.

She knows of the Seal. The time has arrived.

"Go. Now. I never heard you say those words."

"But—"

"GO." She turned her back. "Never mention that to no one else if you value your head."

Stars save us and protect that stupid girl from harm.

The stable-master's thoughts rang through Lia's head as clearly as if they were her own.

The repetitive clanging recommenced with extra force as Lia backed away through the scents of fresh hay and chaff. Theirs wasn't exactly a close relationship, but she hadn't anticipated such a visceral reaction. She was sure the stable-master would laugh in her face and tell her it was an old witch's tale.

Lia's mind raced as she sped back to the castle holding her skirts above the dust and the mud. There had been visible fear in the woman's clenched jaw and urgency to evict her.

What was she so deathly afraid of?

CHAPTER 4

Lia moved through the dimly lit castle corridors lost in thought.

Protect that stupid girl from harm.

She wound through the servant's access passages. A maze of narrow corridors that ran around the lower levels of the castle. Out of sight of the formal rooms of the masters. If she needed to move about the castle during the day time, this was the longer route she must take. No wandering through the rooms like she could do in the middle of the night. These winding narrow passages she knew like the back of her hand. Black stone punctuated with sparse narrow slits of light filtering in. Barely enough to see by.

She started up the narrow stone staircase ahead of her.

A chilling aura crept around her throat before she saw the witch.

Rygor. Captain of the castle guards. A powerful male witch and part of the elite chosen to be in service to the masters.

Mmm. No escape from me here Lia.

His pale gaunt face leered at her from the top of the stairs. Rygor's words burst into her mind like a kick to the stomach. All force and menace. There was certainly no avoiding him this time.

Let me choke your pretty neck and have you begging for mercy on your knees.

She balled her hands into fists. Eyes fixed on the step below her boot. Lewd thoughts of what he wanted to do to her clouded her mind. His silent words sent shivers down her spine.

Such a perfect throat to collar. I'd like to see it bruised beneath my fingers.

Lia did her best to escape his harassment. He was obsessed with her and his thoughts were enough to turn her stomach whenever she had the misfortune to run into him. Fortunately his role as Captain kept him busy and most importantly away from the servants quarters.

His black smoke like tendrils reached towards her, snaking around her stomach and breasts, reaching higher towards her throat, threatening too close.

"Ahh, if it isn't the beauty herself. Where are you rushing off to Idalia?"

A hideous smirk ran across his clammy face. Pale and ghostly, but menacing. Rygor didn't need to be physically intimidating. Without lifting a finger he wielded his dark tendrils of power ruthlessly to immobilise and brutalise. Lia had been told stories of his wrath towards the castle guards who failed in their duties, coiling his power around their necks and snapping them like twigs.

This witch wanted to subjugate and dominate her. Twisted pain that he thought of as pleasure. She had every right to be wary in his presence. Her fire magic and twinkling embers were no match for him.

"Good afternoon, Captain." She bobbed her head. Just play his game and usually it was over soon. Simply a matter of enduring his nauseating thoughts. Her scalp pricked with unease.

How pretty that mouth is. Perfect to fuck.

Lia's stomach dropped in a sickening rush. She pressed her fists into her thighs. Her focus intent on her breath. She needed to anchor herself to something. Anything.

"You really do become more captivating every day. Let me take a look at you." A dark tendril wrenched her chin up. From where she stood, halfway up the steep stairs, she was eye level with his boots.

Ah yes. On your hands and knees for me pet.

A soundless murmur. His twisted sense of satisfaction at looking down on her from above. Unspoken and threatening.

Time to take what is owed to me.

Lia's heart skipped a beat as his thoughts came through dripping in menace. *Shit.* This was completely different to their usual run ins. There was no escaping him this time. She was trapped in a narrow staircase with a madman. The blood drained from her face. Her palms clammy beneath her curled fingers.

"Captain. You are needed in the hall." A guard's voice echoed along the corridor in urgent tones. Those poisonous black tendrils snapped back, relinquishing their hold. Lia quietly prayed her thanks to the Stars for the intervention.

"Such a pity I have to leave with you looking perfect in that... position. You *will* come to me, my dear. I know you feel drawn to my power. And when you do, I will be waiting with eager anticipation."

With that he vanished.

Lia dropped to her hands and knees. Legs shaking. Her stomach threatened to empty itself. That was far too close.

CHAPTER 5

Lia's hands shook as she passed through the doorway to the kitchen. Her body leaden and fatigued as she resumed her post in attendance to the fires and hearths. She clenched her fists in an attempt to return her attention back to the mysterious Seal and wrestled with herself to rid her mind of the run in with Rygor.

Amber flecked eyes. "Let me hear what your pleasure is, my little dragon."

She flooded her thoughts with memories of her *thief*. Her heartbeat slowed with every sucked in breath, every remembrance of his firm hands holding her tight. That caress he softly ran across her skin.

Lia squeezed her eyes shut. She now had a glimmer of confirmation. The *thief* was correct that such a Seal did exist and if it existed within the castle walls it was clearly of the utmost secrecy and importance. It must hold untold value if he had been willing to overlook countless antiques and artefacts that could have easily fetched a pretty penny. This wasn't about thievery for riches. No, it related to something much more. Something much darker.

Now what was she to do? She had a hunter expecting her delivery of a powerful and dangerous *secret* artefact from the House of Elharean in mere hours but she was no closer to obtaining any clues that might help her.

Lia's flames burst forth with a sudden pulse. Clarity hit her with a jolt. It couldn't possibly be that simple? Could it?

The *thief* obviously didn't know what he was looking for! He knew of its name but had asked her to locate it for him last night. He didn't know where it lay within the castle, nor did he have the words to describe it. The artefact he sought was a complete mystery to him, just as it was to her.

Hope gripped her chest and heat flushed across her skin. This was her opportunity and she was damn well going to seize it with both hands.

What if she simply gave him some useless antique tonight and lied to protect herself? By the time he might realise her ruse he would be long gone from here and she would have ample time to inform the guards of an intruder. They would no doubt reinforce security, Rygor was too power hungry to allow his captaincy to be threatened, which would mean no more opportunities for thieves of any kind to slip inside during the middle of the night.

No more amber flecked eyes.

She shook her head, desperate to erase all thought of the wolf that had taken her breath away. She shifted her weight on the wooden stool. *Concentrate.* Where could she find an item to carry out her intended deceit? Lia retraced her nightly steps through the castle in her mind's eye. She cast her glance over the vast assortment of gilded artefacts that adorned each of the grand rooms. Statues, vases, ceremonial weapons, and sculptures all flashed through her awareness.

That was it! She knew exactly what she would use to form her lie.

A blast of commotion hit her like a shockwave when a crush of servants burst into the kitchen. Excitement and shouting spilled across the room as everyone tried to push past one another and crowd at the small window.

"Look!"

"It's the masters."

"They're departing."

Eager faces craned and elbowed at one another for a glimpse of the elusive House of Elharean whom the servants rarely saw in person. All eyes hungrily fixed on the procession of horses and carriages. The masters and their elite advisors preparing to depart.

Lia gasped. Could the Spirits have handed this exact opportunity to her? With everyone distracted by the commotion outside, this was her chance to act swiftly. Quietly she backed out of the kitchen and hastened towards the library. Along the darkened passage and up the narrow stone stairs. A chilling threat lingered silent and ominous where Rygor had stood only an hour before. Like the air itself was tainted by his shadow.

At the top of the steps the corridor led towards the upper gallery overlooking the grand entrance hall. From there her destination lay only a few paces ahead behind a formidable wooden doorway.

She entered the library out of breath and darted straight for the mantlepiece above the fireplace. Every night for fifteen years she had seen it. Unassuming. Hidden among the other antiques. A small gold dagger in its ornamental sheath. The House of Elharean insignia forged into the blade.

Lia had no idea what this powerful Seal was supposed to look like, but neither did her *thief*. And since when had she begun thinking of him as *her thief*?

She stuffed the blade within her skirts to conceal it and slipped quietly back through the servants corridor to the kitchen. The crush of bodies pressed at the window were still fixated on the horses and carriages outside. Lia coughed as she sat down on her stool. Not one eye turned away from the window.

The weight of the small dagger tugged at the waistband of her skirt. Now all she had to do was wait for the midnight hour to arrive. For her handsome *thief* to make his move.

Shadows clung to the castle walls towering overhead where Fehrn stood watching in his wolf form. The witch clearly knew her exact path to reach the walled gardens. She darted between shadowed corners, slipping through the night. His keen eyes watched as his prey moved stealthily towards the gazebo, knowing instinctively to pause. A periodic check of her surroundings for anyone who might be following her. The waxing moon cast an eerie pale glow, but the gardens outside remained shrouded by inky blackness. As she neared he shifted into his human form, but kept himself still crouched in the shadows furthest from the entrance. Ready to strike.

His keen eyes roamed across her body, appreciating the curve of her hips and breasts beneath her dark cape. He had tried to put her out of his mind all day, but his thoughts had kept straying to the touch of her against his lips. Her soft moans and breathless gasps etched into his memory.

If he wasn't sworn to dismantle her dark witch masters and all of her kind, he might have been impressed by her natural gift for moving through the night. He might have been tempted to once again feel her intoxicating heat.

He had a job to do. That was the reason he came here tonight. Or was it? The unfamiliar haze he had been under all day had left him shaken. An elite spy is sworn only to their duty. Even in times when it was necessary to infiltrate and become assimilated with their prey they were to remain completely focused. No distractions.

Walking towards him was an almighty fucking distraction in the form of a dark goddess.

Where he had honed his skill as the cool-headed and rational spy, she was breathtaking in her fire and spark. How the witch had turned to a raging inferno as she came undone beneath his tongue. Her pleasure had radiated heat through him and damn near entirely melted his resolve. Tonight he had to keep his cool. Stick to the plan. Retrieve the Seal. Extract himself and return to his safe lands.

His cool immediately began to waver as soon as she strode across the gazebo towards him, eyes flaring with the same glowing embers he had seen circling her hands the night before. He set his shoulders back and stood at his full height to tower over her diminutive stature.

"It would be a mistake to come here tonight empty handed, little girl." Fehrn warned as she stepped through the archway. His wolf howled with pride inside his chest when the girl didn't miss a beat.

Fierce. Beautiful. Mine.

"I believe, *thief*, our bargain is complete." She spat as a hand thrust beneath her cloak and withdrew a short jewel encrusted gold scabbard. Fehrn's eyes widened. A flicker of surprise caught in his throat.

This was the Seal of Elharean?

CHAPTER 6

No one outside of this castle had seen it for millennia. Lost to the memories of wars and the corrosion of time. Now it was being slammed against his chest by a little witch. A fire raging in her large almond shaped eyes. Her long dark hair curled and flowed freely below her hood, and the calm he had promised himself began to leave his body as her scent wound through the air. Replaced by an entirely different sensation. Raw heat and desire.

"You have no idea how much of a risk I took in stealing this for you. Doing your dirty work." Her forced whisper came through gritted teeth.

"Where I come from our greetings are a touch less acidic, little girl."

Fehrn noted the unmistakable flush gather in her cheeks

and trace the column of her neck. Even wrapped in a cloak of night his supernatural sight saw much more than others. He saw both the external and internal of a being.

The witch wears the scent of arousal and dragon fire.

"Are we done here? You have what you came for. Now if you please I plan to keep my life and my trusted place within the castle." Her tone pitched higher.

Fehrn circled behind her with slow languid movements. He relished toying with the prey now secure within his grasp. His wolf caved to the opportunity to cast an eye over her from all angles.

Need to rid her of that damned cloak.

"Ah, but you cannot be trusted any longer can you?" He purred.

He clicked the wooden door to the gazebo shut. The faint snick of the catch caused the witch to jump and twist around. Embers glowed and hovered in the air just above her palms.

Fuck she is magnificent.

An exquisite tempest of passion he was eager to explore further. To show her the truth and hold onto hope she may one day choose a different future for herself.

"You betrayed your masters without a second thought." Fehrn pressed her as he stalked the edge of the gazebo. Eyeing where the witch remained standing in the centre.

Her gaze followed him unflinching. He could feel the tension as it rippled off her body. A heady mixture of intensity and lust had his wolf nipping his heels to strike.

"Only because you gave me no choice!" Her palms glowed

white hot. Her jaw jutted forward. Her magic flared with electric energy as it swirled to fill the space between them.

Fehrn's lips curled at the edges.

Keep your cool. He sat on the edge of the luxurious day-bed that ran along the far wall. He leaned back on both hands with a casual smile and splayed his legs open towards the witch. In the dim glow emitted by her fire magic he saw her tongue dart out to wet her bottom lip.

His wolf demanded to be let loose at the sensuality of that sight. Such a small motion sending blood rushing south in response. Almond eyes widened ever so slightly as she swept her gaze across his outstretched form. She had no fucking idea how desperate he was to pounce on her.

"We always have a choice, and you made yours very loudly and enthusiastically I might add."

He baited her, Stars knows why. He sensed her rage simmering. But he wanted, needed to know the truth. Did she truly believe, in all ignorance, that the House of Elharean were honourable?

"Tell me, what is to stop your masters torturing every member of the castle staff until they finally wrench the truth from you? What is to stop them punishing every last servant and maid until they find their answer? Turning on all those who serve their twisted agendas?"

"They would never —." Her voice cracked with defiance.

The set of her shoulders stiffened. Her fingers flexed as embers swirled higher. Fehrn knew he continued to push her, but he had long blazed past the point of no return with this witch. He shifted his weight to rest his elbows forward on his knees. Fingers steepled under his chin.

"Oh, but they would. They already have." He raised an eyebrow, studying her expression for any sign of a tell. Time to go in for the kill.

"For hundreds of lifetimes before yours. They wouldn't think twice about tearing your mind from you and stripping your magic to shreds while you lay bleeding."

"No!"

With a cry she lunged for the dagger, unsheathed the blade in a fluid motion, and launched herself at him. Fehrn leapt to his feet, glancing her wrist with his shoulder, and swiftly pinned her against his body. She was now locked tightly in his arms, face to his chest, still clutching the dagger. His wolf bayed, furious with desire at the heat of her pressed hard against his length and unable to wrestle herself from his hold.

The gold engraving of the blade glinted even in the darkness. Its gilded presence hung like a poisoned chalice. Simultaneously adorned in beauty and deadly intent.

"If you want to attack a much larger opponent you're going to need some pointers, little girl." He brushed his lips over her ear, tasting that radiating heat. A muffled protest came from where her mouth was flattened against his shirt. He flexed his fingers around her wrists as her attempt to wriggle from his grip proved futile. The embers from her palms cascaded to the floor like a waterfall.

"First, you need to use your height to your advantage.

Instead of trying to attack the neck you'll need to aim lower and first strike at the knees or the groin." He pulled her tighter against his hips. Her wriggling immediately ceased when the curve of her soft stomach pressed against his hard length. Satisfaction crept over his lips.

Her arousal flooded through his senses. Even if her mind might be intent on attack, her body had other ideas.

"Once you have them at a disadvantage, then you might *choose* to go for the major arteries. The neck is a personal favourite of mine, as you know." He twisted her hand holding the blade in his, turning it until the top of the gold blade pressed against his collar bone.

"But to do that with a short blade such as this would mean having to get close to your opponent. Too close." Her eyes softened in surprise at the now vulnerable position he placed himself in with the sharp point aimed at his own throat. Although he knew she was far too tightly pinned by his arms to leverage any force to break the skin.

"So, what happens next?" Her voice barely a whisper, he could feel the skittering rhythm of her heartbeat. A fiery heat radiated and rose between their bodies with every second.

He flexed his fingers over hers so that the blade pressed harder and his lips hovered closer to hers. Soft pants of her breath mingled with his own.

"You have to be decisive. You have to move swiftly, or else you might lose your advantage."

Fuck. She had him entranced. Bewitched and bespelled. She could stab him now and set him alight with her flame and he would gladly crawl over molten lava to ask her for more.

Her eyes focused on his mouth and he felt her body soften under his tight hold. The dagger hilt slid from her hands as her fingers loosened their grip. He gently removed it from her grasp, all the while keeping his eyes locked on the sensuous lips of his prey.

CHAPTER 7

Lia's fingers hung limp around the handle of the dagger. This man had her completely disembodied within seconds of being in his presence. The heat rippled off her skin like luminescence in the darkness.

She had barely been able to produce a trail of glowing embers. Her power needed time to restore itself after the rigours of the day.

A feeble threat indeed. All spark and no heat.

Apparently all her fire had pooled between her legs in the presence of her *thief*.

The gazebo lay concealed in the walled gardens. At the furthest distance possible from the castle while still enclosed within the grounds. She had made certain to keep to the shadows, wary of anyone following her through the night.

Despite the blackness her embers had cast enough glow to see the sumptuous decor once she stepped inside. Servants rarely had a reason to stray this far from the castle. This might as well have been a small palace, complete with velvet furnishings, priceless antiques, and a golden chandelier hanging unlit from the rafters.

The sight of her *thief* spread out on the day-bed before her had melted her mind. His taunts slashed at her threads of commonsense as if from a swipe of his deadly claws.

There had been no thought behind her launch to attack. No plan. Just raw emotion desperate for release.

She had been resolved to simply deliver the lie and the dagger to him, then flee. But here she was now wrapped in his muscular arms, with no part of her ever desiring to leave. All sense of duty, servitude, and obligation to her masters had been erased from her mind. Instead the heady concoction of his power and desire were drawing her ever deeper. She wanted to be forever in his orbit.

"What do you want to happen next, *little dragon*?" His green eyes blazed with flecks of amber.

"I think... I want to make use of my advantage." Lia swallowed hastily under the caress of his stare.

"Smart girl." His purr rumbled through her body, sending a spiralling wave of pressure ever lower to clench at her core.

He stroked her hair behind her ear and she leaned into the sensation. Those powerful hands she craved so badly. Soft lips met hers with reverence, laced with barely contained intensity that was ready to spring forward.

Her deadly predator. She would gladly offer herself up as his prey for an eternity of his touch.

Lia sucked at his bottom lip, allowing her fingers to spread across his muscled shoulders. His hands roamed across her body and pressed her to him with a fierceness that she craved. No claws in this moment between them, just a meltingly attractive man. His erection jutted against the softness of her stomach, giving her tingles of anticipation. Heat intensified lower in her sex.

Their tongues intertwined and explored one another with increasing passion. She couldn't help but moan against his mouth. His taste was intoxicating, leaving her giddy as her toes barely gripped the ground. Strong hands unfastened her cloak, a sensual slide of material and a brush of fingertips across her shoulders as it tumbled to the floor.

Spirits. Those hands. They cupped and caressed her breasts, her rear. She fumbled at his belt. Her intentions clear. This time she wanted all of him.

He stayed her hands with his own.

"Are you sure, *little dragon*?" He breathed.

That look in his eyes. It spoke of a hunger built over eons.

If only she could hear his thoughts.

She flashed a quick smile. Nervous, yet never more sure. Her fingers continued to work at the buckle. His tongue slid over her neck and she felt the trail of fire flame a path towards her exposed shoulder. As his trousers loosened, she could feel the straining bulge of his shaft responding to her. Making quick work of lifting his shirt over his head, he cast it to the floor. She barely had time to register the rippling muscled chest in front of her eyes before he was wrapped back around her.

"Ahhhh, Stars... I've been dreaming of this." His growl against her neck just about melted her into the floor.

Keep your focus, Lia.

Her fingers shoved at his trousers. His erection sprang forward, breathtaking in size, this was a man who could drive a woman wild with pleasure. Who could drive her wild with pleasure.

A shudder ripped through his corded muscles.

"Better than I could ever have imagined." He groaned as she reached out and took him in hand.

A little uncertain of herself, Lia allowed the desire to wash over her. A heady mixture of tastes and scents of his bare skin. She began to kiss his chest tracing her way down his stomach.

He gripped her arms.

"The only one of us getting on their knees will be me, *little dragon*."

With a swift motion he tugged at the ties on her wrap, dropping the fine cotton beside them. She was now completely bare and his predator gaze hummed across her flesh. Returning his firm grip to her, he pushed her back up against the wall. His hot mouth crushed to hers with urgency.

Need. Fire. Engulfed her wholly.

"Fuck, your skin is addictive ..." He groaned against her lips.

He hoisted her leg high against his hip, wedging her thighs open. She spiralled into the Stars as he slipped his thumb between her sex. Teasing maddening slow circles against that tight bundle of nerves. Lia gripped his shoulders, riding his hand, head thrown back in ecstasy at the return of his touch.

A deep inhuman rumble burst through his chest. His firm body pressed hard against her nipples. She cried out at the rush of sensation. His groan amplifying her arousal.

"I need you, *little dragon*." Teeth softly tugged at her bottom lip. Then moved lower, sucking and licking at the hollow of her neck.

"Oh... I need... I need you, I've been thinking of this.... this..."

A growl interrupted her as he slipped a powerful finger inside of her core. Easing into her in divine circles that had starbursts forming behind her closed eyes. She was swept away, gone. His to pleasure as he saw fit. She might as well be signing her life away, but for this moment right here she didn't care.

"You're so wet for me. Will you have me? Will you open and allow me to please you until dawn?" He purred into her neck. Goosebumps danced across her skin.

Once again she found herself nodding. In complete trust of this man. Her man. Her *thief*. At least for this moment. Willing him to take her, worship her, and bring her pleasure like she had never experienced before.

Strong hands lifted her, his hard cock pressed against her

hip as she wrapped her legs around him. Tingles shot through her at this new sensation and closeness.

He turned and laid her down on the velvet cushions of the day bed. His body covering hers. Fingers flexed against the nape of her neck, cradling her as she drifted down. The same neck he had threatened to rip from her only the night prior.

But if that was the price she paid once he discovered her lies, then send her to join her ancestors now.

Powerful fingers slid across her sex. Heat radiated from her under his caress. One finger pushed inside her, filling her with a friction that had her arching off the cushions below. His mouth closed around her nipple and she moaned, running her fingers through his hair. Gripping him to her. Demanding his attention.

He pinched her other nipple. His tongue flicking a hot wet trail across her breasts. The meeting of her fire and the sensual glide of his tongue. She let out a soft cry.

Two fingers now filled her. A slow deliberate slide in and out. The filthy sounds as he pumped in and out of her wetness filled the night air. Her moans mingled with the sound of his fingers working her tight, wet heat.

She started a spiral towards her edge.

"I'm ... so close." Breathless words stammered from her mouth.

Lia felt his fingers fuck her with deeper intent, but she craved more. Needed him inside and to feel his full length. His thumb circled her clit, while his fingers curled inside her.

Pleasure built and threatened to crash. She bucked towards his hand, her pussy desperate in seeking release.

"You know what I want first, *little dragon*." He dragged his mouth hot and wet across her breast. "Fall apart for me. Let go."

A tremble swept along her body as the coil wound tight. Her nails dug into his shoulders.

"Yes! Just there!" She gasped.

Her walls clamped around his fingers. White flickering flame radiated across her vision. Her orgasm pulsed its rhythm and she cried out again and again.

Make that two of the best orgasms of her life.

As her breath steadied his fingers continued to massage her down. Gentle strokes brought her back into her body. What she would give to hear his thoughts. To know what was running through his mind. Almost as though he could sense her wish, his lips caressed hers. A brief glide, followed by a nip at her bottom lip. His scarred eyebrow arched with devilish intent.

Her body lit up from head to toe in response. Spirits, this *thief* had her set alight under his every touch. Now he had unleashed his sexy, playful side. She needed more of that. So much more.

She felt his hand disappear and watched him shift to rest between her thighs. His hot palm brushed over the sigil tattooed on her hip. Amber flecks pulsed across his irises. Thank the Stars for witches having the gift of spell casting to protect themselves during sex. She certainly desired his thick cock but not any other lasting consequences right now.

Her *thief* stilled. She couldn't drag her gaze away from his eyes. They transformed to full amber with a preternatural glow. His wolf rising just for the briefest moment.

"Please." Lia clutched at his arms. The unfamiliar quiet echoed in her mind. What if he didn't feel the way she did? What if he turned and left again? She couldn't bare to lose him as quickly as last night.

Reaching down he took his length in hand and readied himself at her entrance. He lowered himself onto one forearm and slowly pushed forward. The sensation Lia had fantasised about became the joining of their flesh.

"Ohhh ... Stars that feels so good." She moaned into the darkness.

His forehead pressed against her shoulder. Body tense as he moved slowly inside her. A groan tumbled forth as he filled her to the hilt. The fire in her core slammed through her being and into his.

"You feel... you feel incredible... *little dragon*." He ground his hips slow, giving her another reason to arch off the bed once more. "You're mine, *little dragon*, this will always belong to me."

"Ohhh, just like that ..." Lia murmured. Her eyes fixed on his body. Corded muscles flexed with each thrust forward. "Will you stay? Stay with me?"

He lifted his head. Studying her silently.

"You know I can't... but my heart... will stay here with you... in your hands." He slanted his mouth over hers. A promise. An apology. She didn't know, but no longer cared. He thrust into her over and over. Hitting just the right spot. Decadent friction had her skin tingling. Damp formed with the heat raging between their bodies.

"And my cock ... will be right here inside you... filling you every night... in your dreams." He moved his hips faster, bringing her leg up to open her wider. Her eyes rolled back in her head.

"Say it.... Say you'll always belong to me." His command rasped out. Deep and carnal.

Lia was now sure she had vacated her body. Pleasure coursed through her veins. His gruff intensity caused a new wave of wetness. His thick cock hit just the right place and her fiery coil tightened once more, ready to explode.

"Always." Lia breathed. Eyes clenched tight. Lost to the grip of sensation as it rolled through her core.

"Come for me. Come on my cock, *little dragon*."

At his growling command she fell apart again. Wave after wave rippled through her body. Desperate hands gripped his back, drawing him as deep as possible while he ground against her clit with each hip thrust. His own grunts mingled with her soft cries of pleasure.

"I'm not... going to last... much longer... feels... so good."

With a deep roar his muscles tightened and he released. She could feel his hot liquid against her walls as she floated on her waves of bliss. His sweat slicked chest pressed against hers and he rested his forehead to hers.

Whatever walls he had in place had crumbled. Her *thief's* thoughts now echoed like a cannon shot through Lia's mind.

Mine.

CHAPTER 8

"You really shouldn't be coming this close to the castle. What if the guards see you?" Lia whispered as they walked side by side through the walled garden. Her skin caressed by moonlight as though dipped in shimmering silver.

Fehrn near floated out of his body. His wolf burst with pride at her concern.

"I need to make sure you return safely. Couldn't rest otherwise."

She shot him a shy smile from beneath the hood of her cloak, a faint stain of pink still flushed her cheeks. They paused in the deep shadow at the edge of the courtyard. From here he had a clear line of sight to the door to her quarters. It was closer than he would have preferred and way too exposed in this part of the castle grounds, but his instinct to protect was overriding his training.

She turned to face him, placing her hands over his chest.

"I guess this is where we part ways, *thief*." She playfully dragged her tongue across the word, softly elongating it with tenderness in her voice.

He closed her hands in his, raising one to his lips in silent reply.

"I don't even know your name..." She trailed off gently.

"Best for you not to, *little dragon.*" He reluctantly let go and shifted his weight backwards just a fraction to put an agonising distance between them.

She nodded, drawing her cloak tighter around her and moved out of the shadows towards the castle. His chest wrenched and a low rumble sounded as he fought every instinct that told him not to let her leave his sight. His fingers raked through his hair in frustration. *Fuck.*

She paused as she reached the threshold, turning to face him with one hand on the door. With a slow drift of her fingers she lowered her hood.

"Lia." She breathed softly. Voluntarily sharing her name. As if she could sense he wanted—needed—to retain something that would hold on to her memory. Her long dark hair swayed as it swept down her back, and the trail of her cloak rippled as it disappeared from view.

She was gone.

His heart felt like it had grown wings. He had been through

hell and back over his three hundred years and yet this witch had him in a fluttery mess of emotion. All cool reserve had been incinerated in the wake of her magnificent life force.

Lia.

He ran her name across his tongue.

Fehrn let out a long pained breath. It was for the best they had said goodbye. His world wasn't one for having romantic attachments or commitments. While not explicitly a rule, it was more an act of self preservation. You could be dedicated to a mission for decades if that was how long it took. It was rumoured among the supernaturals that one spy had been undercover for over two hundred years.

This was *definitely* the right decision.

Certainly.

Absolutely.

Not at all terrifying to think that his heart felt like it would burst at the thought of never seeing her smile or feeling her flame tinged skin again.

Crack!

A spark of light, then a dull thud echoed through his skull. Dark splotches started to haze across his vision as something snaked and coiled around his neck. Fehrn felt himself falling as if in slow motion as his knees buckled beneath him. His claws flared and he swiped for his assailant, only to lunge at thin air. A second blow across the back of his head rendered him unconscious.

The last thing to drift through his thoughts was the vision

of intensely glowing embers sparking within large almond eyes.

Lia.

Then nothing.

PAIN SEARED through the side of Fehrn's head. A trickle of warmth ran down his temple. His neck felt bruised and crushed. A metallic taste clung to his mouth. Blood. He attempted to lift his hand to check the damage, but found he couldn't move. Both his arms were restrained in some sort of magically reinforced manacle with chain links connected to the floor. He rolled his weight and struggled to survey his surroundings. His senses were overwhelmed with the pounding waves of scents. The relentless tang of fresh blood, rage, and fear enveloped him.

His right eye was nearly fully closed where it had swelled after the force of one of the blows to his head, or perhaps from damage inflicted after he had blacked out. Eyesight or none, Fehrn had the ability to detect he was not alone. Four, maybe five others were in close proximity but these beings appeared to be wounded.

His instincts were groggy and hardly functioning anywhere near full capacity, but he could still identify supernatural beings and their weaknesses. It was exactly what he had trained for. Isolate the target. Take advantage of any wounding or injury.

Vampire. Shifter. Witch. Vampiress. Fehrn detected the nature of the other captives in the cells alongside him.

Pressing himself up to raise his head, his unobstructed eye quickly acclimatised to the dim lighting. Cell bars appeared to divide each of them. A high slit window in the dripping wet stone walls allowed a small supply of air in. They must be below ground level. No doubt he was being held in the dungeon from the familiar scents of the castle grounds lingering in the air.

Soft keening moans arose from the furthest cell away from him. Vampiress. The others were silent but he could hear an erratic slow heartbeat that must have belonged to either the shifter or the witch. Laboured breathing meant at least one other was inflicted with injuries. How long had he been here? How long had the others been here?

A low rumbling hiss sounded. Vampire. In the distance heavy footfall began to close in on their location. Metal screeched. A key turned with force, followed by a rush of dank mould ridden air as the iron door hinges groaned open. Multiple sets of boots echoed across the wet floor, stopping in front of Fehrn's cell.

"Ahhh, so the pathetic dog lives." *Rygor.*

“Shall we prepare it for your interrogation captain?” A guard flanking Rygor stood ready to unlock Fehrn’s cell.

“Not yet. This is one pet I want to play with a little longer.” Fehrn kept his swollen and bruised eyes closed, relying only on his instinct to tell him all that he needed to know about the situation. His spy training holding firm. This was the risk he took in coming here.

There only appeared to be one other guard with Rygor and none he could detect outside the door. He liked those odds.

“Ready the vampiress. I have a new protégé I want to introduce during our next round of questioning. I think you will find their methods quite, illuminating.” Rygor leaned closer to the bars surrounding Fehrn. “If they prove as successful in their methods as I believe them to be then I shall be happy to extend their usage to the other filth we have down here. Loosen some supernatural tongues.”

Guttural hissing intensified from the vampire. No perceptible sound came from the vampiress. She must already be badly wounded to not put up a fight. Both vampire and vampiress beings alike were renown for their supernatural strength, speed, and healing ability. The only thing to weaken them would be exposure to sunlight, fire, or being unable to feed for an extended period of time. All supernatural beings had rapid healing and recovery powers, making them as close to immortal as you could imagine. Those gifts didn’t exclude them from suffering pain and death.

"Touch her again and you'll pay for it with your head." A snarl came from the other shifter in a different cell.

"Isn't that sweet. The lovelorn mutt speaks his pathetic, empty threats." Rygor paced gleefully in front of the cells, with his hands behind his back as though examining an array of prizes laid out on a shelf for his personal reward.

"There's nothing you can do in here to protect your *mate*, dog. Your own suffering at that fact brings me nothing but immense pleasure."

Fehrn recognised the pained emotion crashing through the air. He could now sense that this other shifter was completely unharmed, yet powerfully restrained. His particular form of interrogation was clear. To suffer watching his mate be tortured repeatedly in front of him with nothing he could do to save her.

Shifters bonded with their mate remained devoted and connected through an unbreakable bond for life. It would be like tearing his soul into a thousand shards. Unbearable for a shifter to experience.

"And how fares our little traitor then?" Rygor was now crouched low peering into the witch's cell. "Not so spiteful without your magic are we?" She must have had her powers stripped from her. Fehrn was aware of the kind of soul death this would cause for a witch. Up to a certain point they could be recovered, but beyond that the witch would be left trapped in a bleak endless void. The process was akin to a death sentence. None he had heard of had ever recovered from that kind of violation.

Had this witch been in servitude alongside Lia? A tightness clenched in his chest at the thought of her being somewhere close by. Had she known all along of this plan? Bile rose in his throat. She had denied all knowledge of the true nature of the House of Elharean when he had questioned her last night. Had she been manipulating him all along? Was she part of this plan to capture him?

His heart thudded harder. His protective instincts howled a seething rage within. The spy in him was trained to be ruthless. Trust no one. Always be anticipating three steps ahead of your target. His heart was telling him she couldn't possibly have been a part of this. She was fierce, yes, but his wolf didn't sense any true darkness within her. Lia had warned him she was a powerful witch when they first met. Was he simply captivated under her spell this whole time?

A metallic tapping drew his attention to the entrance of his cell. Opening his eye, the sight of Rygor's pale twisted grin leered back at him. In his hand, tapping against the bars to his cell, was the golden dagger. *No!* The guards must have searched him when he was captured. Rygor held it up in front of his face and studied the engravings on the blade.

"I'm curious. Why would scum such as you be carrying a blade of the House of Elharean?" Bony pale fingers twisted the dagger in the air. Fehrn could see the gold gleaming within the darkness. "Perhaps you are just a lowly thief after all?"

"I'll rip that Seal from your cold dead hands when we're through here." Fehrn growled.

"You believed *this* to be the Seal of Elharean?" Maniacal laughter poured forth like poison.

Fehrn winced. She had lied to him after all.

Metal clattered to the ground as Rygor allowed the dagger to tumble from his hands. Disdain etched across his face.

"This is nothing but a trinket. A gift in gold to the masters of the House of Elharean from their subjects to show fealty to their rulers."

His wolf howled in agony. Pain seared through his chest at the realisation he had been blinded and double crossed.

"For millennia your people have been trying to find the Seal. All have failed. All have paid with their life, as you shall too. This great house is fuelled by the blood of your kind. I am going to enjoy watching you suffer as you bleed for your new masters."

CHAPTER 9

Three long nights had passed since her *thief* had slipped away into the shadows. Three long nights of replaying over and over in her mind their time together in the gazebo.

Their goodbye.

Lia didn't even know his name and the regret squeezed around her heart. She swirled her glowing embers above her hands absent-mindedly and let loose a half-hearted breath that blew her essence towards the lamps lining the stone corridor. One by one they flared, illuminating the long stretch of dark in front of her.

The narrow world in which she lived suddenly seemed bleak and hopeless. Less than a week ago she had been content with her servitude to the Elharean dynasty, but now there was a restlessness within her soul. He had turned everything she knew inside out.

No longer was she simply grateful to have a bed, shelter, and protection. The hole in her life that represented her independence and spirit as a witch was now glaringly obvious. A restlessness gnawed away at her. What if there was something more available for her that went far beyond this tedium of servitude?

Her bare feet padded against the cool flagstone floor, the coldness of the castle took on a different tone. She still didn't feel the cold, with her skin swirling with heat as always. There was now a chilling sensation that lingered in the air through the dark passageways. It reached into her and wrapped around her soul like a twisted black rope.

Lia paused at the tapestry concealing the servants passage. She lingered a moment to listen for any voices before entering the great hall. All was echoingly quiet. She slipped through and moved on towards the enormous hearth. With a weary breath Lia summoned her magic, infusing her essence into the flames. Watching them dance and flicker under her caress.

The glow licked at her skin as if to taunt her. Their formless freedom a reminder of everything she yearned to experience.

Glancing up at the large mirror above the heavy mantlepiece, she noticed the emptiness in her eyes. Before she used to admire the spark flickering in her reflection. Now she only saw a reflection of how hollow and empty her life was. All the fire in the world couldn't replace the warmth that she had felt curled close to his body. The soothing rumble of his chest as he spoke. The strength she felt within herself. As though she was already powerful on her own but somehow became so much more so when in his embrace.

Lia absently touched her bottom lip with her fingertips. It would have to be a fantasy she only returned to in her dreams. He would be long gone from this place. Returned to his lands. Never to be seen again now that he thought he had what he was searching for.

Dread pulled at her. To even think about alerting the captain of the guard to tighten security around the castle set her stomach swirling.

Maybe she did want her *thief* to come back and hunt her down after all.

From the direction of the library a heavy door crashed closed. Rapid footsteps drew louder as they moved towards the great hall. With a start Lia dashed back into the servants corridor concealing herself behind the tapestry just as two men descended the stone staircase into the hall. Members of the elite household advisors. Both dressed in signature House of Elharean blood red capes over their uniform.

"They will come looking. You know this to be true."

"We can't be sure of anything. The Elharean dynasty has always kept the Seal safe."

Lia's hand shot to cover her mouth. Did one of the men really just mention the Seal? Her heartbeat began thudding hotly in her ears.

"By keeping the prisoners here we are inciting suspicion." The men stopped in the middle of the great hall.

"Let them come. They will see what we do when we capture one of their filthy spies. Let it be a warning to all those who dare desecrate the great house."

"You know the masters prefer interrogation not to happen within the castle. They have instructed the Captain to be merciless but it must occur elsewhere, as per their wishes."

"They won't even know. The captives will be transferred long before they return. Rygor has certain new ... techniques he wants to experiment with. Especially on the vampiress."

"We cannot risk the discovery of the Seal!"

"And so it will be brother. There is no risk here. You worry too greatly. The guards have reinforced their numbers surrounding the chamber, you've seen their might with your own eyes just now."

"It leaves me uneasy. Without the masters here there is always a greater risk."

"They will return with news. Now we must hasten to alert the others to this new threat of spies attempting to infiltrate our ranks."

The giant entrance doors swung on their hinges with a slow groan, as the men disappeared into the night.

Lia stood frozen. What had she just witnessed? Spies? Torture happening here within the castle? The masters approved of this but ensured it happened elsewhere? She reached out to steady herself against the stone wall, her head spinning.

The two men had come from within the library. Lia knew she had to find out where or what this chamber was. If it was as serious as to warrant her *thief*, other supernatural beings, and now a spy attempting to get into the castle, then she knew he could be returning in the future.

Now was the opportune moment to find out more information while the castle was near empty.

Her footsteps scurried across the flagstones towards the grand staircase, she wound her way towards the heavy wooden doors that led to the library. If anyone was to come across her in this early morning hour she could easily defend herself as doing her nightly rounds tending to the castle's fires. It wasn't a perfect plan but she was sure it would be passable enough to get her close to finding some answers.

Lia slowed to a creep as she approached the doorway and paused with her ear pressed against the join to check for movement or voices. Nothing. Silence. These guards protecting the chamber clearly weren't gathered within the library. She pushed the heavy set door ajar just enough to slip inside. All was still and just as she had seen it the night before. She moved swiftly towards the fireplace and blew her embers to have the flames soaring higher to light the space as she scanned the room. Nothing seemed unusual or out of place. The two men had definitely come from here after visiting the chamber. So there must be a secret passage leading elsewhere. Upon first glance, all appeared peaceful and to order in the darkness. Only the flickering firelight spread its glow across the rows upon rows of books.

The heavy set stone walls stared resolutely back, refusing to divulge their secrets. Lia gently moved across the floor and contemplated checking for some sort of trapdoor hidden below one of the large carpets. Could there be a staircase leading below the library? It was possible. There were ancient passages and corridors leading all over this place.

A faint whoosh and a click sounded just over her right shoulder. Lia jumped and spun with a fright expecting to meet the pointed end of a guard's sword. But there was no one. Just the darkness punctuated by the fire light. Hardly daring to breathe she inched towards the direction of the sound. A short freestanding bookcase stood just to the left of the fireplace. Could that be concealing a passageway? She flared her embers above her hand to illuminate the wooden frame. There was another whoosh and the entire structure moved barely an inch as though blown by a breeze from within. The smallest of movements but enough to give away the secret location. Lia reached out and caught the edge of the wooden framework before it shifted back flush with the wall. To her surprise it swung easily in her hand.

Opening it cautiously, she saw nothing but black within the cavity on the other side. A rush of dank odour and cool air filled the space. Her fire magic flared above her palm and she gently crept through into the narrow passageway noting the handle located on the inside of the hidden door. At least she wouldn't be sealed in here if it shut behind her.

Shudder the thought.

The passageway was narrow but tall enough for someone of much larger stature than she to pass through comfortably, albeit in single file. It curved to her left and she realised it formed the start of a spiral staircase heading upwards. With every twist around its winding column she could feel the cold air gust stronger. There must be an opening up ahead. The battlements perhaps?

At the final curve of the staircase she inched towards the doorway at the top, seeing that it had been left propped open. Heart thudding louder in her chest she could see the faint glow of moonlight outside the door. Just as she stepped towards the opening a flash of blood red material crossed her line of vision. A sword held to her throat.

"Well, what do we have here?" One brutish castle guard sneered in her face, while another, equally as burly, restrained her against his blade.

"Out creepin' where you shouldn't be, witch. That'll get you a date with our Captain to decide your punishment." Cold laughter echoed off the stone walls.

Rip that dress from her... See how she begs for it ... Drag her across the roof... Enough meat to share around nicely.

Their lewd thoughts crowded into her brain as they openly gawked at her body.

Shoving aside her disgust, Lia's mind raced to grab hold of a suitable excuse or escape plan. Her *thief's* words from the night before floated through like a shining light in the bleakest storm.

You have to be decisive. You have to move swiftly or else you might lose your advantage.

"You'll unhand me immediately. I am your Captain's personal guest. Rygor invited me to visit him this evening. I am only obliging your Captain's wishes. I am sure neither of you wish to be found going against him now, do you?"

Fuck. Was she really going to hand herself over to the slimy clutches of Rygor to get herself out of this mess?

CHAPTER 10

Flanked by four guards, Lia found herself marched along the battlements towards the castle keep. Heavy boots crunched in rhythm. Trying to think fast in the face of this imminent danger, her mind drew a blank. Before she could make sense of the situation, she stumbled forward through a doorway thanks to a shove at her back. The door then slammed behind her with an ominous thud.

"This witch said you invited her to join you this evening, Captain." Obvious disdain dripped from the guard's tongue.

Rygor stood beside a narrow window overlooking the castle grounds. The perfect high vantage point to observe all that went on below him.

... If I were the one to find the source, the power I would receive ...

Fragments of his thoughts were cut short at their presence.

"Leave us." He commanded.

Lia's stomach churned. This was the last place she wanted to be. Alone in his slimy clutches.

So the witch comes to me at last.

"Witches are truly so clever." His back remained turned to her as he mused to himself. "I had intended to formally invite you to this evening's ... occasion... and yet here you are presenting yourself just for me, as if by divine orchestration."

Occasion? What was Rygor talking about? Lia hastily scanned the keep for any clues. The stone floor bore the insignia of the House of Elharean and red velvet banners hung from the walls. But otherwise it was empty.

"I've always known you were just like me. Drawn to the power. Such potential for destruction running through your veins." Rygor began to circle towards her now, stalking her with slow intent.

I know just the spot to tie you up. My new pet.

"I knew you would come to me. To recognise your own abilities far outstretch anything you busy yourself with as a servant in this castle. You are destined to be here alongside me."

Keep you bound and on your knees like the proper servant you are. That mouth is only good for one thing. Now it will be mine to with do as I please.

Lia flinched as his bony fingers traced a chilling path down her arm. His sickly aura enveloped her from where he moved behind her. A shiver ran down her spine under his lingering gaze. She felt weak and as though her fire was being extinguished by thick black tendrils wrapping around her insides. Twisted, sickening thoughts suffocated her mind as he stared at her.

"What is this place?" She choked out the words. Voice cracking and unsteady.

"You must have been drawn to it. To its majestic power. Only an elite few, chosen by the House of Elharean over the centuries have ever set foot in here." Rygor hovered close to her ear. Bile rose in her throat at his proximity. "Only those who truly align with our masters have the honour of experiencing the Seal of Elharean."

Her mind raced. "This... this is the Seal?"

A bony finger now traced her cheek as Rygor's clammy, pale face and leering smile swam in front of her vision.

"You'll be able to feel its power. The Seal must feed on the powers of those who serve the great house. Don't worry, over time you'll get used to the feeling. It is an honourable sacrifice to make and you shall be greatly rewarded."

"What does it do?" She swayed. Her power draining with every second she remained in this space.

"A doorway to power unimaginable. The House of Elharean has controlled this portal for millennia. It is what allows them to extend their influence across many different dimensions, realms, and worlds. The more lands the House of Elharean can obtain, the greater their power grows. The greater *our* influence grows."

Reeling at this discovery, Lia swallowed heavily. "This portal can open a passageway to other worlds?"

"Yes, yes, and the beings who pledge their loyalty to the House of Elharean across these worlds all give their power in honour of our masters. More and more do so in every moment."

"You mean they knowingly drain their own magic and give it to the House of Elharean?"

"Some do. Many are simply blissfully unaware of their gifts and content to be given work, shelter, and riches. A necessary sacrifice. As yours shall be."

"Forgive me, my Captain. I don't understand." She needed to keep him talking. The words gagged in her throat.

"For millennia the Elharean lineage has kept order. They know what people truly need and that is to be content with their little lives. Every village, every servant, every being dedicates themselves to a much greater cause. This house has a great responsibility to ensure its power is strengthened and sustained. Their subjects happily give that power." Rygor gripped her upper arm.

"Come, we shall see how your talents can truly shine. I have been looking forward to this moment with you stationed by my side for some time now."

Dizziness overtook Lia. Where was he taking her?

THE NOW FAMILIAR sound of boots approaching the dungeon alerted Fehrn to the arrival of guards. With a graunch of metal the door swung open. He could scent six of them filing into the stone chamber. It had been three nights since he first awoke in his cell, but time felt elusive confined within this space. If enchantments were used he could well have been unconscious for longer.

Three nights since he last held Lia in his arms.

Which one of them was to be tortured this time? Suspiciously, Rygor had left Fehrn alone since he had awoken. They seemed to be allowing him to regain his strength while his supernatural healing took hold. However, his restraints were impossible to break. Magical reinforcement held impassable.

Hurt gnawed at him day and night with nothing else to think on except to replay his time with Lia over and over. Seeing all the ways he was manipulated and deceived. Right from those first weeks when he watched her from the shadows, planning his movements to strike, and take her hostage himself. Had she known even then? When she would pause in front of the mirror each night and admire her physique, twisting and turning as the firelight licked her skin in the way he had been so enraptured. Was it all a show to lure him in closer and closer?

Then to discover her lies. He couldn't deny that she had deliberately given him that dagger knowing she would never have to see him again. A brazen act of deceit and never to face the consequences of her decisions.

She had asked him to stay. Asked him to be with her. It had seemed so real and genuine. But a spy was trained in the mastery of manipulation, and she proved to be an expert.

Secretly he kept hoping that it wasn't true. His only remaining thread of hope was that he hadn't seen her appear as part of their torture and interrogations. None of the guards of Rygor had mentioned her name. A foolish, buoyant glimmer flickered in his chest that he might be wrong after all.

The distinctive poisonous aura of Rygor made itself known. Only this time when he followed the guards through the doorway he wasn't alone. Fehrn's eyes flew open as her scent enveloped him.

No, not her... please not her.

His silent plea morphed into an internal yell as he raised his head. His dark haired goddess stood beside Rygor. A mask of cold indifference firm across her face. He was well used to the dim lighting of the dungeon and knew his shifter eyesight was far more skilled than that of a witch. He could see her eyes narrowing as she squinted unseeing at the row of cells in the gloom.

"Now, my beautiful protégé."

Fehrn winced hearing the words ooze from Rygor with noxious pride. His wolf howled for savage retribution.

"I want to introduce you to our guests."

With a sneer Rygor moved his hand to her lower back to guide her to the furthest cell away from Fehrn. To the corner where the vampiress lay bloody and broken after endless torture at Rygor's filthy hands.

His stomach churned. Lia was his protégé. She *had* been part of this all along. It was their plan to trap him using her seduction. How could he have been so ignorant? Three hundred years and he was to be undone by a witch one tenth his age. She may as well have stabbed that damn dagger into his chest.

Fehrn could see that golden blade. It taunted him from outside his cell where it lay in the pooling water mixed with blood.

One by one they stopped in front of each cell. Rygor cooed in Lia's ear, telling her how proud he was to have her by his side. Each prisoner was inspected in turn. Fehrn couldn't stomach seeing her face, seeing her reaction to the suffering. He wanted to keep the memories of his *little dragon* intact as they were from three nights ago. Not this monstrous creature she must have hidden beneath her beautiful exterior.

Closer and closer they came, until finally they stopped at his cell.

"And here we have our most recent treasure. A spy found infiltrating the castle grounds looking for the Seal. He will be a most prized sacrifice for the masters. His shifter blood runs potent and will give us many decades of power as we drain him slowly of his essence." Rygor tucked a strand of Lia's hair behind her ear—*mine*—and encouraged her to step closer.

"Go on. Get a closer look at our achievement, my pet. The dog is restrained so you can get close enough to see him clearly."

She moved dutifully closer. Fehrn locked his eyes on hers as she neared the metal bars. One more step and she should be able to make out his features in the darkness. Eyes flashing with fury, Fehrn fixed his gaze with hers. He would dare her to look at him. He would silently promise vengeance with every moment she neared.

Her eyes focused on him where he knelt bound against the stone floor. He jutted his chin forward in defiance. Despite the madness raging through him his instincts and senses were baying to be near her. His wolf whipped into a frenzy of loathing and longing.

Fuck. He truly had fallen in love with this witch.

How poetic. The spy fell in love with the spineless traitor.

He watched her eyes make out his features in the dark. Her indifference remained cooly fixed in place. Dark and calculating, she surveyed him with a look that slashed his heart open. The warmth of her fire was gone, replaced with ice that would burn all in its wake.

She cocked her head to the side, peering at him bound and on his knees.

"How pathetic, indeed."

CHAPTER 11

Black spots hazed Lia's vision. Seeing her *thief* shackled, beaten, and bloodied in the cell before her was her own personal form of torture. Her mind reeled from the events of the past hour. She barely had time to hold together her composure. Say the right words. Play Rygor's twisted game. Make the Captain believe you are on his side. Think damn it. Think!

"Mmm... yes, a pathetic toy that we shall play with together." Rygor clutched at her arm. "But for now, let's allow you a chance to use your gifts on the vampiress shall we."

Bony fingers steered her back towards the cell furthest away from Fehrn. She locked her neck to focus straight ahead. She didn't dare glance back in case Rygor suspected something. Lia knew the punishments would be beyond anything meted out so far if he had even an inkling of their attachment to one another.

Vengeance... Suffering... Betrayal...

Pain seared through her veins as she heard his thoughts, now clearly in her own mind since their night together. Whatever telepathic shields her *thief* had in place when they first met had dissolved when they made love.

He thought she had betrayed him. He thought she had set this all up and that she had been working with Rygor all along as part of the master's dark agenda. She had lied to him about the Seal and now he knew that.

The witch manipulated me. Lied to me. Set me up to be captured.

A key turned in the lock to the cell in front of her. Keening soft cries came from the shadows in an adjacent cell. Fresh blood and the scent of mould had Lia nearly retching.

Rygor was once again beside her ear, gleefully pressing them both forward into the open cell.

"This one has proved quite immovable in our line of questioning so far. She is restrained of course, but I don't believe she will pose any threat to you, my dear."

A roar bellowed through the darkness from the next cell. Struggling against his restraints a black haired shifter was bound and gagged with wild eyes piercing through her.

Touch her again and the witch will be destroyed. There will be nowhere to hide from my vengeance. I'll tear out every last breath leaving your corpses for the rats.

"Ignore the dog. He quite enjoys these little performances. Sadly, I'm not sure his mate here will have much life left in her after you are finished with her."

Lia's body turned numb. His mate. These monsters were using the vampiress to torture him. Was that what Rygor intended to use her for? Another form of punishment?

"Let's see what a little of your fire might do to loosen some tongues and find our answers."

Horrified, Lia watched Rygor take hold of her hand and turn it to face upwards. He gazed reverently at the inside of her wrist, bent, and kissed her soft flesh. Poison and dread emanated from that garish sight.

"Let loose your flames and let's celebrate this long awaited union, my pet."

No. This could not be happening. There was no way she could do this to another being. She was not one with the masters. She wanted no part in the hideousness that lay before her. Sick guilt churned through her stomach. She had been here for all these years. She had never thought to question the great house. She had never once queried their power, how they achieved it, or the desires that drove them.

"There are those who would take your power and turn it to blackness my little draga."

The words of her grandmother from long ago roared through her mind as clear as if she spoke aloud. This is what she had been warned of. The potential for her magic to be used for both good and for evil. The duality of the fire and the flame. It could burn to provide heat, warmth, nourishment, food, and forge something strong. It could also be used to destroy, obliterate, and torture.

Panic gripped around her throat as Rygor's tendrils circled her, coiling like a python slowly threatening to decimate its prey. She couldn't do this. But she daren't give the Captain any sense that she was betraying him.

Her embers began to circle above her hands. She could now see the vampiress lying on the floor in the glow. Her face and arms were covered in lacerations. She appeared to be skin and bone. The guards must have kept her without nourishment for a long time. Vampires did not usually need to feed frequently. Her frail form lay shackled against the floor. She didn't move as the glowing fire magic lit her cell. Lia gently probed with her telepathic gifts. There was nothing coming from the vampiress in her weakened state but she was still alive. Barely.

At the sudden illumination a savage howl came from the shifter.

No! Get away from her!

He struggled frantically against his restraints. His pain palpable.

Lia swirled her flames above her hands, keeping the fire carefully contained yet buying herself some much needed seconds. Rygor's face in the flickering glow was one of pure lust. Blood lust.

"Do it, unleash your power." He breathlessly urged her on. "She deserves to feel your magnificence and pay for her crimes."

My pet. At last. My weapon to wield.

Suddenly the flames disappeared. Her fingers closed into fists. Only a faint glow of flickering embers fizzled before extinguishing completely.

"What is happening? Burn the vampire now!" Rygor screeched. Tendrils tightened against her neck.

She dares disobey her master!

"I'm sorry my Captain, I don't know what happened. I must need more time to recover after this evening's experience at the keep." She bit down on the lie.

Black tendrils tightened to choke her neck and slammed her backwards against the wall.

"You dare lie to me and you'll feel the consequences. I can just as easily lock you away in one of these cells and take what you owe me." For the briefest second the savage glint of relish flashed across Rygor's features.

Mine!

The word echoed like a bullet through her mind. Her *thief.*

Take your hands off what's mine. Before I remove them.

His agony at seeing her in Rygor's clutches hurtled raw through his thoughts. He might hate her for an eternity but his shifter senses were overriding logical thought.

"Of cour— Of course not. Never, my Captain." She choked out against his grip. "I simply need some time to recharge my powers. I found it overwhelming for my first experience to witness the power the Seal can draw."

"You are young. The Seal is ancient. But you will become used to the effect it has upon you." Rygor sighed, letting her go. She moved hastily out of the cell before she was locked inside herself.

"Thank you. I just need some time to rest, then I am ... eager to please you." Doing her best not to vomit on the words, she heard the silent growl from her *thief's* cell.

Does the witch lie?

Rygor eyed her with a mixture of lust and suspicion. He wasn't convinced. She was going to have to give this the performance of her life.

With an exaggerated sway of her hips Lia moved towards Rygor and reached out to touch the sleeve of his crimson coat.

"I live to please you. I live only to please the great house. I want you to teach me and instruct me in your ways." Numbness swept through her body.

He licked his lips.

"Ahhh, there she is. My beautiful protégé."

There was the slimmest chance she might make it out of this dungeon alive. But would her *thief* ever forgive her?

CHAPTER 12

Wrath simmered and threatened to engulf Fehrn's every sense. He had watched as his Lia purred all over the Captain. Swaying her hips to draw attention to her curves. Jutting her breasts just enough to get her way. Exactly how she had distracted him that night in the library.

Once she was gone, he was left chained to the prison inside his mind where nothing seemed to make sense any longer. He twisted and turned through the events prior to his capture. Churning over every look, every glance, every inflection in her tone. It could so easily have all been different if he had stayed true to his objective in coming here. His own weakness in listening to his instinct rather than cold logic had got him into this entrapment.

Foggy, restless sleep overcame his body and towed him

into the realm of unconsciousness. He dreamed of fiery pools of black water dragging him under and drowning him while also burning through his core.

A faint rustling from the direction of the door brought his attention crashing back to the dungeon. A slow turning of the lock. The door inched open in the darkness then closed softly.

Embers glowed.

A growl from within his throat was echoed by the deep warning hiss of the vampire. Suddenly dark hair and almond eyes appeared as she gripped the bars to his cell, whispering frantically.

"I came as soon as I could."

"To finish what you started?" He spat out the words.

She came back for me?

"I don't have long. I stole the keys from one of the guards. They'll realise any moment."

"What makes you think I would be inclined to trust you. You lied to me. You brought me here."

Her fingers moved fast, fumbling key after key against the lock to find the right one. The scent of burnt flesh stung his nose. His eyes swept her body searching for injury. Whatever had happened she appeared unharmed.

"I lied about the dagger. Yes." Her voice wavered.

"Along with everything else. You were Rygor's pet all along."

"No! I had nothing to do with—"

"How dare you pretend! I saw how you were with him. I saw every look his way. You manipulated me from the start with your bargaining." His jaw clenched tighter. "It takes one to know one, little girl, and I should have known your specialty was deceit the second it paraded itself under my nose."

The cell swung open and she rushed in. He growled and twisted to lurch away from her. His wolf flickered with a glint of hope among his burning fury.

She came back for me.

Flames licked at her palms.

"Hold still. I'm going to remove the magic within these restraints so you can fight when the guards arrive."

His claws flared. A snarl burst from his throat.

"And why should I ever trust a word that comes out of your mouth?" Fury tumbled forth while relief simultaneously washed through his bones.

White hot flame poured along the chains binding him to the floor, incinerating the magic link by link.

"You can't." Her eyes were downcast and her shoulders slumped forward as she focused intently on freeing him.

"I will regret that forever. But I hope you can see to, maybe one day, find it in your heart to think back on me fondly. Once you are long gone from this monstrous place."

With a thud the heavy chains fell to the stone floor. He was freed. She flinched as his claws fully extended. The savage wolf threatened to unleash.

"I understand if you want to seek your vengeance on me... just allow me to free the others while I still have time."

She is yours. Protect her with your life.

Wide eyes snapped up to meet his. Had she heard his thoughts?

Shouts in the distance pierced his keen hearing. Followed by pounding footsteps. Guards running. Too many to count. *Fuck.* Time had run out.

Lia slipped out of the cell and set to work finding the key to free the vampire. Fehrn rose unsteadily to his feet, his shoulders stiffened and bruised. The lacerations through his side had healed but only barely. There was still deeper bruising and damage yet to recover, even with supernatural gifts. He was strong and deadly in combat. He would just have to hope he could last long enough to get to safety.

Chain links dropped against the stone floor of the vampire's cell. Lia rushed to the other shifter who roared through the gag around his mouth. The vampire limped from his cell to stand shoulder to shoulder with Fehrn. Tall with lean muscle on his frame. Vampires possessed immense strength while feeding regularly. This would no doubt be a test of his supernatural abilities after going so long without blood. A nod and silent understanding passed between them. They would be the first line of defence while Lia freed the others.

Fehrn glanced back towards the furthest corner cells. Pulled to search for sight of his witch in the blackness. Fire licked the bars, casting a flickering glow where Lia poured flame on the shifter's restraints.

The door to the dungeon slammed open. A sea of blood red uniforms burst in.

Fehrn lunged forward, claws slashing. He was nowhere near his full strength, but knew he could outmatch these powerless guards. They desperately needed to get out of here before Rygor appeared. The vampire was a blur as he used his supernatural speed to slay the guards closest to him. A furious bellow. A spray of blood to his right. The other shifter had been freed and now unleashed an eternity of fury upon his captors for their torture of his mate.

Lia. Where was she?

His instinct determinedly searched to make sure none of the guards had got past their defence of the dungeon.

There... in the cell at the far corner. As he twisted, wrestled, and clawed at the jugular of each assailant, he saw flames burning from the corner of his eye. Lia worked to free the vampiress with help of the freed witch.

Blinding pain seared through his skull. Fehrn dropped to his knees clutching at his head in agony. The vampire and shifter fell to the ground alongside him in turn. The three trapped in place. Unable to escape.

Rygor.

They were too late. It was futile in the face of this menace. Rygor's magic flowed into the dungeon on his poisonous tendrils. Dark power coiled around their throats, each of them pinned immobile. Their life force choked with crippling intensity of poisonous magics.

"Lia!" He barked out a strangled warning.

I'm so sorry little dragon. I should have been able to protect you. I should have told you I forgave you. I wanted to stay by your side forever if you would have allowed me.

Fehrn's vision began to spot. After three hundred years this was it. He was going to die in this dungeon at the hands of the House of Elharean. Before he had told her how he truly felt.

A flash lit the dungeon with a thundering explosion. A fireball ripped through the air, blasting Rygor in the chest. The vice grip on Fehrn's throat released in an instant. He lurched sideways as another fireball, followed by another, then another, tore across the stone floor. A chaos of wildfire set alight the dead bodies of the guards where they lay strewn on the ground.

Rygor's blood red coat erupted in flame as he fought to shield himself using his magic.

With each searing shot Lia stepped forward, screaming a guttural roar. A rage unleashed that threatened to burn all of them to ash. Fehrn scrambled to get closer to her on his hands and knees. The flames had now engulfed both her and Rygor. His palms singed and skin blistered when he tried to reach out and make contact. To bring her back to him. His wolf clawed within his chest to protect her from her own chaos. His senses rode him harder with every inch that remained stretched out between them.

"Stop! You'll get yourself killed!" The shifter and the freed witch each grabbed him by an arm, pulling him away. The vampire was no where to be seen. He must have escaped immediately after Rygor's spell had broken. The shifter scooped up the limp body of the vampiress. He cradled her to his chest with tears streaming down his blackened face from the billowing smoke, charcoal, and embers now choking the air in the dungeon.

"Go. Get yourselves out of here. Over the walled gardens you can escape into the woods." Fehrn pushed them towards the door, stumbling as the air became so hot he could hardly breathe.

"Lia... listen to me!" Fehrn crawled over the dead bodies of the guards, their gruesome blackened skin burnt under the force of her fire magic. She was blindly pouring forth her fury at Rygor crouched low near the doorway. The Captain cried out as he fought to keep shielding himself.

Lia was boiling him alive. Her eyes full glittering obsidian streaked with white flames.

"You don't want to kill him! It will only make you more like them. I know your heart. You are kind and courageous and powerful." He choked on the thick ash as he tried reaching towards her arm, his fingers burning.

"You don't want to live their life filled with hatred and vengeance."

He let out a roar, gritted his teeth and lunged to make contact with her wrist. His skin blistered and charred.

"Please. Please. Come back to me, *little dragon*."

At his touch the flames receded. Lia stood eerily calm with her palms extended and white hot tendrils of fire spreading from each hand. She appeared completely unharmed but everything around her was incinerated or burning.

Rygor lay on the floor, chest heaving. Lia reached down and picked up the dagger that had been laying outside Fehrn's cell. Gold now smeared with splattered blood and caked in ash.

"You're right. I don't want to live this kind of sick, twisted life. But I protect what is *mine."* With a flick of her wrist she encased the dagger in a bolt of white flame and plunged it into Rygor's stomach.

"You most likely won't die before someone finds you, but you can suffer a fraction of what you have inflicted on others. You and your masters took my life and my power from me. Drained me every day. Now you will know to fear me, for I will torch you all."

Rygor screamed in agony as the dagger burned and seared through his flesh, sunk as far as it would go, and wrapped in white fire that continued to burn as his blood spilled over the ground.

"Lia, we need to go. Please." Fehrn crept towards her warily. She wasn't fully aware of her surroundings he was sure of it. No white was visible in the full blackness of her eyes. He didn't want to startle her.

Gently taking her by the shoulder, he guided her along the passageway and out into the dawn.

The blue haze of morning light cast a glow across the castle courtyard. After coughing on the thick acrid smoke they both gulped in the fresh air. Fehrn surveyed the grounds. They could make a run for it. More guards would be coming.

"The walled garden. Can you run?" He touched her face. Was his *little dragon* still in there or had he lost her entirely to the flames? She nodded, clutching his forearm. He groaned in agony and she jerked back her hand.

"Oh, you're ... I burned you... I'm so sorry." She gaped at his blistered skin.

"It doesn't matter right now. We have to run for it." As he turned he felt her collapse under his hands. The surge of otherworldly magic she tapped into had surely ripped her apart. He tried to pick her up but his injuries prevented him from moving freely. They were sitting targets out in the open. Panic reared up his spine. He had no chance of getting them to safety. Even if he shifted into wolf form he would still be too injured to carry her. Dragging her in a half limp, he started for their escape route. Just make it to the walls. Get her into the forest.

Distant shouts began echoing through the battlements of the castle. More guards had seen the smoke billowing from the dungeon. They would capture them easily. He tried to run with Lia hooked around his neck. Pain seared along his body. He stumbled and they both dropped to the ground metres from the section of wall they needed to scale. How was he going to get them both over and into the freedom of the forest on the other side?

Footfall crunched to his right. Inhuman. Fehrn wheeled around flaring his claws ready to defend and protect.

A great white wolf. Majestic and like none he had ever encountered before.

Lowering its forequarters to the ground, the wolf nudged its snout against Lia's shoulder. Fehrn understood and carefully laid her onto the wolf's back.

"Hold tight, *little dragon."* He wrapped her hands in the wolf's mane. Once she was secure he shifted himself.

The two wolves sprang up and over the stone wall, then hurtled on into the forest. Fehrn could feel his injuries slowing him down but determinedly kept pace behind Lia where she clung to the back of the white wolf.

They reached the first clearing and saw two bodies bent over something on the ground. The shifter and the witch. He cradled the head of the vampiress, stroking her matted hair and murmuring. The witch was casting healing spells along her broken frail body. Her hands shook with the exertion as she offered what little healing magic she could muster.

Fehrn shifted back to his human form as they neared. Wincing and holding his side he checked that Lia was still gripping tightly to the other wolf's mane.

"Thank you," he addressed the wolf. "This means more than you will ever know." The great white head nodded in silent acknowledgement.

"Can you carry her? We have to move quickly now." Fehrn spoke now to the shifter and motioned to the vampiress in his arms.

"I'm unharmed. Let me carry you both, if you'll allow

me?" The shifter spoke softly to the witch crouched beside him.

"I can hold her and try again as we travel." The witch agreed.

Fehrn helped the witch position the vampiress on the back of her mate, now shifted into his wolf form, then ensured she too was secure.

"You have lost your power?" He could feel the witch tremble as she seated herself. Her face deathly pale. Gaunt eyes stared down at the broken body laid across her lap.

"Much has gone. Been taken from me. But there are fragments that remain. I will give whatever I can to aid her healing." Tears rolled down the witch's face.

Fehrn nodded solemnly to the others, then shifted.

They disappeared into the cover of the trees as the golden light of dawn began to filter through the forest above them.

CHAPTER 13

Lia floated in and out of consciousness for days. She could tell they had travelled an enormous distance. Stopping for no more than a few hours rest at a time. The mysterious white wolf gently carried her the entire way. She recalled seeing the familiar green and amber flecked irises of another wolf ever present beside her when she mustered enough strength to open her eyes for the briefest of moments.

Finally she found herself with enough strength to rouse from her haze. Strong arms enveloped her where she lay on a bed of moss. The light of a full moon illuminated the clearing where Lia and her *thief* lay wrapped together. She felt his body stir behind her and she twisted to face the source of familiar warmth surrounding her.

"You came back to me. I missed you, *little dragon."* The familiar voice rumbled softly.

She reached up to brush a hand down the side of his face, now healed of his wounds and bruises. Lines of weariness creased his features.

"Where are we?"

"On the outskirts of our lands. We are safe here, we crossed the borders earlier today. As long as we remain within this realm we are protected."

"Are the others..." She trailed off as the memories of the battle at the castle came rushing in.

"Safe, thanks to you... and they are healing, slowly." He ran his thumb gently over her bottom lip.

"You saved us all." Her *thief* pulled her tighter towards his chest.

Mine.

Lia's shoulders sagged. Relief coursed through her veins on hearing his thoughts. After everything, perhaps there was a chance he could forgive her?

"I don't know what happened. I had never experienced that kind of magic before. The rage, it engulfed me. It was as though once I knew the truth about it all I was able to finally access something that had been kept hidden from me."

I would have burned the world to get to you. To keep you safe. If they touch you again, they'll die.

Lia felt his strong hands flex against her skin.

"Without you we would all certainly be dead." His voice soft, yet his hold was possessive and fierce.

"It scared me. I lost myself within the fury of it all. I could have easily turned into a monster just like them."

He grasped her chin and turned her face to meet his.

"I promise we will find answers when we reach our destination. We can find out more on how your gift with the fire truly works, *little dragon.*"

Movement stirred behind her back. Lia immediately stiffened.

"Shhh... there's nothing to fear here." He pushed her hair back from her face.

"Would you like to try eating or drinking something?"

"Some water perhaps." Lia pushed herself up into a sitting position as her giant protector fitted himself behind her, supporting her back and cradling her head against his shoulder.

Her eyes widened at the scene before her. Across the other side of the clearing, no more than twenty feet from where she sat with Fehrn, three women huddled together talking in low whispers. The vampiress and the witch she had freed from the cells. The third woman with them had flowing snow white hair tucked in a loose bun. The stable-master. Lia's mouth dropped open.

"The scrap of coal dust awakens." Friendly, teasing eyes met hers in the moonlight.

"You? You are—were—have been a shifter all this time?"

"That's right. It has been my duty to operate as a spy within the castle for over two hundred years."

Two hundred years? Lia felt her mind begin to race.

"How..."

"Perhaps a story for another time." A deep grumble rose from the chest pressed hard behind her.

"Fehrn here has been more than a little concerned when you wouldn't wake." The witch rose and slowly moved forward to pass her a flask of water.

Fehrn? My thief. Her heart tripped over itself.

"I'm Nell. Thank you for saving us. We had been in captivity for... quite some time." The young witch gave a shy smile that attempted to hide the pain in her eyes.

Lia smiled back and gratefully sipped at the water. Her eyes flicked to the vampiress who sat with her arms curled around her legs, staring up at the full moon.

"That's Melinkya. She is still healing. She hasn't recovered the use of her vocal cords or her gifts yet. It will take a long time before she might fully be herself again I'm afraid." Nell returned to sit holding the hand of the vampiress who didn't seem to register they were talking about her.

"What happened to her mate? Did he survive?"

"He made the difficult decision to leave once we reached the safety of the border. He couldn't remain near her knowing the suffering she had endured. He blames himself. Their time in the dungeon... it broke both of them in different ways." Another deep murmur against her neck, followed by a gentle kiss.

"But she is his *mate.* How could he leave her?"

The white haired woman, who she had only ever known

as the stable-master, moved across the clearing to hand Lia some berries wrapped in a cloth.

"Enough questions. Here. Eat."

"Thank you. I suppose it made sense as a spy to never reveal your true identity to others at the castle? You know the other servants always speculated how long you had been the stable-master." Lia let out a brief chuckle.

The stable-master wiped her leathered hands against her slacks.

"My real name is Thena." She cocked an eyebrow in Lia's direction in the moonlight. "And I said that was enough questions, coal face. You need to rest." She motioned with her head over Lia's shoulder.

"Fehrn here will start growling again." With a roll of her eyes she turned back to the other two women.

Lia's heart skipped another beat. *My thief's name is Fehrn.*

Strong hands rubbed up and down her arms.

"Come, walk with me. You need to stretch your legs a little after so long travelling."

I'm never letting her go.

Taking his hand Lia stood to her feet, wobbling to gain her balance. Strong hands wrapped around her waist and steadied her as they walked beyond the clearing deeper into the forest. Sweet scents of pine and earthy moss caressed her senses. A trickling sound of water drifted on the breeze from a gentle stream up ahead.

They walked on in silence, his hand wrapped around hers, following a path leading closer to the source of the running water. As the trees cleared up ahead they stopped at the bank of the stream. Lia felt soft grasses cushion beneath her feet. Moonlight reached down through the gap in the tree tops to caress her skin.

"Fehrn... your name is Fehrn?" Lia squeezed his hand. Amber flecks glowed intensely in response to his name on her lips.

"It is."

"It suits you. Better than calling you *my thief* for the next hundred years." She reached up to touch his scarred eyebrow.

She wants to stay with me for a hundred years? I'll follow her to the ends of this world for eternity.

Firm hands grasped her hips to draw them closer together. Desire and hope for a future intermingling as their bodies pressed against one another. Fehrn slanted his mouth across hers, their tongues meeting in a slow, sensual kiss. Filled with quiet promises.

Never letting you go.

A flick of her tongue across his sent flares of heat tangling through her core. Lia sucked his bottom lip and pulled back just enough to look into his eyes.

"I have to tell you something. I'm a telepath. I can hear your thoughts."

His wolf appeared for the briefest second in his eyes. That amber glow punctuated the night.

"Oh, can you now?" He pinched at her hip. "Tell me then, what am I thinking?" The corners of his mouth ticked up.

You'll not be leaving my bed for a month. More like a year.

"Deplorable, despicable thoughts." Lia flashed a grin. "I couldn't hear them when we first met but then after the night in the gazebo, something changed. They just started coming through."

"What can I say. You've broken down my walls, stolen my heart and my mind."

"And I want you to know, you are the *thief* of my heart. The brightest flame burning within my soul." On her tiptoes she stretched up to kiss his chest. Lia felt her fire begin to dance with delight. Her core smouldered under his caress across her back and around her hips. Powerful hands moved lower, blazing a trail of ecstasy across her skin.

"I want to make sure you are alright. We have plenty of time now. There's no need to rush into anything while you're still healing." He whispered against her neck.

But I ache for you, little dragon.

"I ache for you too." Lia pressed her forehead to his chest.

"Fuck. This telepathy thing is going to get me into all sorts of strife, I can already tell." Fehrn rumbled with laughter as he licked slowly up the side of her neck. "You'll know every time I look at you exactly just how stimulating it is for me."

"Well, I can tell you that taking time for healing or not, there's more than just my usual fire going on for me right now."

"Tell me how I can help with that, *little dragon.*"

"Touch me, Fehrn. Please." She rolled her head back. An invitation. Her skin rippled with heat.

Growling with pleasure, he shifted his hands below her rear and lifted her off the ground. Her legs wrapped around his waist. Fehrn's hand slid beneath her hem, the other bracing her against him. His fingers stroked at her sex. Gentle and with a sensual pace. With his thumb he circled her clit, fingers spreading her.

"Mmmm... so beautiful." He murmured against her lips.

Lia twisted her hands in his hair to pull him down hard against her mouth. Demanding more. His hips thrust against her as he stroked her towards the release she so craved from him.

"I want you inside me." She gripped his shoulders. "Please."

All day and all night long.

He shifted his weight so they were wrapped together on the ground. Fehrn quickly removed his belt, freeing himself. His long, hard shaft positioned at her entrance.

"I love you, *little dragon.*" He sank slowly inside her.

Stay with me. Forever.

Heat erupted along Lia's spine. His cock thrust in shallow rhythm. Her walls stretched as he filled her with delicious friction.

"You are *mine.* And I am *yours.* I'll always stay." Her breathless whisper hot against his ear.

Fehrn groaned and plunged forward to sink all the way inside her. His hips slowly moved in and out. Their bodies in unison. Fitting together with perfection. Heat pooled and coiled low. Her fingers dug into his lower back. She urged him deeper. Harder.

"Yes... more. Please, Fehrn." She moaned.

Fuck. My name on your lips is addictive, little dragon.

Lia let out a sob. His thoughts brought on a flood of wetness. Her walls clamped around his cock in response.

He reached down to press his thumb against her clit. Pressure that danced a flame straight to her core. Sparks erupted across her vision. Lia's climax barrelled through her. His followed straight after with a shuddering groan.

Their chests rose and fell together in time with one another. Lia placed her hands against his chest to feel his thudding heart. He wrapped his arms tighter around her. Protective and certain.

Gazing up at the full moon hanging in the sky above them, she knew no matter what was to come she could trust this man with her heart, her mind, and her magic.

Her *mate.*

"I love you, Fehrn." Lia pulled him towards her, kissing him deeply.

Heat engulfed them both, melting away all that had separated them. Forging their bond. Sealing their souls into one.

Mated.

THANK YOU FOR READING

I hope you loved Lia and Fehrn's romance. If you want a peek into a little more of their story, including seeing Lia become an elite supernatural spy alongside Fehrn, you'll meet them again in Book Two of the Nocturnal Hearts series: IN DARKNESS WAITS DESIRE

Come join *The Cauldron*, my reader group for Nocturnal Hearts exclusives!

If you enjoyed this book as much as I adored writing it, please consider leaving a review on your favourite book website.

Reviews are crucial for any author and even just a few simple words can create incredible ripples of impact in helping this book and the Nocturnal Hearts series reach other lovers of paranormal romance.

Want to get your hands on bonus scenes from the extended Nocturnal Hearts world? You can download them at:

https://www.elliottroseauthor.com/bonuses

Acknowledgments

These characters and their story arrived in a chaotic whirlwind while I was in the midst of writing another book in the Nocturnal Hearts series. Lia and Fehrn's romance poured onto the page over the space of about two weeks and I am so incredibly grateful to the soul family in my life who helped me make this novella happen so incredibly fast.

Lazz - My rock and guide through the ups and downs of authorship. Thank you for believing in this book (and this entire series) from the very first moment before words even hit the page.

Dazz + Marz - I love you. Thank you for always supporting my vision and dreams.

Inca, Shilo, and Bert - My constant companions through the wild journey that writing can entail.

Thank you to my incredible behind the scenes team who have helped bring this book to life. Kerryn Hewson my editor and Sandra at Maldo Designs.

To my beta and advanced readers - The way you support these stories and characters gives me so much joy. Thank you for being here on this wonderful, magical journey. Thank you for your time spent giving feedback, sharing about this book, and helping her travel far and wide. You are incredible!

And finally, to you - the reader - thank you from the bottom of my heart.

ELLIOTT ROSE

paranormal Romance · nocturnal hearts Series

If you want to return to the Nocturnal Hearts world...

Keep reading for a sneak peek at the first two chapters of

In Darkness Waits Desire

Next in the Nocturnal Hearts Series

Book Two

~ In Darkness Waits Desire ~

Determined, gentle, and running from unspoken terrors of her past. Belle yearns for the freedom to be her own person, released from her life of enslavement and servitude.

One night will change everything, leaving her questioning what is real.

When she is hunted and nearly killed, Belle is thrust into a world she never knew existed. Alternate realms, supernatural beings, and a discovery of her unique powers... as a witch.

A witch with magic the likes of which hasn't been seen for centuries.

As she learns to navigate this new life and unravel the

questions from her past, she becomes tempted by the mystery of the fierce Guardian watching from the shadows.

Her protector.

The one keeping himself at a distance from everyone. Especially her.

Despite his cold exterior and stern glare that follows Belle into her dreams, she starts to feel something crack open the barriers she has long placed around her heart.

But when the secrets they both hold are brought to light the truth could destroy them all.

***

Aloof, reserved, and disciplined. Lachlan of Nocturne lives out his binding duty as Guardian of the Soterian Realm.

Beneath his brooding mask lies a dark secret. His plan for vengeance has been his sole focus for two hundred years... until he meets her.

A witch with the rarest of abilities, evil chasing her, and a fated destiny connecting them.

Trouble is, he has sworn to carry out his plan no matter what. To keep his dark secrets hidden away to himself. Making amends for nightmares of the past.

He'll ensure the necessary arrangements are in place to protect her. But having a *fated mate*?

That's a weakness.

The kind he cannot afford to indulge.

But day by day, his every fantasy that he daren't dream could become reality–a fierce beauty wrapped in a silk dress–breaks down his walls. Now he'll have to admit the truth he's denied for too long.

She's his.

Even if it will cost him everything.

CHAPTER 1

Blood pounded in Annabelle's ears.

She flattened her back against the stacked wooden barrels and willed herself to merge with the alleyway's long shadows. Ominous, twisted shapes thrown by the night lanterns where they hung in the darkness. The flickering amber light reflected on the wet cobbles below her boots.

She daren't breathe. The slightest noise might reveal her location.

Their presence had closed in on her all week. A menace that drew ever nearer. No matter how quickly she moved on to each new town, the shadows chasing her lingered around every corner.

Tonight she had been so desperately close. Nearly making it to the safety of the tavern when she felt the familiar chill sweep up the back of her neck. Instead she found herself fleeing down this darkened back alley in an attempt to shed her pursuers.

Crimson. Splattered and shining wet. Blood coating her hands. Stuck beneath her fingernails. Clogging her senses with its foul smell.

Belle squeezed her eyes shut. A futile attempt to block out the nightmare from six days ago.

Chilling tendrils of fog swirled towards her ankles. Her heart skittered faster at the sight of it reaching for her, like misshapen claws.

They had come. The fog was their disguise.

Her hand clamped over her mouth to stem her silent scream. Inch by inch she slid her back along the rough brick-work of the alleyway. Body braced to run. It was her only option left.

Might as well face death knowing she had tried every possible means of escape.

She pushed off the wall just a fraction, clutching her satchel tight against her chest. The tavern lay only half a mile from here. She listened intently for any hint of noise above her panicked heartbeat.

Silence, for now.

Time to lay her trust at the feet of the Goddesses.

On the count of three. Don't look back. One. Two. Thr—

She lurched forward into the pooled fog, bolting for the far end of the alley. Adrenaline spiked to urge her legs in a sprint away from the street. Out there she would be vulner-able in the open. Easy prey. These narrow passages behind the brick terraced houses would all connect somehow. If she followed their winding path it would lead her to sanctuary for the night.

The alley disappeared up ahead into a sharp right bend. She threw herself around the corner blindly.

Oooof. With a gnarly thud Belle collided into something —someone—at full force. A solid frame and large chest towered over her. The wind knocked out of her lungs. A gasp echoed through the dark as she tumbled onto the wet cobbles. Her body sprawled sideways with the force of the fall. Knees hit the ground first. Palms scraped across the grime-covered stones. A sharp sting of broken skin where the ground roughed across flesh. Her satchel flew out of reach with its meagre contents spilling forth into grimy puddles.

NO! Her eyes flew wide. With a painful motion her body dragged itself forward in a half crawl, half limp. She lunged desperately to grab at the leather handle.

"Watch where you're going, witch."

On all fours with her desperation laid bare, Belle stiffened from head to toe at the deep whiskey tone coming from directly behind her.

Did he just say witch?

Her mind desperately wanted to scream for help, but she was too winded to utter a word. Fear drowned out the urge, reminding her that she would be a fool to trust anyone. Her body raced with adrenaline as she carried on a painful crawl forward. Her burst satchel might as well have been an ocean away rather than mere feet.

The stranger would no doubt carry on his way into the night. This was a cold, cruel world as Belle had found out in the most heart wrenching of ways. You could only rely on yourself.

Fuelled by willpower blazing like a furnace she pushed herself to keep going. Inch by inch towards safety. This moment might be her final breaths, or if she could just keep fighting she might yet have a glimmer of hope to make it through til tomorrow.

A pair of charcoal leather boots came into view—expensive looking but well worn, blocking her from reaching her few possessions.

The stranger crouched down on his haunches meeting Belle at eye level and held her in a fierce stare. Searing aquamarine eyes met hers. Indifferent and cold. Unnatural against the inky grey damp of the night air. No hint of emotion crossed his face. His chiseled features were covered in trimmed dark stubble and thick brown hair, short but tousled, framing his face. The hint of some marking on his skin, tattooed up his neck, reaching from beneath his shirt. A heavy dark coat with a high collar almost moulded him into the night.

Her mouth went dry. She was held immobile as though hypnotised by that preternatural gaze. Like he saw right into her soul.

Suddenly she realised her fingers clutched the cracked leather handle of her satchel. The firm material heavy where it materialised beneath her scraped palms. How had it appeared in her hands? Did she hit her head and black out for a moment?

Belle didn't know how many seconds had passed and right now she didn't care. There was no time. She needed to get out of there. With a start she pushed off her knees, blindly stumbling away further into the night. Leaving the stranger to disappear in the fog behind her.

Don't look back. One foot in front of the other. Keep pushing.

Pain seared up her shins from the fall. Intensifying with every heavy thud of her boots against the cobbles. A limping run was the best she could muster. She reached out to steady herself against the brick wall to her right as she turned into the next alleyway. She winced as the roughness dragged across the fresh wounds on her palm, the gashes opening wider.

The fog whipped around her body. Damp lashed at her skin and plastered the edges of her long dark hair against her face. A chill sunk deep into her chest, boring in with a frightening intensity. *Evil.*

Looming in the fog were dark shapes, visible against the cloak of grey they shrouded themselves within. Ever so slowly and deliberately they closed in.

She had run out of time. The last grain of sand in the hourglass had begun a descent to the other side. A final voyage to the underworld.

So, this is what it feels like to meet with death.

As the fog thinned to reveal the edges of the forms

hunting her, a scream caught in her throat at the horrific sight appearing before her.

These were not the men she feared.

This was her every nightmare come to life. Her hands shook uncontrollably. It couldn't be real.

Skeletal creatures, grey skinned, and with sunken black holes where their eyes should be. Calculated. Efficient hunters. Long claws extending from bony fingers had blackened where they were caked in dried blood.

Two crawled on all fours and two more prowled upright. Somehow human in form, yet ghoul-like in appearance. Four mouths twisted into horrifying silent undead screams. The gaping maws appeared to be sewn closed.

Belle felt her chest seize up as though pinned in a vice. Her face drained of blood. A roaring in her ears hurtled forth as vertigo claimed her in its spiralling clutches.

There was no escaping this fate. She was trapped. Immobile. Frozen.

The first one lunged forward with a shriek and tackled her to the ground. The others followed. Enclosing her with their putrid stench. With a scream she tucked her knees trying to make herself into a ball, desperately shielding her head with the leather bag. Talons swiped at her cloak, shredding the fabric and wrenching it from her shoulders. Another vicious swipe and her satchel was cut to ribbons. She wrapped her head in her arms for futile protection, sobbing at the knowledge this would be it. *No no no no no.*

A savage scream erupted from her throat. Searing pain

tore through her side. Razor sharp claws dragged through flesh. Her entire right side felt as though it boiled her alive. Warm liquid gushed down her back where her dress and body had been ripped open.

Her right arm exploded in agony. Screams echoed into the empty night. More lacerations as claws tore open flesh and shattered bone. Red seeped into the blackened pool of water beneath her face, coating the cobblestones in a macabre sheen of violence.

Claws dug into her left calf, piercing the skin and gripping tight, dragging her further into the dense fog. Her arm hung twisted and mangled. With the other she clawed at the cobbles. Crying out in vain.

There was no one. Nothing that could save her from these monsters.

All she had wanted was to live a life of freedom. To one day be her own master. She had dreamed of being able to decide her own destiny and no longer be controlled by another person. Maybe this was all her destiny was to be. A short miserable life filled with heartbreak and hollow emptiness. The girl who had belonged to her wealthy aunt. Presented to the world as though part of the nobility, but in private she was controlled and abused. Enslaved as nothing more than a wretched servant.

Six days ago she had stared into her aunt's lifeless eyes. Shaking as she surveyed the gruesome scene. No memory of what had happened. Perhaps she was a murderer? Perhaps she deserved her own violent end.

But what would it have been to live a life of her own choosing? To have known true happiness. To have loved. To have experienced the love of another.

Her head went limp. Tingling numbness spread through her extremities. A metallic tang filled her mouth, running over her tongue.

This would be her fate. A sadistic and torturous finale.

Her eyes rolled back in her head at the blinding pain from her broken body. The fog encased her and amplified the sickening screeches filling the night air.

Out of nowhere a bolt of blue light filled the alleyway. Jagged lightning crackled through the fog like a whip. She felt the weight of the creature's pressure on her leg vanish. Its claws wrenched from where they pierced her skin. The four figures thrown backwards by an unseen force.

The fog began to swirl and compress into a tight ball surrounding each ghoul, lifting their horrific bodies into the air. Their foul clawed hands scrabbling at their throats as if being suffocated by the very fog they lurked within.

Belle rolled onto her side and pressed shaking fingers against the blood where it seeped through the bodice of her dress. There was too much. It gushed against her hand. Black spots crept in at the edges of her vision.

Charcoal leather boots stepped in front of her hazy vision. Long strides stalked towards the creatures with intent. Reaching under his coat, the stranger withdrew a short blade in each hand. Instead of silver metal these glowed with a bright blue flame.

His tall, broad stature was a towering physique before her. All muscle and a foreboding kind of strength. The kind of imposing power that held a steely facade and potential to strike, if necessary. Masculine beauty disguised a cold beast within.

And he had his prey in his sights.

The ghouls writhed and twisted where they each hung in the air. Grotesque choking filled the silence.

Belle's vision blurred. Unconsciousness dragging her under. It was far too late. But she could die in this moment safe in the knowledge she had been avenged.

The last thing she saw was four severed heads thudding to the ground in a flash of blue flame. Splatters of black blood oozed forth as the decapitated bodies crumpled in a heap behind them.

Then she was gone.

CHAPTER 2

Lachlan of Nocturne was many things to many different supernatural beings. Protector, defender, wise counsel, Guardian. What he was not was a sentimental fool.

From the moment he crouched down to help the girl sprawled on all fours on the cobblestones, he had sensed it. The whisper had come in undeniable and insistent from Source.

She is yours. Your fated mate.

Fuck. No. This would not be happening to him now. After two hundred years his plan had come together and he was not going to allow the fates of the Universe to derail his vengeance.

Vampires, shifters, and fae would most commonly have a *mate* fated to them. An instinctual drive and lifetime bond that could not be denied once awakened. Despite their strength and mystical gifts, it was a weakness that could always be exploited.

Witches had the power to choose, and Lachie chose to go it alone.

He growled to himself as he wiped his blades clean of the snatchers' blood. He turned as he sheathed them in their holsters below his coat. The sight of her mangled body lying in a pool of blood clenched something long iced over within his chest.

She was clearly working as a servant. Perhaps she had been one for the House of Elharean, judging by her ragged appearance. Lachie knew all too well the squalid conditions those in service to the powerful dark witches affiliated with the House of Elharean endured.

The girl—witch—seemed to be running from something or someone.

That didn't mean she was any of his concern. Most definitely not *his*. Certainly not his *fated mate*.

Lachie was regarded as the most powerful witch within his home realm. The chosen Guardian from an ancient lineage of practicing witches. He had been chosen to lead and protect his community. To safeguard supernaturals from the threat of the House of Elharean, a legion of dark witches who sought to enslave both supernatural and everyday people. Their dark agenda fed on the power within all who fell under their control. Lifetimes of servitude taken by force or coercion from all those who pledged their allegiance to the House of Elharean.

All beings here in this world had the potential for magic lying within them. The vast majority living outside of the supernatural community going about their normal, regular people lives had either forgotten the old ways long ago or their ancestors had deliberately turned their backs on magic.

His elite group of supernatural beings who served as his most trusted were highly trained and skilled in the art of spying, intelligence, and combat. They were also experts in covert operations here in the non-magical world, crossing the threshold between realms to eliminate packs of snatchers. Those ghoulish souls trapped in limbo and commanded to roam the non-magical world searching for newly awakened supernatural beings to deliver to their House of Elharean masters. He'd been tracking this pack, only they had behaved strangely tonight. Usually opportunists and scavengers, he hadn't witnessed such a direct hunting of any supernatural beings before. This was different. Unsettling in the way they had evaded him and managed to attack her before he could intervene.

They weren't going to kill her but their blood thirsty nature wouldn't stop them from savaging the witch before dumping her body with the House of Elharean.

Crouching down, he hovered his hands two inches in the air above her gaping wounds. One above her arm, the other moving over the largest lacerations on her side. Heat gathered in his palms as the healing spell took hold. Knitting bones back together and repairing the slashed open skin. A triage style enchantment would have to do to prevent her from bleeding out. A faint trace of magic still clung to her aura which meant she was alive, even if a mortal might have succumbed to these kinds of injuries by now.

He scowled to himself. He hated places like this. The narrow back alleys where only grime and menace could ever be found after dark descended. His magic roiled around inside of him. The air reeked of misery. No wonder the snatchers were drawn to these places. Where hope had long been extinguished from the vocabulary of the mortals suffering out their lives in overcrowding and destitution.

The last of her wounds closed over beneath his gaze. Porcelain soft skin now covered in gruesome welts. The evidence of untold savagery ran across her torso and arm as angry, red slashes. Back in his realm magic and healers would be able to do the rest now that he could safely move her.

Footfall crunched, moving towards him in the darkness. For a moment he tensed, ready to strike, before hearing a familiar voice call out.

"There he is. The prince of charm himself!" A hand clapped him on the shoulder, "I see you've also enjoyed happy hunting this night."

Ceranthe. A non-magical being—mortal—and a long-standing trusted ally in this strange world. His tussled sandy hair and lazy grin allowed him to move around with an easy charm. A perfect ear to the ground when rescuing supernaturals newly awakened to their magic.

"Oh shit! What happened?" He peered down at the figure twisted on the ground. "Will she live?"

"The pack got the drop on me. Never happened before." Lachie muttered through clenched teeth. "A witch. I'll portal her back with me."

"Aye, and best be soon from the look of those wounds. I finished off two others of the bastards. Found them lurking close to the tavern." Ceranthe slung his crossbow across his shoulder.

Lachie nodded sternly. "They seemed to be drawn to her. Hunting. I can't explain it."

Ceranthe's brow drew into a frown. "We've done all we can here tonight. You best be on your way, Lach."

"Are you sure you don't have any magic within you? Dispatching two like that on your own?" Lachie turned to eye his companion sternly. "That was reckless. I'll not be having you get yourself killed when you could—should—have waited for me."

"Is it so hard for you witches to believe that maybe I'm just that good? Mortal or not. My aim is true." Ceranthe shrugged his shoulders nonchalantly.

With a grunt Lachie shifted his weight and with an effortless motion scooped the limp frame of the woman into his arms. She suddenly consumed his every sense. Her soft curves beneath his fingertips. Plump mouth tinged with blue and slightly parted as she drew the shallowest of breaths. The heavy wet dress clung to her, shredded across her waist like a shipwrecked sail. The heavy material might as well have drowned her alive. Long brown hair hung in a single braid with the edges framing her face loose and plastered across her deathly pale cheeks.

Dragging his attention from her body cradled in his arms, Lachie fixed Ceranthe with a glare.

"You'll not do any more hunting without one of us to fight alongside you here. Or watch me come through the threshold to wring your neck myself."

Raising both hands in quiet surrender, yet with eyes crinkling in a smile, Ceranthe knew better than to say anything while Lachie was in this kind of mood.

Lachie tightened his grasp on the body in his arms. The rain and the wet cobbles of the alleyway began to dissolve as though into a thick smoke. It swirled closer around him, billowing and seething as the weightlessness took hold. Lachie drew her in tight, pressing his precious cargo to his chest. Closing his eyes, they both disappeared from the alleyway just as he heard the ethereal words ring loudly through his mind.

Protect her.

Also by Elliott Rose

THE NOCTURNAL HEARTS SERIES

Sweet Inferno

In Darkness Waits Desire

The Queen's Temptation

Vicious Cravings - August 2023

Brutal Birthright - November 2023

With more to come...

About the Author

Elliott Rose is an indie author of paranormal and dark fantasy romance. She lives in a teeny tiny beachside community in the south of Aotearoa, New Zealand with her partner and three rescue dogs. Find her with a witchy brew in hand, a notebook overflowing with book ideas, or wandering along the beach.

- Join her reader group *The Cauldron* for exclusive giveaways, BTS details, first looks at character art/inspo, and intimate chats about new and ongoing projects.
- Join her Newsletter for all the goodies and major news direct to your email inbox.

Illustration de couverture : *Mandala* de Kumagusu MINAKATA et *Kumano kodo,* chemin de pèlerinage au cœur des montagnes et forêts sacrées de la péninsule de Kii.

Photo au dos de la couverture : maison de Kumagusu MINAKATA à Tanabe (Japon).

Satoshi OHARA
Jean-Christophe VALMALETTE

MINAKATA Kumagusu

L'émergence d'une pensée écologique entre Orient et Occident

Golden Nihon Collection / AnimaViva multilingüe

Anima Viva
Multilingüe

Golden Nihon Collection

dirigée par Jacques KERIGUY

déjà paru dans la collection :

IKKYÛ. L'impertinence au service de la foi
par Sôshô YAMADA, 2012, ISBN 978-99920-1-966-5

L'Étrange voyage de Confucius au Japon
par Olivier ANSART, 2015, ISBN 978-99920-68-07-6

Penser le nucléaire. Autopsie d'une illusion
par Hiroaki KOIDÉ, 2015, ISBN 978-99920-68-06-9

AnimaViva multilingüe S.L.U.
AD700 Escaldes-Engordany, Principat d'Andorra
www.animaviva-publisher.com

Traduction du japonais : Myriam DARTOIS-AKO pour la partie Satoshi OHARA

Couverture et mise en page : Alberto JORGE

Impression : Bod GmbH, Norderstedt, Allemagne

ISBN livre imprimé : 978-99920-68-21-2
ISSN : 2305-8455
E-Pub: 978-99920-68-22-9
MobiKindle 978-99920-68-23-6
Dépôt légal : British Library, U.K.

Table des matières

3e Partie

Avertissement

En japonais, on nomme habituellement les individus par leur patronyme, que l'on fait suivre du prénom. Nous avons fait le choix de ne pas utiliser cette convention dans le présent ouvrage et, pour désigner le personnage qui fait l'objet de cette étude, d'accorder la préférence au prénom, Kumagusu, en raison de son caractère symbolique qui apparaîtra au fil du récit.

Golden Nihon Collection
dirigée par Jacques Keriguy

Who can do justice to Japan without sympathy ;
and how many writers on Japan have a grain of it ?...
But what a horribly difficult thing is to write about Japan !
The effort in itself dries me up.

Lafcadio Hearn, Letter to W. B. Mason,
1st of November 1892.

Cette collection se propose de jeter un regard sur l'ancrage spirituel, social, littéraire, artistique et culturel du Japon ; chaque volume la composant est consacré à un personnage qui, par ses actions, éclatantes ou furtives, par ses mots, exaltés ou secrets, par l'élan qu'il a impulsé, frénétique ou fragile, a introduit une rupture dans les pratiques intellectuelles ou sensibles de ses contemporains et a contribué à modeler l'imaginaire nippon. Ces éclats d'érudition ont pour objectif de bâtir une trame sur laquelle, depuis ses lointaines origines, se noue la mémoire d'un pays qu'un amas de clichés dérobe à la vue de l'étranger.

Appartenant à différentes écoles de recherche ou d'enseignement, les auteurs, japonais ou occidentaux, ont en commun la complicité qu'ils entretiennent avec le sujet de leur étude : non contents de l'insérer dans l'époque où il s'est épanoui, ils cernent les traces de sa mémoire auprès des générations qui se sont succédé jusqu'à nos jours. C'est, me semble-t-il, une façon de mettre en relation les modes de pensée de l'Orient Extrême et de l'Occident, que l'on considère trop souvent encore comme opposés, sinon inconciliables.

Provocatrice, paradoxale, atypique, polémique, les adjectifs ne manquent pas pour qualifier la personnalité de Kumagusu Minakata (1867-1941). Qui, mieux que lui, a incarné l'esprit d'ouverture, la quête de savoirs ? Qui a davantage pressenti et symbolisé les mutations scientifiques, politiques et sociales de l'ère Meiji ? Ces mutations, il les a rassemblées pour parvenir à une conception subtile de l'écologie, science alors émergente, et lui conférer une dimension proprement extrême-orientale. Le présent ouvrage invite à suivre le cheminement de cet autodidacte solitaire, né dans les forêts de Kumano, situées au cœur de la spiritualité japonaise. Il quitta son Japon natal à l'âge de dix-neuf ans. Quinze années d'errance lui permirent de parcourir les États-Unis, les Caraïbes, l'Amérique latine, puis de s'installer à Londres avant de regagner le village natal. Dans ce pays où le sentiment de la nature touche au sacré, Kumagusu construisit un itinéraire intellectuel singulier : il se consacra d'abord à la botanique, puis tenta de bâtir une ethnologie englobant Orient et Occident ; il développa ainsi une vision originale de la logique scientifique à la veille du grand bouleversement que subit la science contemporaine au XXe siècle. Tout ce temps, il le mit à profit pour élargir son horizon intellectuel et acquérir des connaissances très disparates. Ses voyages et ses vagabondages dans l'espace intellectuel le conduisirent à fréquenter de nombreuses personnalités marquantes avec lesquelles il tissa des liens d'amitié profonde et durable. Parmi elles, Sun-Yat sen, fondateur de la Chine moderne qui lui promit la création d'un parc botanique au mont Loufu, ou Ueshiba Morihei, fondateur de l'aikidô, un art martial qui porte son empreinte. Dans un Japon marqué par une hiérarchisation sociale implacable, ce personnage excentrique et provocateur parvint à séduire le jeune empereur Hiro Hito, qui lui consacra un haiku.

Kumagusu était encore mal connu dans son pays il y a quelques années : son refus de se plier aux règles académiques lui fit ombrage, sans doute, mais l'audace et l'originalité de sa pensée commencent à être reconnues.

Parmi les premiers, il a contribué à introduire les principes de la science occidentale au Japon ; à l'inverse, il fit connaître la pensée orientale à des chercheurs qui en ignoraient l'existence. Précurseur, il l'a été, dans plusieurs domaines : la botanique et l'entomologie, bien sûr, mais aussi la sociologie comparative, l'éthnologie, dont il a dessiné les premiers contours, sans oublier l'écologie, à laquelle il a donné une dimension sociale et spirituelle. Il a aussi livré des réflexions sur la philosophie bouddhiste et sur l'évolution politique de son pays. Ses archives sont conservées à Kii-Tanabe et un musée lui est consacré dans le district de Nishimuro-gun.

Les auteurs, Satoshi Ohara et Jean-Christophe Valmalette, tous deux universitaires, ont souhaité faire connaître à l'Occident, qui l'ignore, le personnage de Kumagusu. Ils ont consulté et exploité les documents disponibles parmi les archives abondantes ; ils ont recensé son œuvre immense et composite ; ils l'ont analysée ; ils nous en livrent dans cet ouvrage leur interprétation ; ils la situent dans les mouvements de pensée qui ont éclos tout au long du XXe siècle et la projettent dans la modernité la plus novatrice. Derrière leurs propos transparaît une fascination que, loin de masquer, ils justifient avec conviction et transmettent sans peine au lecteur.

La collection Golden Nihon, qui accueille leur ouvrage, le premier consacré à Kumagusu MINAKATA en une langue autre que le japonais, remplit la mission qu'elle s'est fixée de faire connaître des aspects méconnus de la culture japonaise, et répare une injustice.

Jacques Keriguy

Source: *Minakata Kumagusu Archives.*

Kumagusu Minakata (1867-1941) est un homme excentrique, considéré comme un génie dans son pays, où l'anticonformisme fascine. Issu de la province de Kii (l'actuelle préfecture de Wakayama), il est un autodidacte hors du commun, auteur d'un grand nombre de publications scientifiques, dont cinquante parues dans la prestigieuse revue *Nature* et trois cent vingt-trois publiées dans la célèbre revue de sciences humaines *Notes and Queries*. Son œuvre prolifique embrasse des domaines très variés : la biologie (en particulier la mycologie), l'astronomie, l'archéologie, l'anthropologie, l'ethnologie, la philosophie. Il maîtrise treize langues et ses travaux de recherche ont pour champ le monde entier. Le regard de cet encyclopédiste japonais oscille entre Orient et Occident, entre passé et présent. Il nous invite dans un cheminement inattendu et souvent complexe à mieux comprendre les transformations du monde dans ce qu'il a de permanent et d'universel.

Kunio Yanagita, l'un des plus grands ethnologues japonais, disait de lui qu'il « avait repoussé les limites des Japonais ». Kumagusu apparaît aussi comme une figure pionnière de l'écologie moderne par les liens qu'il révèle entre facteurs biotiques et pratiques folkloriques, tous deux ancrés dans un territoire commun. Si son action est fortement engagée dans la protection de l'environnement sur l'archipel, ses idéaux sont le rapprochement des sciences de la nature avec les sciences humaines et sociales et le respect de la nature et de la diversité, autant de grands axes susceptibles de guider l'humanité au XXIe siècle.

Outre la présentation d'un cheminement scientifique singulier, produit d'une alchimie entre philosophies orientales et occidentales, le présent ouvrage serait incomplet s'il ne présentait un portrait de l'homme reposant sur des anecdotes singulières, parfois savoureuses, et s'il n'évoquait les riches amitiés qu'il a cultivées. Plutôt qu'une présentation académique de son œuvre, le lecteur est invité à suivre le regard croisé de deux scientifiques contemporains, l'un japonais, l'autre français, sur l'un des derniers « encyclopédistes » dont la vie et les pensées balancent entre Orient et Occident. Cet ouvrage, qui peut parfois paraître partial et passionné, doit être considéré comme une première présentation de Kumagusu au public occidental.

La démarche semble utile, indispensable même : au Japon, le nom de Kumagusu Minakata émerge des ténèbres de l'oubli vers la fin des années 1980 seulement ; il figure aujourd'hui dans certains manuels scolaires. Le personnage est devenu héros de mangas et l'on a même donné son nom à un astéroïde qui se promène quelque part entre Mars et Jupiter. À l'étranger, son nom apparaît parfois dans des revues d'ethnologie, d'écologie ou encore de biologie, mais les références sont rares ; elles ne présentent d'ailleurs qu'une facette du personnage. La première contribution en une langue autre que le japonais revient à Carmen Blacker, de la British Academy, spécialiste du folklore et de la religion du Japon à l'université de Cambridge. En 1983, elle a publié dans la revue spécialisée *Folklore* un article intitulé « Kumagusu Minakata, le génie japonais ignoré ».

Enfin, alors que l'on croise son nom dans les biographies de nombreuses personnalités sur lesquelles il a exercé une influence majeure et qu'il existe aujourd'hui de nombreux ouvrages en langue japonaise sur sa personne et son œuvre, on ne peut que regretter le manque de documents permettant aux lecteurs non japonophones d'appréhender sa pensée. La vie de ce personnage complexe, parfois excentrique mais assurément en avance sur son temps, gagne à être mieux connue en Occident. Le mot célèbre de Buffon « Le style est l'homme même » semble, à la lumière de la vie, de la pensée et de l'action de Kumagusu, avoir été écrit pour lui.

LES CRÉPITEMENTS DE LA PASSION

L'éveil du tengu

Kumagusu Minakata voit le jour le 15 avril 1867, à la veille de l'ère Meiji (*Meiji-Isshin*, 1868-1912) qui marque une profonde transformation dans l'organisation politique, sociale et économique du Japon. Il est le fils cadet d'une famille de marchands aisés de Tanabe, petite ville de la péninsule de Kii, à la bordure des montagnes sacrées de Kumano (« pays des ours »), haut lieu de la spiritualité du Japon. Lieu favorable s'il en est : Tanabe se trouve non loin de la capitale Nara où s'est installée la cour impériale entre 710 et 184. Il est également proche du mont Kôya, centre du bouddhisme de l'école Shingon ainsi que du grand sanctuaire shintô d'Ise. À peine plus loin se trouve la riche cité d'Ôsaka, parfois considérée comme la Venise de l'Orient, située au fond de la Mer Intérieure du Japon, qui connaît en cette deuxième moitié du XIXe siècle une extraordinaire croissance industrielle et devient pour quelques décennies la première ville du pays. Le père de Kumagusu, Yahei Minakata, à peine lettré, a déjà bâti l'une des plus importantes fortunes de la province de Wakayama en faisant le commerce de matériel de quincaillerie. La famille est bouddhiste, profondément ancrée dans l'école Shingon. Elle nourrit le jeune enfant de textes et de contes bouddhistes qui vont l'influencer durablement.

Sculpture d' Ojizo sama, *pris dans le tronc d'un* sugi *(cèdre) plusieurs fois centenaire dans le cimetière du mont Kôya. Ces sculptures sont traditionnellement déposées après la mort d'un bébé ou d'un enfant.*

Un premier épisode marque profondément son existence. Dès son plus jeune âge, une gastrite chronique sévère fait planer des doutes sur ses chances de survie, mais, grâce aux prières de guérison adressées par son père au majestueux et millénaire camphrier (*kusunoki*) sacré du sanctuaire Fujishiro que vénère la famille Minakata, l'enfant se rétablit. C'est d'ailleurs le nom de cet arbre qui fournit l'un des deux caractères chinois choisis pour le prénom du jeune Kumagusu.

Camphrier millénaire du temple Fujishiro (ville de Kainan) sous lequel son père conduisait Kumagusu atteint d'une maladie digestive pour obtenir sa guérison.

Le garçon court la campagne autour de Tanabe. Bon marcheur, il est, semble-t-il, capable de parcourir sans effort jusqu'à cinquante kilomètres par jour en terrain accidenté. Cette aptitude lui vaut, dans son enfance, le surnom de *Tengyan*, diminutif affectueux de *tengu*. Cette créature légendaire, mi-homme mi-oiseau qui vit dans les montagnes, est censée kidnapper les humains ; elle demeure très présente aujourd'hui encore dans l'imaginaire japonais.

Le signe du kusunoki (楠)

Toute la vie de Kumagusu est placée sous le signe du camphrier (*kusunoki*), l'arbre vénéré qui veille sur le moindre sanctuaire shintô. Ce n'est donc pas par hasard que ses parents, guidés par le prêtre, choisissent à sa naissance de le prénommer Kumagusu (熊楠). En effet, selon la tradition japonaise, la signification des *kanji* accompagne l'enfant durant sa vie entière. Le premier *kanji* (熊) signifie « ours » et le second (楠) désigne le camphrier (« arbre 木 du Sud 南 »). Les *kusunoki* millénaires protègent des attaques de la foudre et des insectes la myriade de petits sanctuaires shintô villlageois. En retour, les sanctuaires, espaces sacrés, lieux de transition entre culture et nature, préservent les *kusunoki* par leur présence. Comme par un effet de miroir, le *kusunoki*, abri d'une biodiversité exceptionnelle, a guéri le très jeune Kumagusu alors qu'il était atteint de maladie chronique ; à leur tour, nombre de ces immenses *kusunoki* échapperont à l'abattage grâce à l'action de Kumagusu contre la politique de regroupement de cette multitude de petits sanctuaires.

Ce surnom de *Tengu* trouve également une autre origine : totalement absorbé par la collecte d'échantillons pour son herbier, Kumagusu passe fréquemment plusieurs jours dans les collines sans rentrer chez lui, oubliant de manger comme de dormir. Il suscite ainsi l'inquiétude de sa famille qui craint qu'il n'ait été enlevé par un *tengyan*. L'enfant reçoit un autre surnom : le *Ruminant*. Comme les vaches qui remâchent leurs aliments, il se montre capable en tout lieu et à toute heure de régurgiter volontairement sa nourriture.

Kumagusu se passionne pour l'étude dès son plus jeune âge. En 1873, il entre à l'école primaire Ono, établissement public fondé par le gouvernement de Meiji pour promouvoir l'instruction moderne. Dans le même temps, il fréquente aussi des établissements privés survivants de l'époque d'Edo ; il étudie la morale dans un cours néo-confucianiste et les classiques chinois dans un cours d'études chinoises. Il reçoit de ce fait une double éducation, classique et moderne.

Ni l'école ni les cours privés ne suffisent pourtant à étancher sa soif de connaissances. Durant ces années, Kumagusu manifeste un fort intérêt pour les animaux et les plantes ; lorsqu'il trouve un spécimen intéressant sur le chemin de l'école, il avale sur-le-champ son déjeuner pour vider la boîte à bento qui le contient et y fourrer grenouilles et crabes, afin de les observer. Et quand il joue dehors avec des camarades, il les quitte soudain pour aller cueillir seul des champignons dans les collines ou des algues au bord de l'eau. À cette époque déjà, son immense curiosité et sa mémoire surhumaine sont à l'œuvre : il veut apprendre par lui-même. Dès l'âge de sept ans, il écume les maisons de ses camarades et les librairies à la recherche de livres rares qu'il lit, mémorise et, de retour chez lui, il recopie tout ce qui lui tombe sous la main. Pour commencer, il s'attelle à la retranscription des cent cinq volumes de la célèbre encyclopédie de la période Edo *Wakan sansai zue*. Suivent bien d'autres ouvrages également fondés sur des encyclopédies chinoises ; il s'agit là d'une prouesse incroyable pour un enfant de cet âge. Leur lecture nécessite le déchiffrage de plus de dix mille *kanji*, pour la plupart obsolètes dans ce Japon qui, en généralisant l'usage des *kana*, permet aux adultes moyennement instruits de se contenter de la connaissance d'environ deux à trois mille *kanji*.

Kumagusu passe cinq ans à reproduire le détail des notices illustrées sur la faune et la flore, puis, en à peine une année, les cinquante-deux volumes du dictionnaire de botanique *Bencao gangmu*. Mais sa curiosité est loin d'être satisfaite. À partir de douze ans, il se plonge dans la description précise de plantes et de leur usage médicinal qu'il trouve notamment dans l'herbier chinois du XVIe siècle *Pen-tsao kang mu*. Il recopie le *Yamato honzô* (« Précis de botanique japonaise »), un autre herbier du début du XVIIe siècle, que l'on doit au philosophe néo-confucianiste japonais Kaibara Ekken, considéré comme l'« Aristote japonais », ou encore le *Nihongi* (« Annales du Japon »), le *Shôkoku meisho zue* (« Recueil illustré de lieux célèbres »), l'encyclopédie populaire Ôzassho, le dictionnaire *Setsuyôshû* et même le *Taiheiki* (« Chronique de la grande paix »), soit en tout une cinquantaine d'ouvrages.

Cette boulimie pour l'écriture lui est certainement inspirée par le plaisir que procure le geste même de la calligraphie : outre sa valeur picturale, le mouvement qu'elle inspire est chargé d'une forte densité poétique. Kumagusu savoure très jeune cet instant où le *sumi* (le bâton d'encre) fraîchement frotté sur le *suzuri* (la pierre à encre) humecté, permet au pinceau de révéler la subtilité de la lumière comme dans un délicat camaïeu. Le processus de lecture, incluant la mémorisation et la retranscription, permet ainsi à Kumagusu d'accumuler, dès ses années d'écolier, une foule de connaissances. Il gardera toute sa vie cette mémoire et cette ténacité exceptionnelles qui lui vaudront d'être qualifié d'« encyclopédie vivante ».

© J-C Valmalette

Nécessaire de calligraphie de Kumagusu : fude *(pinceau),* sumi *(encre),* suzuri *(pierre à encre). Source: Minakata Kumagusu Museum.*

Ses activités de copiste font parler de lui ; on le considère comme un enfant prodige. De fait, il obtient son certificat d'études primaires à l'école Ono en trois ans. Son père, Yahei, qui tient près du château de Wakayama un commerce florissant, la boutique Saikaya, semble avoir tout d'abord considéré Kumagusu comme peu digne de la lignée familiale de marchands.

Saika

Le nom propre *Saika*, dont s'inspire celui de la boutique du père de Kumagusu, *Saikaya*, est fort répandu à Wakayama. Sa déclinaison la plus connue est sans doute le Saikashû, qui désigne un groupe de combattants de l'époque Sengoku (milieu du XVe siècle – fin du XVIe siècle) issu des environs de la ville de Wakayama. Sous l'autorité de Magoichi Suzuki, il a opiniâtrement résisté à Oda Nobunaga (1543-1582), premier unificateur du Japon, à ce titre déterminé à mettre le pays entier sous sa coupe ; il est aussi le groupe armé le plus puissant de l'époque. Le Saikashû rassemble non les grands seigneurs guerriers et leurs vassaux, mais des gens du peuple, pêcheurs et agriculteurs, pour lesquels la liberté a plus de prix que le pouvoir et la richesse, sans doute parce que, grâce aux abondants bienfaits de la nature tirés de la mer, des rivières et des montagnes de la région de Wakayama, grâce aussi à un climat doux, l'environnement était propice à la vie humaine. Les habitants de la préfecture de Wakayama possèdent un tempérament que l'on peut qualifier de généreux, si l'on cherche à le mettre en valeur, ou, dans le cas contraire, de nonchalant. Leur générosité et la chaleur du terroir ont sûrement contribué à modeler le caractère de cet anticonformiste qu'était Kumagusu.

Yahei se ravise cependant : Kumagusu est peut-être la réincarnation du frère aîné de sa défunte épouse, féru d'études. Yahei a en effet été adopté par les Minakata, la famille de sa première femme, selon la tradition. En partie pour témoigner sa reconnaissance à sa famille d'adoption, il décide de respecter les vœux de son fils et lui fait suivre des études, ce qui est encore rare pour un fils de marchand en ce début d'ère Meiji. De ce fait, comme il le souhaitait, Kumagusu intègre l'école Shôshû, puis, en 1879, à la disparition de cet établissement, le nouveau collège de Wakayama. Mais dans cette institution, Kumagusu n'est plus l'enfant prodige d'autrefois, ses notes laissent à désirer. En effet, aux leçons ennuyeuses et parfois inexactes, il préfère l'observation des êtres vivants dans leur milieu naturel, la lecture et la retranscription, activités bien plus intéressantes à ses yeux. Kumagusu est convaincu qu'il « suffit de travailler juste ce qu'il faut pour obtenir le diplôme. La vie est courte, il n'y a pas de temps à perdre avec des matières détestables. » Il n'aime pas le collège, à une seule exception : les cours dispensés par Hiraku Toriyama, qu'il appellera « maître » toute sa vie, avec déférence. Toriyama, aujourd'hui connu en tant qu'auteur des paroles de *Warship March*, l'une des trois plus grandes marches militaires du monde, est un intellectuel préoccupé d'études nationales *kokugaku*, géographie et études occidentales ; il enseignera plus tard à l'école Gakushûin.

L'instruction de Kumagusu était jusqu'alors axée sur des connaissances asiatiques, issues de la Chine et du Japon. Mais les savoirs nouveaux venus d'Europe, auxquels il accède à travers ce professeur, le stimulent fortement et renforcent sa soif de connaissances. Sous la direction de Toriyama, il rédige à la main une Étude des animaux en s'appuyant sur des originaux anglais qu'il compare avec des ouvrages sino-japonais. Ce manuel, réalisé en autodidacte, avec son classement systématique de la faune, préfigure les articles scientifiques ultérieurs pour lesquels Kumagusu puisera dans ses vastes connaissances asiatiques et occidentales. Par ailleurs, les encouragements de Toriyama, qui lui conseille de faire des études d'histoire naturelle, considérant qu'il fera un bon chercheur, émeuvent profondément Kumagusu et renforcent encore son intérêt pour cette discipline : ne lui laisse-t-elle pas entrevoir, par l'oculaire du microscope, un monde inconnu et fascinant ?

En puisant abondamment dans la littérature classique chinoise et sa représentation du monde, qui s'articule entre « Ciel-Terre-Homme » et dans laquelle tout objet trouve sa place, le savoir du jeune adolescent se structure à l'écart du nouveau modèle académique de l'ère Meiji. Entre 1639 et 1868, le gouvernement shôgunal avait appliqué le *sakoku-rei* (« politique isolationniste »), qui punissait de mort tout contact avec les Occidentaux, à l'exception des Hollandais, contenus dans le mince îlot de Dejima. Par son intermédiaire furent importés parcimonieusement quelques reflets de la science européenne, qui donnèrent naissance au *rangaku* (« études hollandaises »). La restauration de l'ère Meiji, à l'inverse, s'emploie à construire la conscience nationale sur le fameux slogan *wakon yosai,* « esprit japonais, talent occidental » lancé par Yoshikawa Tadayasu l'année même de la naissance de Kumagusu. Les pratiques traditionnelles sont systématiquement remplacées par les modèles occidentaux « supérieurs » dans tous les domaines de la société : organisation politique, modèle économique, éducation, relations sociales, technologie et organisation militaires. Kumagusu n'a que quinze ans lorsqu'il écrit que « son but ultime est de concevoir, à l'échelle de la planète, une encyclopédie unifiant les connaissances japonaises, chinoises et occidentales sur le cosmos, la Terre et l'homme, sous la forme d'un mandala. »

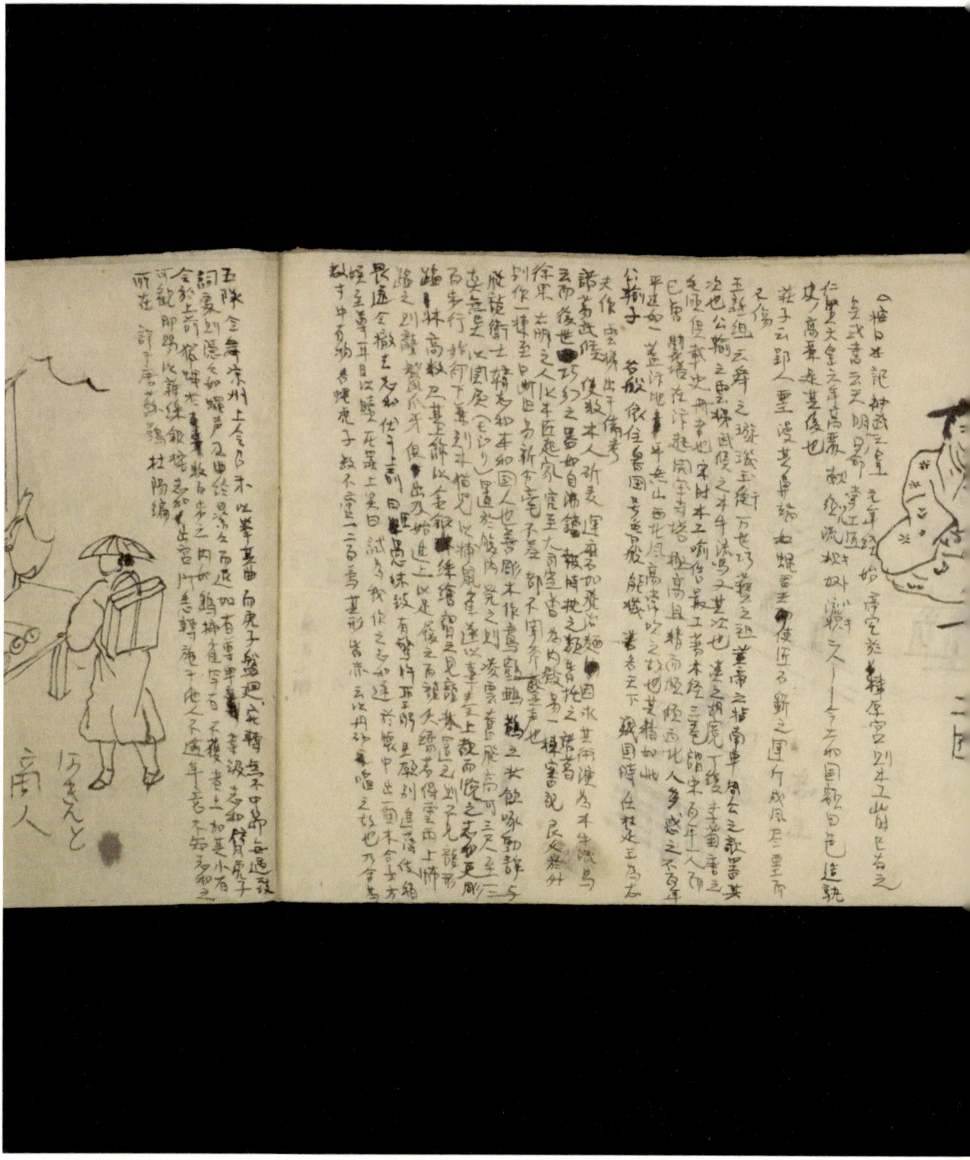

Illustration réalisée par Kumagusu (âgé de huit à douze ans) à partir de la célèbre encyclopédie illustrée sino-japonaise Wakan Sansai Zue, *publiée en 1712, durant la période Edo. Source: Minakata Kumagusu Archives.*

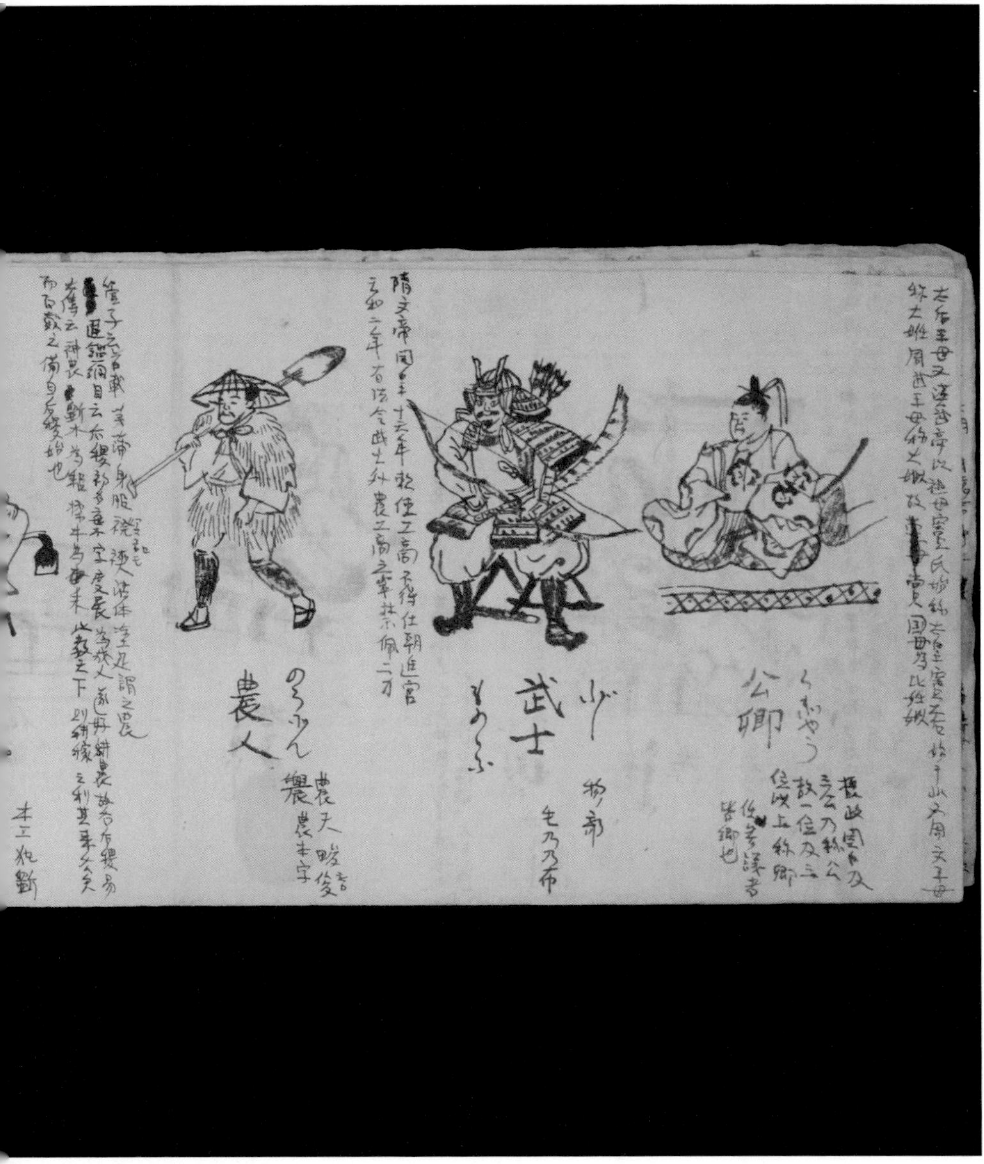

くわぎやう
公卿
武士
もののふ
のうにん
農人

« *Je ferai connaître le Japon au monde entier* »

En 1883 (an 16 de l'ère Meiji), Kumagusu, diplômé du collège de Wakayama, intègre l'école Kyôryû dans le quartier de Kanda à Tokyo. Cet établissement ouvre la porte à l'école préparatoire de l'Université de Tokyo. Creuset du mouvement de modernisation, la nouvelle capitale est une ville immense où flottent les effluves du monde occidental, mais ses habitants ont encore une mentalité campagnarde ; Kumagusu n'y trouve guère l'esprit de défense des libertés et des droits du peuple auquel il s'attendait. Par ailleurs, les cours dispensés à l'école Kyôryû le laissent sur sa faim : en sciences naturelles notamment, il considère qu'aucun professeur ne possède plus de connaissances que lui. Comme l'on pouvait s'y attendre, il passe plus de temps à la bibliothèque qu'en classe, pour y lire avec avidité. Il fait néanmoins une exception notable pour les cours d'anglais du directeur de l'école, Korekiyo Takahashi (futur premier ministre), qui, pour faire rire ses camarades, surnommait *Nanpô* cet élève assidu. Le patronyme Minakata peut en effet également se lire *nanpô*, « méridional, tropical ».

À l'époque, Kumagusu a déjà décidé de consacrer sa vie à la biologie. Quand il apprend dans le journal que Miles J. Berkeley, un botaniste britannique qu'il respecte, a recueilli avec l'Américain Curtis A. Moses six mille spécimens de *fungi* et qu'ils ont publié le premier herbier de champignons au monde, Kumagusu s'enflamme : « Je mettrai ma fierté d'homme à faire mieux, et je ferai connaître le nom du Japon au monde entier avec sept mille échantillons. »

Un an plus tard, Kumagusu réussit brillamment le difficile concours d'entrée à l'école préparatoire. Cet établissement a pour vocation la formation des élites de l'ère Meiji, bâtisseurs de l'université moderne appelée à transformer en profondeur la société japonaise. Il provient du regroupement d'anciennes institutions du shôgunat Tokugawa où s'assimilait la science occidentale sur fond d'isolationnisme. Cette école préparatoire deviendra trois ans plus tard l'Université impériale puis l'Université impériale de Tokyo, et enfin la très prestigieuse Université de Tokyo.

À cette époque, Kumagusu fréquente Shiki Masaoka, avant qu'il ne devienne l'un des quatre maîtres japonais du haïku, et Natsume Sôseki, le romancier qui fera découvrir les auteurs occidentaux aux Japonais. Parmi ses camarades figurent aussi de futurs grands noms, comme l'écrivain Bimyô Yamada, le vice-amiral Saneyuki Akiyama, le professeur de l'Université de Tokyo et spécialiste de littérature japonaise Yaichi Haga ou encore Kôtarô Honda, professeur de l'Université du Tôhoku et premier directeur de l'Institut de recherche sur les métaux. Surnommé le roi du fer, autorité mondiale dans le domaine de l'acier, Honda est l'un des plus grands chercheurs en matériaux du Japon, inventeur du plus puissant aimant permanent de l'époque.

Malgré leurs qualités, les cours de l'école préparatoire, rêves de toute l'élite japonaise, ne trouvent pas grâce aux yeux de Kumagusu. Aux cours magistraux, il préfère la bibliothèque : il y poursuit inlassablement la transcription d'ouvrages. Il se passionne aussi pour les musées, les jardins botaniques ; il observe, dessine, prend des notes et collecte des échantillons dans les parcs qu'il fréquente plus assidûment que les bancs de l'université. Lui qui ne sait qu'adorer ou détester n'est pas fait pour ce système d'éducation sélectif où il faut avoir la moyenne dans chaque matière pour passer à l'année supérieure. Ses résultats sont très inégaux. En particulier, il semble n'avoir pas supporté les cours de gymnastique dispensés par un professeur français : il n'y assiste pratiquement jamais.

À l'époque, Kumagusu s'enthousiasme également pour l'archéologie ; il se consacre à des fouilles aux alentours d'Ômori et de Suzugamori (situé dans le Grand-Tokyo), où l'on trouve des outils en pierre, des poteries et des ossements anciens. Il va aussi à Enoshima et Kamakura (préfecture de Kanagawa) pour ramasser des échantillons de coquillages. Pendant les grandes vacances, avec des amis, il pousse jusqu'à Nikkô (préfecture de Tochigi), où il cueille des plantes pour son herbier.

Kumagusu déteste l'école mais il aime les études et semble bien profiter de sa jeunesse : il mange de la viande de bœuf, boit de la bière à satiété, prend du bon temps avec ses camarades, va au spectacle et fréquente les salles de *rakugo*, où un conteur récite des historiettes littéraires humoristiques qui autorisent parfois la vulgarité. Il se passionne pour ce style de théâtre.

Kumagusu n'est pas particulièrement obnubilé par la gent féminine, mais ses écrits en japonais, des simples missives aux articles scientifiques les plus sérieux, sont parsemés d'allusions salaces. Le commentaire qu'il accole à un spécimen de champignon « parfaitement semblable au pénis avec le prépuce rétracté », n'en est qu'un avant-goût ; une missive officielle adressée à un cadre de l'entreprise Nippon Yusen donne des explications sur les positions sexuelles, et il régale un membre du gouvernement de l'histoire d'un remède souverain pour séduire les jeunes filles vierges. Les anecdotes paillardes liées à Kumagusu sont légion. Il existe deux raisons susceptibles de justifier son goût pour la grivoiserie. La première est qu'il s'agit d'un moyen de captiver son auditoire car, dit-il, « en règle générale, les Japonais se lassent facilement des longs discours et sans une grivoiserie ou une blague entre deux explications, ils ne restent pas concentrés tout du long. » La seconde est que Kumagusu place le sexe à la base de l'étude anthropologique. Plus tard, il critiquera d'ailleurs vivement son ami Kunio Yanagita en ces termes : « Scruter les régions où pullulent les pratiques indécentes, c'est ça l'étude du folklore, nulle vraie recherche n'est possible si on exclut ce domaine. »

Bien entendu, le quotidien insouciant d'étudiant de Kumagusu à l'école préparatoire à l'Université de Tokyo ne dure pas longtemps. D'après son bulletin de notes, il obtient aux examens de fin de deuxième année une moyenne insuffisante, notamment en algèbre, matière qu'il goûte peu. Le règlement de l'école, très strict, prévoit le redoublement en cas de note inférieure à la moyenne ne serait-ce que dans une seule matière, et ce, quelle que soit la moyenne générale.

Kumagusu n'est pas parvenu à trouver sa place dans ce système académique et c'est sans surprise que ces deux années se soldent par un échec à l'examen final ; sur les cent treize élèves de sa promotion, quarante -sept redoublent. Son camarade Masaoka, qui redouble deux fois, parviendra à décrocher son diplôme en six ans, mais Kumagusu, en février de l'année suivante, quitte l'établissement sur ces mots : « Pas question de rester dans cette école qui fait redoubler des génies comme moi. » Il n'a aucun regret, ni sur sa vie à Tokyo ni sur ses études à l'école préparatoire ; une éducation élitiste fondée sur le bachotage ne l'intéresse pas. Il invoque auprès de sa famille d'atroces maux de tête et des insomnies pour justifier son échec aux examens et, sous prétexte de prendre du repos, il rentre à Wakayama en compagnie de son père.

De retour dans la maison familiale, migraines et insomnies imaginaires guérissent en quelques jours. Kumagusu passe des nuits blanches à classer les échantillons rassemblés pendant son séjour à Tokyo et parcourt inlassablement les forêts à la recherche de myxomycètes et de lichens, entre autres. Les myxomycètes, que l'on classe aujourd'hui parmi les protistes, sont des organismes vivants surprenants, qui ont longtemps échappé aux classements des biologistes en raison de leurs caractères relevant à la fois du règne animal et du règne végétal et semblant passer de l'un à l'autre en l'espace d'une nuit. Pour Kumagusu, les observer revient à rechercher les fondements de la vie, et cette intrusion dans le sacré le fait vibrer. « Mon rêve n'est pas l'école préparatoire ni même l'Université impériale. C'est la Terre. Je veux parcourir le monde, étudier toutes les disciplines, observer la nature et comprendre les mystères de la vie ».

Décidé à partir aux États-Unis, il s'ouvre de ce projet à son père. Mais la restauration de Meiji en est à ses balbutiements et, pour un parent, le départ à l'étranger est synonyme d'adieux éternels ; bien entendu, Yahei s'y oppose fermement. Kumagusu est préparé à cette réaction. À force d'explications sur la signification de ce voyage et d'exposés enflammés sur ses rêves d'avenir, huit mois plus tard, sa famille finit par céder devant son enthousiasme. Il évoque ses espérances dans un poème composé dans le genre populaire *dodoitsu* en honneur à la fin d'Edo :

Moi aussi je vais étudier
et après mon voyage à l'étranger
je laisserai derrière moi l'Amérique
et repartirai pour le lointain Japon.
Ma grande mission accomplie,
je veux qu'on dise de moi quel grand homme.

Errances américaines

Kumagusu se trouve à l'étroit sur cet archipel pourtant en profonde mutation. Son père, qui a un sens aiguisé des affaires, se réjouit finalement d'envoyer son fils cadet vers le continent qui promet de bâtir le siècle qui vient : l'Amérique. Le 22 décembre 1886 (an 19 de l'ère Meiji), le fringant Kumagusu embarque à Yokohama, avec la somme considérable de 8000 yens, sur le vapeur *City of Peking* à destination de San Francisco, où il arrive le 8 janvier de l'année suivante. Il intègre tout d'abord le Pacific Business College de San Francisco, mais en très peu de temps, il réalise que le sens du commerce de son père lui fait cruellement défaut ; il abandonne au bout de six mois. En août 1887, il poursuit vers l'est pour rejoindre la Michigan State School of Agriculture à Lansing, mais là non plus, il ne parvient à étancher sa soif de connaissances. Comme à l'école préparatoire à l'Université de Tokyo, Kumagusu ne suit guère les cours, passant son temps à la bibliothèque ou par monts et par vaux, à collecter des cryptogames, *fongi,* lichens et autres spécimens.

Il découvre l'œuvre du naturaliste suisse de la Renaissance, Conrad Gessner, homme de terrain, souvent considéré comme le premier zoologiste des temps modernes, également précurseur de la bibliographie et de la linguistique. Kumagusu décide de faire de cet universaliste son modèle pour le reste de sa vie et s'oppose résolument à la spécialisation en vogue auprès des scientifiques de cette fin de XIXe siècle.

Le caractère de Kumagusu est emporté ; on le retrouve à plusieurs reprises en état d'ébriété dans des bagarres qui tournent mal. À cette époque, il se fait des amis parmi les étudiants japonais : Genzô Murata, membre du même dôjô que le fondateur du judo, Jigorô Kanô, plus fort que lui, et Mishima Katsura, futur responsable des cérémonies officielles du Ministère impérial, bagarreur invétéré. Des étudiants américains, imprudents auteurs d'un mauvais tour joué au fougueux trio dans les dortoirs, s'exposent à des représailles dignes d'une bataille rangée. Kumagusu semble en fait avoir laissé l'action à ses deux vigoureux comparses, se contentant de les soutenir en paroles. La vie à la résidence universitaire finit par s'apaiser et l'hiver arrive au Michigan. La veille du départ en vacances des internes, la chambre des étudiants japonais est le théâtre d'une fête arrosée au whisky, en compagnie de deux camarades américains. Tous aiment boire, en particulier les trois Japonais qui, lorsqu'ils commencent, ne savent plus s'arrêter. Les cadavres de bouteilles s'entassent, une sorte de roulette russe est improvisée, avec pour gage de vider son verre cul sec. Le sort désigne souvent Kumagusu, qui, gorgé de whisky, est ivre mort ; il a trop chaud, il se déshabille entièrement, sort dans le plus simple appareil et finit par s'endormir dans un couloir, les bras en croix. Manque de chance, le très strict directeur de l'école, venu faire sa ronde dans les dortoirs, le trouve dans cette tenue ; révolté par ce comportement honteux, il sanctionne tous les participants à la fête. Voyant là une bonne occasion de quitter l'établissement, Kumagusu endosse l'entière responsabilité de cette beuverie et abandonne l'école d'agriculture au bout d'un peu plus d'un an.

Kumagusu et l'alcool

Les prouesses et déboires de Kumagusu en relation avec l'alcool sont nombreux. Déjà à l'époque de l'école préparatoire, il buvait beaucoup, et à Londres, où il se rend après les États-Unis, il écluse de la bière jusqu'à plus soif. « Depuis que je suis à Londres, j'oublie de manger tellement j'étudie, mais je n'oublie pas de boire », confie-t-il à un ami ; il semble qu'il faisait la tournée des pubs qu'on trouve à chaque coin de rue. Le goût de Kumagusu pour l'alcool pourrait également avoir tenu à son caractère, car il était timide. En réalité, il n'aimait pas s'exprimer devant une assistance fournie et, plus d'une fois, il est apparu ivre à des conférences. Il buvait aussi un verre, paraît-il, avant une rencontre ou une discussion importante ; l'anecdote rapporte que lors de sa première rencontre avec Yanagita Kunio, alors que ce dernier avait fait le déplacement jusque chez lui, il l'a d'abord renvoyé à son auberge, puis est allé l'y rejoindre après avoir ingurgité une bonne dose d'alcool.

Les liens profonds entre Kumagusu et l'alcool ne tiendraient-ils pas en partie au fait que le commerce familial était une brasserie ? Son père a créé en 1884 la brasserie de saké Minakata et, six ans plus tard, c'est Tsunegusu, le frère cadet de Kumagusu, qui en a repris les rênes. L'entreprise existe toujours ; elle a changé de nom en 1971 pour s'appeler Sekai Ittô. Aujourd'hui, l'établissement a inscrit dans sa production un saké baptisé *Kumagusu.*

Après son départ de Lansing, Kumagusu s'installe à Ann Arbor, ville universitaire du même État, le Michigan, mais sans s'inscrire à la faculté ; il fréquente la bibliothèque universitaire et les musées, où il consacre tout son temps à lire et à recopier des ouvrages comme il sait si bien le faire. Stimulé en particulier par la biographie de Gessner, l'esprit libre qu'est Kumagusu décide de « devenir le Gessner japonais » ; c'est à ce moment qu'il choisit la voie de l'étude solitaire, libérée de tout carcan. À Ann Arbor, il rassemble en un *Recueil des fungi de l'État du Michigan* les échantillons de cent cinquante et une espèces de *fungi* collectés jusqu'alors au cours de ses déplacements : il effectue ainsi son premier travail de biologiste. Par ailleurs, le quotidien de Kumagusu à Ann Arbor est égayé par sa correspondance avec l'avocat William Calkins, qui mène des recherches sur les *fungi* et lichens à Chicago. C'est le premier véritable chercheur que Kumagusu rencontre aux États-Unis ; la simple relation épistolaire ne lui suffisant plus, il va lui rendre visite à Chicago. Calkins, valeureux colonel de l'Union pendant la guerre de Sécession, se réjouit de cette rencontre et lui serre la main avec amabilité. Il lui montre sans réserve sa collection de spécimens. Bouleversé, Kumagusu voit là « la véritable étude. » La passion de Calkins pour les *fungi* et les lichens le gagne instantanément. Lorsqu'ils se quittent, celui-ci l'incite vivement à aller en Floride, une terre restée sauvage, véritable réservoir de lichens et vivier inépuisable de plantes inconnues même aux chercheurs américains.

Petit microscope transportable utilisé par Kumagusu pour l'étude des spécimens biologiques. Source: Minakata Kumagusu Museum.

Kumagusu, en proie à l'excitation, décide sur-le-champ de s'y rendre. Il achète aussitôt microscopes, filets à insectes, herbiers, trousse à pharmacie, pistolet, et le 29 avril 1891 il prend le train de nuit à destination de la Floride, à quelque deux mille kilomètres de distance. L'après-midi du 2 mai, le train arrive enfin à Jacksonville, à la base de la péninsule, et le travail de terrain de Kumagusu en Floride débute. Même s'il bénéficie d'une pension envoyée par son père resté au Japon, les versements deviennent irréguliers et parfois insuffisants. Kumagusu loge dans l'épicerie d'un Chinois de Jacksonville, Jiang Shengzong, pour lequel il travaille durant la journée et, le soir venu, il identifie, dessine, classe, range et naturalise avec soin les spécimens recueillis durant le week-end. Le généreux Cantonais éprouve un profond respect pour Kumagusu qu'il voit étudier toutes les nuits, l'œil rivé à son microscope jusqu'à l'aube. Il finit par appeler son employé « maître » et le soutient dans la mesure de ses moyens. Kumagusu peut enfin se consacrer sans relâche à sa collecte d'échantillons de plantes et d'insectes. Épaulé par Jiang, Kumagusu a la chance de découvrir dans un étang de la ville une algue verte, la *Pitophora Oedogonia vaucherioides*, qu'il présente dans une courte note à la revue scientifique mondialement connue *Nature*. Le directeur d'un musée national de Washington, informé de cette découverte, écrit à Kumagusu et lui demande un échantillon de son spécimen d'algue verte.

Encouragé par la publication de cette note dans *Nature*, Kumagusu décide de se rendre à Cuba, à cette période pays de jungle et de fièvre jaune, en proie à la rébellion des autochtones contre le joug des colonisateurs espagnols. Passant outre l'opposition de Jiang, son bienfaiteur, Kumagusu achète un nouveau pistolet pour sa protection et quitte Jacksonville en juillet pour Tampa. Il se rend ensuite à Key West, à l'extrémité méridionale des États-Unis, où il reste un mois, puis gagne La Havane en septembre. Cependant, sur l'île sauvage qu'est Cuba, la collecte de lichens et de *fungi* n'est pas tâche aisée, même pour le remarquable marcheur qu'est Kumagusu, dévoré par les tiques : l'expédition s'avère une longue lutte acharnée et Kumagusu trouve l'occasion de se servir de son arme lors d'émeutes raciales, comme il le raconte dans une lettre à son ami Takesaburô Kitahaba : « Deux nuits plus tôt, il y a eu un combat dans les rues de la ville entre «Blancs» et «Noirs» et des troupes US se sont rassemblées. La nuit dernière, trois «Blancs» ont été blessés et il y a eu cinq coups de feu. La bataille s'est déroulée environ à un mile de là où je suis. Il y avait environ une centaine de «Noirs», trois cents «Blancs», cent miliciens et cinq cents soldats. J'ai prévu d'aller sur le champ de bataille ce soir pour observer. Je suis en train de préparer mon pistolet. »

Mais Tarô Nakayama, biographe de Kumagusu, affirme qu'il a fait plus que préparer son arme : « Jeune homme au sang chaud, Minakata s'est montré sensible aux sentiments patriotiques des révolutionnaires, il a alors pris un pistolet non chargé et s'est joint à eux. Il a tenu à se battre à leurs côtés ici et là, mais cela cessa lorsqu'il fut touché à la poitrine par l'ennemi et qu'il dut être soigné à l'hôpital ».

À La Havane, Kumagusu rencontre plusieurs Japonais affiliés à une troupe du cirque italien Chiarini. Pour des raisons pécuniaires, il se joint à elle. Pendant deux mois environ, il s'occupe des éléphants et suit la tournée, qui le conduit à Port-au-Prince, à Caracas, en Colombie et en Jamaïque, tout en poursuivant son travail sur le terrain. Il semble qu'il lisait aux femmes de la troupe les lettres reçues d'admirateurs du monde entier et rédigeait à leur place des mots d'amour en réponse, pour se faire de l'argent de poche. À l'époque, le niveau d'anglais de Kumagusu est déjà excellent, et il finira par maîtriser aussi le français, l'allemand, l'espagnol, le grec, l'arabe..., un véritable tour de force qui n'avait, semble-t-il, rien d'exceptionnel à ses yeux. Au cours de son périple aux Antilles, où qu'il aille – en Haïti, au Venezuela, en Jamaïque,... –, il maîtrise la langue en un rien de temps, grâce à sa mémoire exceptionnelle.

Kumagusu et les langues

Kumagusu apprend seul les langues étrangères qui lui sont nécessaires pour découvrir l'histoire de l'art, la littérature, la philosophie, la religion, la biologie, l'anthropologie, la sociologie, la psychologie, l'ethnologie, la géographie. Il lit indifféremment les langues anciennes (japonais médiéval, chinois classique, latin, grec, perse, arabe), les langues modernes (anglais, français, italien, espagnol, allemand, portugais,...) mais il se lamente fréquemment des difficultés qu'il rencontre pour apprendre le néerlandais. C'est d'autant plus surprenant que c'est par l'intermédiaire des Hollandais qu'ont été introduites les sciences occidentales (*rangaku*) au Japon, à partir du comptoir installé sur l'île de Dejima à Nagasaki.

Son anglais est excellent et surpasse même celui de certains érudits britanniques de l'époque. Sa qualité, particulièrement louée, semble beaucoup devoir aux conseils bienveillants de ceux qui deviendront ses amis proches durant son séjour londonien, l'écrivain Morrison, et deux conservateurs du Bristish Museum, Franks et Douglas. Tous trois ont permis à Kumagusu de progresser jusqu'à atteindre un niveau qui les émerveillait.

C'est dans ce contexte que Kumagusu découvre de rares lichens calcaires jamais vus, dont il prélève des échantillons qu'il envoie à Calkins à Chicago. L'honnête Calkins les fait parvenir au professeur Nylander, botaniste mondialement reconnu résidant à Paris. C'est ainsi que Kumagusu apprend que ce lichen appartient à une nouvelle espèce, encore inconnue. Nylander la baptise *Gaylecta cubana* ; elle attire immédiatement l'attention de la communauté scientifique et le nom du Japonais Kumagusu Minakata parvient aux oreilles des botanistes du monde entier.

Au-delà de cette découverte, en vérité assez mineure, c'est davantage son contexte, et le symbole qu'il représente, qui frappent la communauté. Il s'agit en effet de la première découverte au monde en biologie faite par un Asiatique dans un territoire sous la domination des « Blancs », selon la terminologie de l'époque.

Tout comme il l'avait ressenti aux États-Unis, Kumagusu n'est pas vraiment séduit par le tempérament des Américains présents dans les Caraïbes. Par comparaison avec les autres peuples qu'il a rencontrés lors de ses voyages, il écrit de ces gens qu'ils sont « particulièrement brutaux et grossiers ». Mettant un terme à son travail de terrain à Cuba, Kumagusu retourne à Jacksonville en juillet 1882 où, toujours avec le soutien de Jiang, il se plonge dans le classement des spécimens recueillis dans les Caraïbes. Au cours du mois de juin de l'année suivante, Jiang liquide son affaire.

Au bout d'environ six mois passés à naturaliser trois cent soixante-sept espèces de *fungi*, la soif de connaissances de Kumagusu est toujours vive. Les États-Unis sont une nation encore trop jeune pour satisfaire son appétit. « À l'épicentre de la culture mondiale, je veux affiner mes connaissances auprès de savants exceptionnels, à la lumière de leurs travaux », s'enflamme Kumagusu, dont le regard passionné est déjà tourné vers Londres, capitale des sciences. Il décide de rejoindre New York d'où il embarque sur le *City of New York* en septembre à destination de Liverpool.

La consécration au cœur de l'Empire britannique

Le 14 septembre 1892 (an 25 de l'ère Meiji), à New York, Kumagusu monte à bord du *City of New York* à destination de la Grande-Bretagne. Il débarque sept jours plus tard à Liverpool, s'y repose quelques jours et arrive le 26 septembre à la gare terminus d'Euston à Londres. Il loge dans diverses pensions bon marché avant de se fixer dans le quartier de Kensington où il loue pour dix shillings par semaine une modeste chambre au-dessus d'une écurie, au 15 de la rue Blithfield. C'est à cette époque un quartier bon marché, mal desservi par les transports publics, où vivent émigrants et Juifs. Kumagusu a vingt-cinq ans et, dans les premières semaines suivant son arrivée à Londres, il rencontre un vieil ami de la famille Minakata, Yoshikusu Nakai, qui lui remet une lettre de son frère cadet, Tsunegusu, lui annonçant que son père s'est paisiblement éteint à l'âge de soixante-quatre ans. Kumagusu est effondré. En réponse aux dernières volontés de son père, qui souhaitait « voir le résultat de ses longues études rassemblé dans un livre », Kumagusu décide de travailler d'arrache-pied, mais avec ce décès, les envois d'argent cessent. De ce fait, sa vie à Londres commence par la recherche d'un travail rémunérateur. Il devient veilleur de nuit dans un théâtre et se nourrit principalement de concombres marinés. Mais dans sa misère, la chance lui sourit soudain. Sur le chemin de retour de la grande parade organisée à l'occasion du mariage de George V, petit-fils de la reine, il croise un compatriote, Takijirô Mitsuda, appartenant à une troupe de cirque. Grâce à son expérience acquise avec le cirque Chiarini, il se lie d'amitié avec Mitsuda, qui l'invite à dîner chez lui. Kumagusu apprécie le somptueux repas japonais qui lui est offert : un festin auquel il n'a pas goûté depuis longtemps. Il fait la connaissance de Masayuki Kataoka, que l'on appelle aussi le *Prince Kataoka*, un marchand d'antiquités japonaises. Kataoka, époux d'une riche Anglaise, parle un anglais parfait qui suscite l'admiration de Kumagusu. Au cours de leur conversation, le *Prince* est frappé par l'érudition du jeune Kumagusu, qui contraste avec son allure devenue peu à peu miteuse. Sa personnalité intrigue l'homme respectable qui décide de le prendre sous son aile et lui écrit une lettre de recommandation auprès de son richissime ami Sir Augustus W. Franks, figure du British Museum : « Je vous présente Kumagusu Minakata, un drôle de Japonais qui sait tout sur tout. » Franks a été nommé conservateur du département des antiquités en 1851 et, en 1866, il a créé le département d'archéologie et d'études folkloriques, qu'il dirige. Plus grand collectionneur de l'histoire du British Museum, il a fait don au musée d'une immense collection, notamment de céramiques d'Iznik et de *netsuke,* objets souvent de grande valeur servant à tenir dans la ceinture le cordon attachant une boîte à médicaments, une pipe ou un nécessaire à écrire. Ce don fait de lui l'une des figures fondatrices du British Museum. Personnage-clé de l'institution, il va sur ses soixante-dix ans. D'abord surpris face à Kumagusu, vêtu d'une redingote élimée mais recommandé par le *Prince*, puis, séduit par son savoir encyclopédique et son enthousiasme, il tombe vite sous le charme. Franks traite avec respect ce jeune Asiatique dépourvu du moindre diplôme, le qualifiant de « remarquable scientifique », et l'autorise à consulter les documents du British Museum. Par ailleurs, il met à contribution sa prodigieuse érudition en lui demandant conseil sur les arts orientaux.

Kumagusu n'oubliera jamais l'accueil chaleureux que lui réserve Franks. Il fréquente également le Southern Kensington Museum of Art, le Natural History Museum et de nombreuses galeries. Son cadre de travail à

Londres est ainsi établi, mais sa vie quotidienne reste placée sous le signe de la pauvreté. À cette époque, il apprend que la revue scientifique *Nature*, dont il est un lecteur assidu, lance un appel à la publication d'articles scientifiques sur la composition des constellations. Il décide immédiatement de répondre. Armé d'un dictionnaire hors d'âge emprunté à sa vieille logeuse (dans le style excessif qui est le sien, l'ouvrage est tellement abîmé que si les sections A à Q sont bien présentes, il manque les pages R à Z, arrachées), il passe un mois à rédiger un article intitulé *The Constellations of the Far East* (« Les Constellations de l'Extrême-Orient »), qu'il envoie à *Nature*. Peu après, le nom de Kumagusu Minakata se trouve au centre de l'attention mondiale. En effet, sa contribution, la plus brillante de toutes, a été publiée. C'est la première fois qu'un article rédigé par un non-Occidental paraît dans cette revue faisant autorité ; de plus, son style et son érudition remarquables lui valent d'être largement repris dans les quotidiens, à commencer par *The Times*.

La publication dans une revue scientifique de premier ordre de la contribution d'un jeune homme inconnu, sans diplômes ni statut, n'a peut-être rien d'exceptionnel en Europe et aux États-Unis, mais dans la société savante extrêmement hiérarchisée du Japon d'alors, elle paraît impensable.

Kumagusu se voit invité dans les salons londoniens, il est reçu par le consul du Japon. À la même période, plusieurs personnalités se rendent, pour des discussions savantes, dans la modeste pièce qui lui sert de logement. C'est le cas notamment du baron Carl Robert Osten-Sacken, l'un des plus grands entomologistes de l'époque. Tous ces éminents visiteurs sont surpris par le caractère misérable de l'endroit et saisis par l'odeur d'urine et de crottin de cheval provenant de l'écurie située en-dessous de sa chambre. Le premier à se réjouir de ce succès est Sir Franks : il invite chez lui Kumagusu, toujours dépenaillé, et organise en son honneur une fête magnifique. La générosité de Franks, membre de l'aristocratie britannique et chercheur d’un statut supérieur, bouleverse le jeune Oriental, qui savoure pour la première fois la liberté et le statut social qui accompagnent le savoir.

Durant cette période londonienne, Kumagusu consacre presque tout l’argent dont il dispose à l’achat de livres qu’il assimile avec une rapidité exceptionnelle. Les trajets quotidiens qui le conduisent ou le ramènent du British Museum à Kensington lui offrent l’occasion de s’immerger dans la diversité ethnique de son quartier. Il prend le temps de faire de longues haltes pour écouter attentivement ces fameux orateurs de Hyde Park qui interpellent les passants, se livrent tantôt à des monologues, tantôt à des joutes verbales sur tous les sujets de morale, de politique ou de philosophie susceptibles de susciter la controverse. Le jeune Japonais éduqué dans le confucianisme et l’acquiescement implicite à l’autorité découvre en ces instants les vertus du dialogue et de la confrontation d’idées.

© J-C Valmalette

London bashô *(« Notes et copies durant la période à Londres »), volume 2 : copie par Kumagusu d’un extrait du livre de Jean Moura intitulé* Le Royaume du Cambodge, *1883. (Londres, le 6 juin 1895.) Source: Minakata Kumagusu Archives.*

En cette fin de XIXe siècle, Londres est le cœur du plus grand empire du monde et ses universités mesurent la nécessité d'attirer les étudiants les plus brillants provenant des colonies. C'est également à cette époque que s'accélère la rivalité entre les grandes universités américaines, britanniques et allemandes. C'est ainsi par exemple qu'elles font progressivement évoluer leurs examens d'entrée, en remplaçant le grec par le chinois, le hindi ou l'arabe classique pour les ouvrir à une « élite mondiale ».

Le 24 janvier 1896 est fondé le Cambridge Club dans lequel se rassemblent les étudiants japonais. Le diplomate et spécialiste du Japon, Sir Ernest Satow, y est invité le 12 mai 1898. La figure emblématique du cercle est Dairoku Kikuchi, le premier et le plus jeune des étudiants japonais à avoir réussi l'examen d'entrée à Cambridge. Après son retour au Japon, ce mathématicien contribuera à restructurer la prestigieuse Université de Tokyo et deviendra ministre de l'Éducation.

Si les universités allemandes se concentrent sur les connaissances dans le seul objectif d'une recherche académique, les universités britanniques consacrent une large part à l'éducation des individus dans leur globalité. Les étudiants japonais de Cambridge forment un véritable réseau qui se développe dans le contexte de l'importante alliance anglo-japonaise signée le 30 janvier 1902. Après le départ de Kumagusu, cette alliance se fixera pour objectif de limiter l'expansion russe vers l'Asie orientale en renforçant la position du Japon. Quelques années plus tard plusieurs de ces anciens étudiants japonais seront envoyés auprès des nations occidentales pour obtenir leur soutien dans la guerre russo-japonaise. Ce modèle britannique, qui repose sur une tradition chrétienne, a pour objectif de former de futurs *gentlemen* à même de conduire la société. Contrairement à ces principes, pourtant, la transformation de la société japonaise se fera dans le respect du système impérial. De cette situation particulière va émerger une confrontation des différentes conceptions du système d'éducation japonais, reflets de la distinction nécessaire ou non entre modernisation et occidentalisation. Kikuchi écrit en 1910 : « À cette période, nous sommes entrés en contact avec les nations occidentales, nous avons observé combien les capacités des Occidentaux étaient supérieures à celles des Japonais. Il me semblait que si nous, Japonais, voulions bénéficier d'une égalité de traitement avec les Occidentaux, ou, en d'autres termes, si nous voulions maintenir le Japon comme nation indépendante, nous avions à acquérir leurs connaissances et leurs technologies qui sont à l'origine de leur puissance. Ainsi, nous nous sommes appliqués à suivre l'enseignement des sciences occidentales avec sérieux et enthousiasme. Par la suite, le résultat s'est manifesté de manière remarquable lors de la récente guerre russo-japonaise. Ceci a surpris les gens du monde qui n'avaient pas prêté attention au Japon dans le passé. » (*Shin Nihon*, Fuzanbo, 1910, p. 1-2.)

Mais Kumagusu reste en marge du cercle des étudiants japonais et ne fréquente que rarement ses membres. Néanmoins, il y a des exceptions avec les étudiants qu'il apprécie et sa gentillesse peut devenir envahissante. L'une de ces exceptions est Tajima Tan, premier étudiant de l'université Waseda, alors nommée *Tôkyô senmon gakk*ô, à partir étudier à l'étranger et à obtenir le diplôme de Cambridge.

Tan Tajima

Tan Tajima est issu d'une famille de riches commerçants de Hiromura dans le Kishû (aujourd'hui Hirogawa dans la préfecture de Wakayama), les Hamaguchi, par la suite installés à Chôshi, dans la préfecture de Chiba, où ils ont prospéré de génération en génération dans la fabrication de sauce de soja (l'actuelle Yamasa Corporation). Son père, Gihei Hamaguchi, est célèbre pour avoir sauvé les habitants du village de Hiromura d'un puissant tsunami, en 1854. Le journaliste et écrivain Lafcadio Hearn, qui a pris, au Japon, le nom de Yakumo Koizumi, admiratif de l'acte de Gihei, l'a dépeint dans *A Living God* « Un Dieu vivant », ouvrage publié à l'étranger où il a suscité beaucoup d'émotion. L'histoire de « L'incendie des gerbes de riz », qui figurait dans les manuels scolaires de toutes les écoles primaires japonaises avant-guerre, est une traduction réalisée d'après l'œuvre de Hearn réintroduite au Japon. En voici la teneur : « Le chef du village, Gohei (Gihei), qui vit sur les hauteurs, voit la mer se retirer au large après un puissant tremblement de terre ; il comprend qu'un tsunami va frapper. Pour avertir du danger les habitants plongés dans les préparatifs de la fête du village, il saisit une torche et enflamme des gerbes de riz fraîchement récoltées dans ses propres rizières. Sous les yeux des villageois accourus pour lutter contre l'incendie, le tsunami se déchaîne. Tous sont sains et saufs grâce à l'ingéniosité et au sacrifice de Gohei. »

Pendant ses études à Londres, sur les conseils de Kumagusu, Tajima donne une conférence sous son ancien patronyme, Hamaguchi. À l'issue de son intervention, une Anglaise se lève et demande si le conférencier, qui porte le même nom que le Hamaguchi du *Dieu vivant* de Hearn, a un lien de parenté avec celui-ci. Lorsque l'organisateur explique que ce M. Hamaguchi est précisément le fils du célèbre Gohei, applaudissements et cris d'admiration fusent. On reconnaît bien là l'esprit facétieux et la générosité sans bornes de Kumagusu.

La personnalité de Kumagusu est très éloignée de celle de cette future élite du Japon, dont le doyen de Cambridge de l'époque, Henry John Edwards, dit : « Ils [les étudiants japonais] sont tous calmes, polis et disciplinés, mais ils réagissent peu en classe et ont tendance à rester entre eux. » Le caractère de Kumagusu est en tous points aux antipodes de celui de ces étudiants qu'il ne fréquente guère.

Il choisit de demeurer cet immigrant vêtu de haillons, réservant ses modiques sommes d'argent à l'achat de livres et de bières. Ce mode de vie n'est pas seulement une liberté qu'il veut se ménager, mais aussi une manière d'accumuler une expérience « ethnographique » sur le regard des Londoniens, sur la manière dont on lui parle ou dont on parle de lui, et probablement une forme de défiance vis-à-vis de toute forme d'institution sociale.

La diversité des relations qu'il engage prouve ce refus de s'enfermer dans un milieu social : à la fin du mois d'octobre 1893, Kumagusu fait la connaissance de Dogi Hôryû, son aîné de treize ans, qui sera son ami pour la vie. Représentant du bouddhisme japonais au Parlement mondial des religions à Chicago, ce moine de l'école Shingon du mont Kôya s'est arrêté à Londres sur le chemin du retour au Japon. Kumagusu, exigeant dans ses relations, est immédiatement attiré par la figure de Hôryû ; il ne le quitte pas un instant pendant son court séjour d'une semaine. La journée, il lui fait fièrement visiter le British Museum et le soir, il s'invite chez Hôryû où ils débattent du bouddhisme du Grand Véhicule et de diverses religions. L'entente a sans doute été parfaite car, de façon surprenante, ils discutent jusqu'à l'aube sans se lasser. Après Londres, Hôryû gagne Paris où il visite le musée Guimet avant de repartir pour le Japon ; la volumineuse correspondance qu'échangeront les deux hommes tout au long de leur vie commence dès ce séjour à Paris et se poursuivra alors que Hôryû sera en charge du célèbre monastère du mont Kôya, centre du bouddhisme Shingon, auquel est rattachée la famille de Kumagusu.

© J-C Valmalette

Cimetière du mont Kôya : représentation des cinq éléments du bouddhisme de l'école Shingon-shû dans lequel a été élevé Kumagusu. Depuis le haut : l'Espace, le Vent, le Feu, l'Eau et la Terre.

Le mont Kôya et l'école Shingon

Situé au nord-est de la préfecture de Wakayama, le mont Kôya culmine à environ 900 m d'altitude. Sur ses hauteurs se dresse le sanctuaire principal du bouddhisme Shingon fondé par Kûkai (Kôbô-Daishi) dans les premières années du IXe siècle. Depuis l'édification du premier temple au début de l'époque Heian (XIIIe siècle), le mont Kôya est l'une des montagnes sacrées les plus fréquentées par les Japonais et, depuis quelques années, par les étrangers. Le bouddhisme Shingon (de la « Vraie parole ») a pour idéal suprême l'avènement dans ce monde du paradis terrestre dans l'éveil du Grand Bouddha Solaire Dainichi Nyorai, et l'accession pour chacun au statut de bouddha de son vivant par la grâce que celui-ci peut accorder au fidèle adepte de l'ascèse (*yoga*). Ryôtarô Shiba, auteur de romans historiques, écrit à propos de cet enseignement : « Par exemple, supposons que le vent souffle fort. Le ressentir à travers notre propre perception physique, à travers le mouvement des branches des arbres autour de nous ou mesurer la vitesse du vent avec un anémomètre, c'est la compréhension exotérique. En comparaison, la compréhension ésotérique est totalement différente ; l'un des objectifs de l'ésotérisme est de transcender la connaissance et la perception pour devenir le vent lui-même. »

À la différence des autres écoles bouddhiques, le bouddhisme Shingon voit l'appétit sexuel d'un œil favorable, en lien direct avec la vision positive de la vie et des désirs humains propre au bouddhisme ésotérique. À propos de la conception du sexe dans cette doctrine, Kumagusu écrit : « Max Nordau [1849-1923, médecin et critique sociologique, auteur entre autres de *Dégénérescence*, auquel il est ici fait allusion] soutient, paraît-il, que la parure de l'extérieur trouve son origine dans la relation charnelle entre un homme et une femme, mais je ne le pense pas, le fondement de la morale se trouve dans l'amour conjugal, cet amour dans lequel, au plus fort de l'acte, l'homme voit la femme jouir et la femme voit l'homme jouir. Le bouddhisme appelle cela l'extase, et voir le visage de l'autre dans l'extase est réservé au couple. »

Malgré l'étendue de ses connaissances et sa puissance de travail hors du commun, Kumagusu ne s'intègre toujours pas au système académique.

La publication de l'article « The Constellations of the Far East » publié dans *Nature*, dont il lit presque tous les numéros depuis son séjour aux États-Unis, apporte à cet autodidacte une grande confiance en lui et lui ouvre les portes de la société savante londonienne. Dans le sillage de ce premier article, il en publie plusieurs autres dans *Nature*, trente-six en tout durant son séjour en Grande-Bretagne. On en trouvera la liste complète en annexe.

Le titre de chaque contribution est intéressant et montre l'étendue des connaissances de Kumagusu. L'un de ses premiers articles sur les croyances orientales relatives aux abeilles et aux guêpes a été écrit en soutien à la théorie de l'entomologiste Osten-Sacken. Celui-ci s'intéressait au récit de l'Ancien Testament consacré à Samson découvrant des abeilles dans la dépouille d'un lion ; il entendait prouver scientifiquement que les insectes vus par Samson étaient en fait une sorte de mouche, des syrphidés de la famille des tabanidés, et non pas des abeilles, arguant de la forte ressemblance entre ces insectes. L'article sur les croyances orientales relatives aux abeilles et aux guêpes y fait écho, de même que ceux qui touchent aux théories chinoises sur l'origine de l'ambre et aux superstitions des Bugonia et la présence en Inde de l'éristale gluant, variété de mouche semblable à l'abeille mélifère, ainsi que de nombreuses missives privées. Osten-Sacken n'est pas seulement une autorité en matière d'entomologie, c'est aussi un membre de la noblesse russe et un diplomate important, qui a notamment exercé les fonctions de consul général de Russie à New York. Il n'est pas étonnant que, lors de la visite qu'il rendait à Kumagusu, le vieux baron, sidéré par la saleté de la pièce où traînent partout des livres et par l'odeur nauséabonde qui se dégage des échantillons soigneusement conservés dans du fumier de cheval provenant de l'écurie située sous le logement, Osten-Sacken goûte à peine le thé que son hôte lui a servi d'une main peu assurée dans une tasse à la propreté douteuse, lui exprime sa gratitude et reparte aussitôt.

Les recherches conjointes avec Osten-Sacken, alliant entomologie et études folkloriques, sont l'occasion pour Kumagusu de s'atteler sérieusement à l'étude du folklore. Il poursuit inlassablement ses recherches au British Museum. Il trouve dans la revue *Notes and Queries* un outil qui lui convient parfaitement. Cette revue, créée en 1849, fonctionne à la manière d'un groupe de discussions actuel sur Internet avec un éditeur qui remplit le rôle du modérateur. « Ainsi, nous souhaitons faire de cette modeste publication une sorte de carnet de notes, un concentré de tout ce que font les hommes qui, écrivains ou lecteurs, se consacrent à l'étude de sujets aussi divers que les objets antiques, les arts, les sciences, l'histoire, les contes populaires et la généalogie, c'est-à-dire, en bref, un recueil traitant de tous les sujets autres que ceux qui, dans le discours populaire, sont qualifiés de politiques ou de polémiques, réunis en une juxtaposition propre à donner libre cours à toute attraction ou répulsion naturelle, de sorte qu'elles puissent devenir lieu de rencontre obligé entre des affinités qui se cherchent. » Des personnalités issues du monde académique mais aussi des amateurs éclairés livrent leurs découvertes ou leur opinion sur la littérature, le folklore, l'histoire et les mythologies, partagent leurs questionnements et suggèrent de multiples interprétations. Les textes publiés suscitent des échanges qui se prolongent parfois même sur plusieurs décennies.

Son érudition incommensurable va conduire Kumagusu à devenir l'un des contributeurs les plus actifs de *Notes and Queries*. Cette forme de dialogue le stimule dans sa quête de rapprochement de domaines en dérive les uns par rapport aux autres tels des continents du savoir qu'il voudrait unifier. Les sujets qu'il traite sous la forme de notes courtes nous renseignent sur son éclectisme.

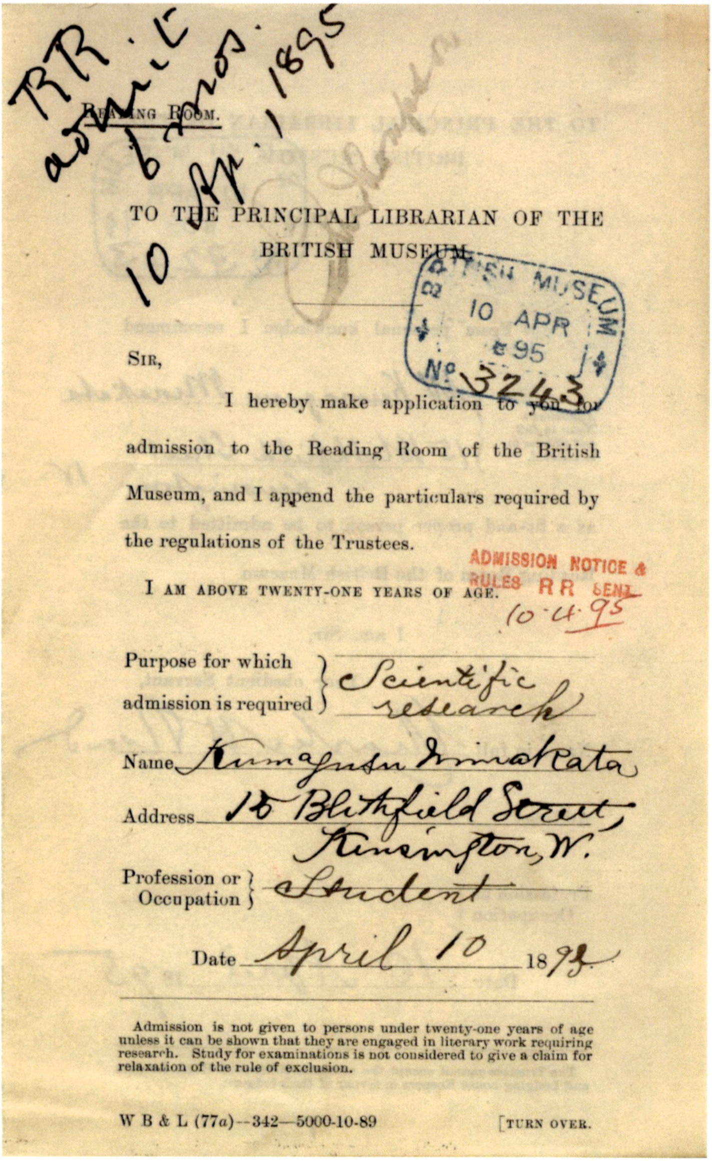

RR admit 6 mos. 10 Ap. 1895

READING ROOM.

TO THE PRINCIPAL LIBRARIAN OF THE BRITISH MUSEUM.

BRITISH MUSEUM 10 APR 95 No 3243

SIR,

I hereby make application to you for admission to the Reading Room of the British Museum, and I append the particulars required by the regulations of the Trustees.

I AM ABOVE TWENTY-ONE YEARS OF AGE.

ADMISSION NOTICE & RULES RR SENT 10·4·95

Purpose for which admission is required } Scientific research

Name Kumagusu Minakata

Address 15 Blithfield Street, Kensington, W.

Profession or Occupation } Student

Date April 10 1895

Admission is not given to persons under twenty-one years of age unless it can be shown that they are engaged in literary work requiring research. Study for examinations is not considered to give a claim for relaxation of the rule of exclusion.

W B & L (77a)--342--5000-10-89 [TURN OVER.

Certificat d'admission de Kumagusu à la salle de lecture du British Museum (10 avril 1895). Source : British Museum.

Le 10 avril 1895, officiellement autorisé à utiliser la bibliothèque du British Museum, Kumagusu est émerveillé par la majestueuse salle de lecture ronde et se réjouit de pouvoir y travailler tout son soûl. Il y passe toutes ses journées à consulter de précieux ouvrages du monde entier et recopie ceux qui éveillent son intérêt. Ses cahiers de l'époque sont couverts de passages dans des langues variées, extraits de livres sur l'archéologie, l'anthropologie ou encore la théologie. Ces *Carnets londoniens*, transcriptions de textes en neuf langues sur plus de cinquante grands cahiers, constitueront une importante base pour ses travaux académiques ultérieurs. Par ailleurs, en parallèle avec ses recherches, Kumagusu aide l'équipe de Sir Robert Kennaway Douglas, conservateur en charge du tout nouveau Department of Oriental Printed Books and Manuscript, à établir le *Catalogue of Japanese Printed Books and Manuscripts*. C'est sous la responsabilité de Douglas que le British Museum a fait, trente ans plus tôt, l'acquisition d'un grand nombre d'ouvrages japonais anciens, de manuscrits richement illustrés, de cartes et de croquis. Ces documents ont été achetés à Alexander Siebold, qui les tenait de son père, le célèbre médecin allemand Philipp Franz von Siebold, qui demeura à deux reprises à Dejima (Nagasaki) pour le compte de la Compagnie hollandaise des Indes orientales. Frappé par l'étendue des connaissances du jeune Japonais, il lui propose peu après un poste au British Museum, mais Kumagusu refuse l'offre en expliquant qu'il y perdrait sa liberté. Douglas publie cette même année son *Catalogue of Japanese Printed Books and Manuscripts* dans la préface duquel Kumagusu est dûment remercié, tout comme Sir Satow, pour sa contribution abondante.

À la même époque, Kumagusu fait la connaissance de Frederick Victor Dickins, directeur de l'Université de Londres. Dickins a séjourné à Yokohama immédiatement après l'ouverture du port, en qualité de médecin militaire dans la Marine britannique, avant de devenir avocat. Il est retourné au Japon en 1871, où il s'est consacré à l'étude de la littérature et des arts japonais jusqu'à son départ en 1879. De ce fait, Dickins est le plus fin connaisseur britannique du Japon, qui le fascine. Il s'enthousiasme pour ce remarquable et dynamique savant venu seul d'une petite île d'Extrême-Orient jusqu'à la capitale de l'Empire britannique, et invite Kumagusu à l'Université de Londres. Mais leur première rencontre, dans le bureau de Dickins, tourne à la dispute. En effet, Kumagusu lit la traduction anglaise du *Conte du coupeur de bambous* à laquelle Dickins a consacré de longs efforts, et lui signale sans hésiter des erreurs de traduction. Dickins s'emporte et les deux hommes se séparent fâchés, mais à tête reposée, il s'aperçoit de la justesse des remarques de Kumagusu et regrette sa conduite. Kumagusu n'a pas hésité à défendre le point de vue du savoir, sans céder à la flatterie face à lui, représentant du puissant Empire britannique. Impressionné par ce courage, Dickins reconnaît son erreur et lui présente ses excuses. Par la suite, une amitié indéfectible liera les deux hommes.

À Londres, Kumagusu ne fréquente pas que des savants. Parmi ses amis japonais figurent Dogi Hôryû ou encore le marquis Yorimichi Tokugawa, quinzième Tokugawa de la branche de Kishû. Il se lie aussi d'amitié avec des non-Japonais, comme l'auteur de romans policiers à succès Arthur Morrison et le réfugié russe anarchiste Kropotkine. Toute sa vie, sans se limiter à son séjour londonien, Kumagusu sera en relation avec de nombreux personnages illustres, mais la plus étonnante de ces amitiés est sans doute celle qui le lie au révolutionnaire chinois Sun Yat-sen, considéré comme le père de la Chine moderne.

Sun Yat-sen (Sun Zhongshan, 1866-1925)

Sun Yat-sen naît en 1866 dans une famille de paysans pauvres du sud de la Chine. Tout jeune adolescent, il rejoint son frère émigré à Hawaï et fonde « Les trois principes du peuple », en écho à la célèbre phrase d'Abraham Lincoln : « Le gouvernement du peuple, par le peuple, pour le peuple. » Après l'obtention de son diplôme de médecine à Hong-Kong, il se tourne vers l'action politique en créant le Xingzhonghui (« Société pour le redressement de la Chine »). En 1895 il échoue dans sa tentative de coup d'État contre le gouvernement impérial Qing. Il est alors contraint à un exil politique qui va durer seize ans. La première étape de cet exil le conduit à Londres où il rencontre Kumagusu.

Sun Yat-sen arrive à Londres le 1er octobre 1896. L'ambassade de Chine demande immédiatement son extradition mais celle-ci est refusée par le ministère des Affaires étrangères britannique. Le 5 décembre de cette même année, il visite pour la première fois le British Museum.

En mars 1897, Sun et Kumagusu sont présentés l'un à l'autre dans le bureau de Douglas au British Museum. L'entente est immédiate : le médecin en exil, préoccupé par la construction d'une identité nationale chinoise, et l'érudit japonais autodidacte s'estiment profondément. Sun a tout juste trente ans, Kumagusu en a vingt-neuf. Chacun suit une voie différente, l'un dans les sciences naturelles sociales et humaines, l'autre dans l'action politique, mais c'est sans doute l'amour de la patrie et leur aspiration commune à un « Orient nouveau » qui les réunit. Leurs rencontres sont fréquentes durant le printemps de cette année. Kumagusu les mentionne scrupuleusement dans son journal, qu'il tiendra toute sa vie durant, en précisant les lieux, les heures et les autres personnes éventuellement présentes. On peut imaginer que Sun Yat-sen puise chez Kumagusu une connaissance encyclopédique vivante qui stimule sa réflexion sur le destin de la Chine qu'il va bientôt refonder.

Les deux amis fréquentent des milieux anticoloniaux de Londres, parmi lesquels Volkhovsky, dissident révolutionnaire russe échappé d'un camp de Sibérie et fondateur du communisme libertaire, Mulkern, un nationaliste irlandais qui sert de garde du corps à Sun et sera plus tard à ses côtés en Chine. Ces cercles informels reçoivent les témoignages des actions menées par l'homme d'affaires et impérialiste Cecil Rhodes en Afrique du Sud et son coup d'État manqué au Transvaal. Certains historiens ont noté que Kumagusu portait déjà avant son départ en Amérique un intérêt au mouvement des droits des peuples (*jiyumenken undo*) parfois à l'origine d'incidents violents. Plusieurs de ses amis deviendront des socialistes engagés.

© J-C Valmalette

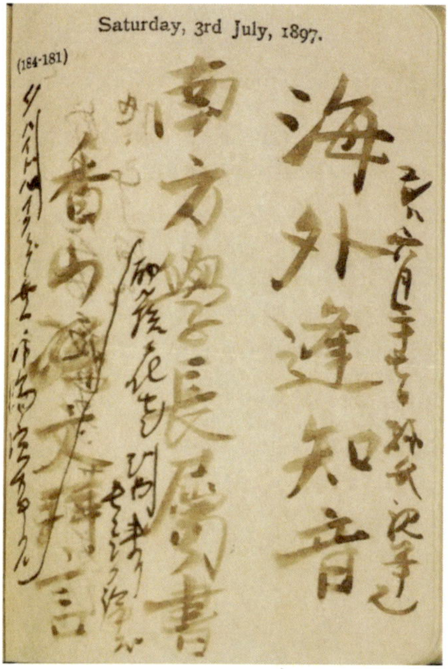

Message laissé par Sun Yat-sen, avant son départ de Londres, sur l'agenda de Kumagusu : « Meilleurs amis rencontrés dans un pays étranger ». Source: Minakata Kumagusu Museum.

Mais, par-delà les supputations, force est d'admettre que l'on ne sait que peu de choses sur la nature des relations entre Sun et Kumagusu : contrairement à ses habitudes, Kumagusu ne dévoile rien du contenu de leurs discussions dans son journal dans lequel figurent pourtant une trentaine de rencontres avec Sun. On peut imaginer que leurs discussions alimentent le sentiment d'une identité chinoise, voire pan-asiatique, chez Sun Yat-sen. De son côté, Kumagusu perçoit-il le sens politique hors du commun chez celui qui, après son asile politique au Japon, fondera le Kuomintang et deviendra le premier président de la Chine moderne ?

Des recherches récentes ont permis de découvrir le rôle de Kumagusu dans le soutien que recevra Sun Yat-sen lors de ses séjours ultérieurs au Japon. Kumagusu en effet convaincra les industriels japonais et des personnalités politiques d'accorder leur soutien financier et matériel à la révolution chinoise. Anecdote révélatrice : à la question « Quelle est ton ambition ? », Kumagusu aurait répondu : « Mon souhait est de voir les Asiatiques chasser une fois pour toutes tous les Occidentaux d'Asie. » Cependant, les historiens s'accordent à dire que Kumagusu a toujours gardé ses distances vis-à-vis de la Dai-tô-a Kyôeiken, *Sphère de coprospérité de la Grande Asie extrême-orientale.*

Quoi qu'il en soit, le médecin en exil, entièrement préoccupé par la construction d'une identité chinoise, et le chercheur autodidacte nourrissent un profond respect mutuel. C'est une amitié brève mais intense, qui débouche sur des serments solennels, Sun promettant à Kumagusu qu'« après l'avènement de la révolution, il fera du mont Luofu à Canton le plus grand parc botanique du monde, pour lui. » L'heure de la séparation venue, Sun trace dans le journal intime de Kumagusu cinq caractères chinois, qui signifient : « Mon ami pour la vie rencontré à l'étranger ».

Sun Yat-sen (assis au milieu) lors de son exil au Japon rend visite à Kumagusu (debout à gauche). Source: Minakata Kumagusu Archives.

Plus tard, en 1900, Sun fomente une deuxième insurrection, qui se solde de nouveau par un échec. L'année suivante, exilé au Japon, il rend visite à Kumagusu à Wakayama. En 1911, Sun fait aboutir la Révolution Xinhai et assume le poste de président provisoire de la République de Chine mais, en vertu de l'accord Nord-Sud, il cède le pouvoir à Yuan Shikai. En 1913, après l'échec de la deuxième révolution, il se réfugie une nouvelle fois au Japon ; il souhaite alors rendre visite à Kumagusu, mais celui-ci est malade et la rencontre n'a pas lieu. Ensuite, en 1919, Sun devient président du Kuomintang, avant de mourir six ans plus tard à Pékin. Son existence mouvementée n'a rien à envier à celle de Kumagusu.

Kumagusu, quant à lui, ne deviendra pas un leader politique, mais on peut penser que l'influence exercée par Sun Yat-sen est réelle, notamment dans l'action qu'il mènera quelques années plus tard dans sa lutte contre la disparition des temples villageois shintô, au motif de la préservation de l'environnement et d'une certaine écologie sociale.

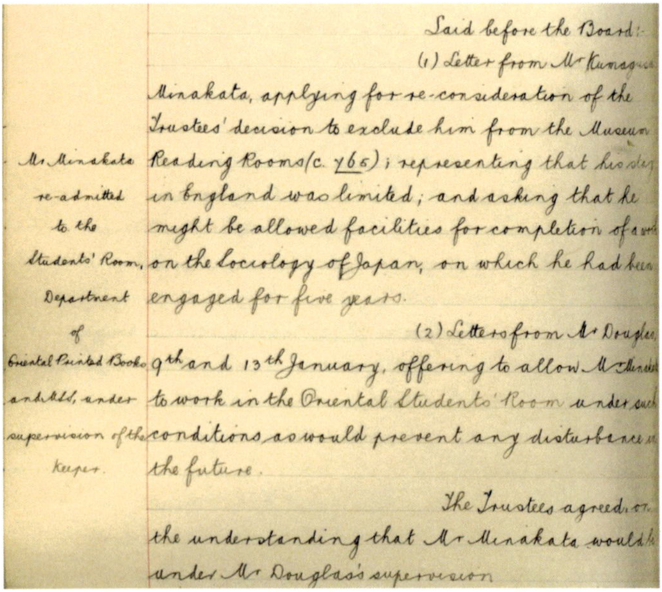

Mr Minakata re-admitted to the Students' Room, Department of Oriental Printed Books and MSS, under supervision of the Keeper.

Laid before the Board:–
(1) Letter from Mr Kumagus
Minakata, applying for re-consideration of the Trustees' decision to exclude him from the Museum Reading Rooms (c. 765); representing that his sta in England was limited; and asking that he might be allowed facilities for completion of a wo on the Sociology of Japan, on which he had been engaged for five years.
(2) Letters from Mr Douglas, 9th and 13th January, offering to allow Mr Minak to work in the Oriental Students' Room under such conditions as would prevent any disturbance in the future.
The Trustees agreed, on the understanding that Mr Minakata would under Mr Douglas's supervision

Compte rendu du Bristish Museum. Source : Bristish Museum.

À Londres, la situation financière de Kumagusu est de plus en plus délicate. Après le décès de son père, son frère cadet Tsunegusu lui a de temps à autre fait parvenir de maigres sommes d'argent, mais vers 1897, ces envois cessent complètement. Les difficultés financières aidant, le 8 novembre de cette année, toujours imprévisible, il crée un incident dans la salle de lecture du British Museum. Un rapport du responsable mentionne que Kumagusu y agresse un lecteur du nom de G. St Leger Daniels et que son expulsion est difficile. Kumagusu présente ses excuses dans un courrier, en prenant soin d'indiquer qu'il a été provoqué. Nouvel incident le 6 décembre de l'année suivante ; nouvelle suspension : faisant valoir que son séjour est limité dans le temps, il demande à pouvoir être admis à nouveau pour terminer son travail sur la sociologie du Japon auquel il se consacre depuis cinq ans. Deux lettres de Douglas des 9 et 13 janvier 1899 l'autorisent à accéder à l'Oriental Students Room à condition qu'il ne provoque plus de perturbations. D'autres incidents sont signalés : un coup de poing décoché en pleine face d'un employé, du nom de Thompson, qui lui fait le reproche d'être trop bruyant et qui, déjà, se serait plusieurs fois moqué de lui et du Japon. Bénéficiant une fois encore de l'indulgence de la direction, Kumagusu voit son droit d'accès à la salle de lecture suspendu durant deux mois. Mais, par la suite, les tensions avec certains utilisateurs anglais s'exacerbent et une nouvelle dispute avec le même Thompson aboutit cette fois à son expulsion du British Museum. Les efforts dévoués de Morrison, Franks et Douglas auprès du prince héritier, le futur Édouard VII, alors membre du conseil d'administration du musée, de l'archevêque de Canterbury et du maire de Londres, aboutissent à une réintégration conditionnelle : Kumagusu n'est admis désormais que dans le bureau de Douglas, ce à quoi ne peut se résoudre sa fierté de chercheur et de Japonais. Il remercie donc Douglas et quitte cette institution qu'il a fréquentée de façon quasi quotidienne après avoir retranscrit plus de six cents ouvrages et accumulé cinquante-trois gros volumes de notes manuscrites. Cependant, il fait don au British Museum de plusieurs ouvrages dont certains se trouvent maintenant à la British Library. Ironie de l'histoire, ces deux incidents provoqués par Kumagusu font connaître Sir Douglas au Japon en raison de l'amitié qu'il entretient avec lui. À l'inverse, Douglas tombera injustement dans l'oubli en Occident.

Kumagusu poursuit désormais ses études en solitaire, notamment au Natural History Museum et au Victoria and Albert Museum à South Kensington, mais son quotidien est de plus en plus difficile. Dickins fait tout son possible pour créer à Cambridge ou Oxford une chaire de langue et littérature japonaises qu'il voudrait voir attribuée à Kumagusu. Ce dernier semble avoir placé certains espoirs en ce projet, mais hélas, sous l'effet de la guerre des Boers, toutes les universités voient leurs budgets réduits et le projet échoue.

Durant cette période, Kumagusu occupe donc divers petits emplois ; le plus original de tous est celui de courtier en estampes *ukiyo-e*, entrepris avec son ami Kinichi Takahashi, un personnage interlope, allergique au travail et grand buveur. Cette activité, engagée peu après l'incident du coup de poing, dure environ deux ans. Les commentaires un peu farfelus rédigés en anglais par Kumagusu pour accompagner les estampes achetées à crédit par Takahashi rencontrent un immense succès auprès des gens fortunés et des savants qui s'arrachent les tableaux, parfois pour plusieurs fois leur prix de départ. Mais cet argent facilement gagné disparaît tout aussi vite dans la mousse des bières, ne laissant dans son sillage qu'une multitude d'anecdotes d'ivrogne. Cette vie d'excès et de débauche afflige Kumagusu, qui noie dans l'alcool sa frustration vis-à-vis de ses travaux scientifiques.

C'est dans ce contexte de trop-plein éthylique qu'il prend la décision de rentrer au Japon. Au même moment, il croise le destin d'un de ses anciens camarades de l'école préparatoire à l'Université de Tokyo, Natsume

Sôseki, qui vient d'être envoyé à Londres par le gouvernement japonais pour y étudier la littérature anglaise. Cependant, Sôseki renonce à étudier à Cambridge pour des raisons financières et dit-on, pour avoir été choqué de voir lors de sa visite des étudiants s'exercer étrangement sur des terrains de sport au lieu d'étudier. Il résumera ainsi ses deux années londoniennes : « Mes années passées à Londres ont été les plus désagréables de ma vie. J'ai vécu parmi les gentlemen anglais comme un pauvre chien égaré au milieu d'une meute de loups. »

Kumagusu est certes dépité, mais c'est transformé par quatorze années d'itinérance occidentale qu'il embarque le 1er septembre 1900 à Liverpool sur le *Tambamaru* pour regagner un Japon qui a maintenant entamé l'une des transformations les plus rapides de sa longue histoire.

Le retour dans la péninsule de Kii

À l'aube du 15 octobre 1900 (an 33 de l'ère Meiji), le *Tambamaru* accoste à Kobe avec à son bord un individu transformé, bien différent du jeune homme fringant qui quitta quatorze ans plus tôt la baie de Yokohama à la conquête de nouveaux horizons botaniques. Kumagusu a alors trente-trois ans. Son frère Tsunegusu, averti par télégramme, est venu l'accueillir au port de Kobe ; il est sidéré de voir débarquer son aîné dans des vêtements à l'occidentale, en haillons, accompagné de quantités de malles d'ouvrages et de spécimens. Le retour soudain de Kumagusu, à l'issue de tant d'années en Occident au cours desquelles il n'a pas décroché le moindre diplôme, n'est guère apprécié par les Minakata, notamment par l'épouse de Tsunegusu, qui l'accueille fraîchement. De ce fait, Kumagusu n'est pas hébergé dans la maison familiale de Wakayama, occupée par son frère et sa belle-sœur. Tsunegusu, qui a hérité de l'affaire de son père, préfère tenir son frère à distance. Il lui trouve un abri à Wakanoura, au petit temple Enju-in du mont Atago tout proche. Le supérieur, un vieillard affable nommé Kanchû, lui donne une chambre plus grande que la sienne et le traite généreusement, le laissant même boire de l'alcool dans l'enceinte du temple. Sur place, la chance sourit à Kumagusu. Il découvre une nouvelle espèce de myxomycète sur un cerisier de l'entrée principale et aussi, dans un baquet d'eau intouchée, la première espèce d'algue d'eau douce jamais trouvée au Japon, la chrysophycée *Ochromonas vischeri*.

À la même période, Sun Yat-sen, alors réfugié au Japon pour échapper au pouvoir des Qing, vient lui rendre visite à Wakayama. Les deux hommes sont ravis de se retrouver et Kumagusu organise une grande fête pour Sun dans le meilleur établissement de Wakanoura, l'auberge Ashibeya. Lorsqu'ils se quittent, Sun ôte son panama blanc apporté de Taiwan, en coiffe Kumagusu, et les deux hommes échangent une poignée de main. Kumagusu, enivré par la tournure favorable des récents événements, ne trouve rien de mieux que de profiter de l'absence du supérieur pour manger du *sukiyaki*, une fondue à la viande de bœuf, dans sa chambre du temple. Manque de chance, Kanchû, de retour plus tôt que prévu, le surprend en plein repas, en train de déguster sa viande avec un verre d'alcool. Le moine, indulgent mais fidèle à ses vœux, ne peut réprimer sa colère devant ce spectacle et Kumagusu est chassé du temple. Avec l'aide de Tsunegusu, il choisit de s'installer dans une succursale de l'entreprise familiale dans la région de Kumano, à Katsuura (l'actuelle ville de Nachi-Katsuura, préfecture de Wakayama). La raison de ce choix tient à son vif intérêt pour Kumano, région encore inconnue et vierge.

© J-C Valmalette

Kumano kodo, chemins de pèlerinage dans les monts Kii.

Kumano est le monde des ténèbres où s'est réfugiée Izanami, déesse de la création et de la mort ; les montagnes y sont peuplées d'esprits. Baigné dans une atmosphère d'outre-tombe, Kumano a vu se développer, après l'introduction du bouddhisme, le culte des Trois montagnes protectrices de la région (Hongû, Shingû et Nachi). Se livrer aux pratiques d'austérité dans le massif de Kumano était censé conférer des pouvoirs surnaturels ou permettre d'accéder à l'état de bouddha vivant : ces croyances se sont répandues dans tout l'archipel. À l'époque Heian, le culte s'est amplifié, drainant une foule considérable appartenant à toutes les couches sociales, depuis les membres de la famille impériale et de l'aristocratie jusqu'au peuple. Pour désigner ce pèlerinage vers cet outre-monde sacré, on parle même de « la procession des fourmis à Kumano » tellement les visiteurs sont nombreux. L'objectif est de porter en terre dans ce pays des morts son moi ancien souillé par le monde profane, afin de renaître, neuf. Pour les gens du Moyen Âge en proie au désespoir, le pèlerinage à Kumano ouvrait la voie à la résurrection de soi. Kumano, sa nature et son culte, font aujourd'hui partie du Patrimoine mondial de l'Unesco, sous la dénomination de « sites sacrés et chemins de pèlerinage dans les monts Kii ». Il représente avec le mont Kôya l'un des hauts lieux touristiques de la préfecture de Wakayama.

Hongū-taisha, grand sanctuaire shintô de Kumano.

Après son installation dans cette région mystérieuse de Kumano, Kumagusu s'attelle immédiatement au travail de terrain, sans s'impliquer le moins du monde dans l'entreprise familiale. Et les lieux répondent à ses attentes, en particulier la forêt primaire du mont Nachi, chaude et humide : elle constitue un environnement idéal pour l'étude des lichens.

© J-C Valmalette

Cascade de Nachi, lieu de symbiose entre la nature et le sacré qualifié de lieu de « surprise essentielle » par André Malraux.

À Nachi, la montagne est insondable, si bien que Kumagusu lui-même, quand il part en expédition, s'adjoint par prudence la compagnie d'un guide local et d'un porteur. La collecte d'échantillons dans les montagnes de Kumano, véritable réservoir d'espèces végétales, dure en tout trois ans. Durant cette période, Kumagusu, la conscience aiguisée, fait l'expérience de nombreux phénomènes surprenants, notamment des rêves prémonitoires. Intrigué par ces étranges phénomènes surnaturels, il se lance dans l'étude de la « psychologie anormale ». Sur les indications de son défunt père qui lui apparaît en songe, il découvre une orchidée sauvage qu'on croyait disparue, la *Cymbidium lancifolium*. Il identifie également une algue extrêmement rare qui n'avait encore jamais été observée en Orient, la *Pitophora Oedogonia vaucherioides*. Kumagusu en avait découvert le premier spécimen en Floride, après quoi personne n'en avait plus jamais observé. Ses découvertes remarquables ne s'arrêtent pas là : à Kumano, il trouve aussi une espèce de volubilis, l'*uchiwa-kazura*, jusqu'alors signalée seulement à Okinawa et dans les îles Ogasawara, ainsi qu'une algue microscopique extrêmement rare, répertoriée uniquement en Allemagne et en Grande-Bretagne, la *Stephanosphaera*. Kumano est également le lieu d'une rencontre importante et inespérée avec Koaze Shirô, vingt-huit ans, directeur du bureau de Kobe de la célèbre compagnie maritime Nippon Yusen. Koaze, amateur d'orchidées, est venu en cueillir à Kumano lorsque par hasard, au pied de la cascade Nachi-ichinotaki, les deux hommes engagent la conversation. Plus tard, fasciné par Kumagusu, Koaze deviendra son meilleur disciple en matière d'étude des myxomycètes ; cet homme de bien non seulement l'aidera toute sa vie dans ses recherches, mais lui apportera aussi un soutien financier constant.

Enfin, à la même époque, Kumagusu achève avec Dickins, à Londres, la traduction en anglais du *Hôjôki,* « Notes de ma cabane de moine », mais sous le titre « Un Thoreau japonais du XIIe siècle ». Composé en 1212 par le moine Kamô no Chômei, ce texte livre, dans la pure tradition bouddhiste, des réflexions sur l'aspect éphémère et transitoire des choses de ce monde à partir des malheurs, séismes, famines, incendies, qui se sont abattus sur Kyoto au début de la période dite Kamakura (1185-1333). L'œuvre de traduction de Kumagusu est immense et délibérément ancrée dans la modernité. Grâce à sa collaboration avec F. V. Dickins, les textes fondateurs de la littérature japonaise sont libérés de leur traduction littérale. La relation mutuelle entre ces deux hommes ouvre cette littérature à l'Occident.

Actif sur le terrain comme dans ses travaux de rédaction, Kumagusu met un terme à sa récolte d'espèces végétales à Kumano et s'installe à Kii-Tanabe, aujourd'hui Tanabe. Simple bourg de province, Tanabe a néanmoins toujours prospéré grâce à son port naturel, qui en fait un passage obligé, et aux nombreux riches marchands qui animent la localité. Tanabe est aussi la ville natale de Toriyama, le professeur de collège que Kumagusu respectait profondément, et du fondateur de l'aïkido, Morihei Ueshiba.

Morihei Ueshiba (植芝 盛平) ***1883-1969***

Morihei Ueshiba est le fondateur de l'*aïkido*. Originaire de Tanabe comme Kumagusu, il reçoit également l'enseignement bouddhiste de l'école Shingon durant une enfance menacée par une santé fragile. Il est le petit-fils d'un ancien samouraï très réputé dans la région. Dans les années 1909-1910, il apporte son soutien à Kumagusu dans le mouvement de protestation, parfois violent, contre le regroupement des sanctuaires shintô imposé par le gouvernement Meiji. Ueshiba est profondément influencé par cette rencontre avec Kumagusu, de vingt-six ans son aîné, qui lui révèle sa conception d'une nature où chaque « chose » évolue par son interdépendance aux autres (*in en* 因縁), qu'elle soit un lichen, un myxomycète, un *kusunoki*, un oiseau, ou un homme qui va à la rencontre des *kami* au sanctuaire de son hameau. Il dira quelques années plus tard de Kumagusu qu'il a été le l'homme le plus important qu'il ait jamais rencontré.

Ce n'est qu'ensuite qu'il fait la rencontre du grand maître du jujitsu Sokaku Takeda dont il devient le disciple. Quelques années plus tard, sa vie se lie à celle de Deguchi Onisaburô, meneur charismatique de la secte internationaliste Ômoto-kyô, nouvelle forme de shintô.

Enfin, c'est sous ces influences diverses qu'il fonde une nouvelle forme de *budô* (« voie du combat ») qu'il appelle *aïkido*. Sa réputation s'accroît à la suite des défis qu'il remporte face aux plus grands maîtres de *budô*. Dans les années 60 il tente la transformation ultime de l'« art de la guerre » développé initialement par les samouraïs en un « art de la paix » (*shobu aïki*).

Morihei Ueshiba.

C'est également dans cette ville que vit Takesaburô, le meilleur ami de Kumagusu depuis l'époque du collège à Wakayama. Takesaburô, médecin, consacre son temps et son argent à la recherche sur les maladies endémiques, mais c'est aussi un grand buveur, simple et avenant, ce qui lui vaut une certaine popularité. Les deux hommes au caractère bien trempé, avides de spiritualité, s'entendent très bien et se respectent mutuellement. D'ailleurs, une fois installé à Tanabe, Kumagusu épouse en 1906, sur les recommandations de Takesaburô, la quatrième fille du prêtre du sanctuaire Tôkei, Matsue Tamura. Takesaburô, qui joue le rôle d'entremetteur, selon la tradition japonaise de l'époque, semble avoir arrangé le mariage avant même que Kumagusu comme Matsue n'en soient informés. Pour commencer, Kumagusu est formellement opposé à cette idée : pour lui, « une épouse serait une gêne dans [ses] recherches », mais lorsqu'il voit la menue Matsue devant le grand portique du sanctuaire, son joli visage intelligent le fait brusquement changer d'avis et il est déterminé à « se marier contre vents et marées. » Dans sa fougue, son premier cadeau à la jeune femme est un fût de soixante-douze litres rempli de livres. Le mariage est arrangé ; Kumagusu a alors trente-neuf ans et Matsue vingt-huit. La cérémonie du *sansankudo*, lorsque les futurs époux partagent la même coupe de saké à plusieurs reprises, se déroule normalement en silence, mais Kumagusu qui, jusque-là, s'était tenu coi, l'air grave, n'y tient plus et s'exclame à voix haute « Versez-moi une coupe pleine ! » Tancé par sa sœur aînée adorée, qui tient le rôle des parents du marié, il se fait tout petit, pétrifié comme une souris devant un chat. Cet épisode cocasse est caractéristique des dérapages du personnage.

Alerte sur le petit sanctuaire villageois

Kumagusu partage maintenant son quotidien avec Matsue qui, comme on peut l'imaginer, n'a pas la vie facile, et ce, dès les premiers temps de leur mariage. Si elle range le bureau de Kumagusu, elle se fait réprimander parce qu'il ne retrouve plus ses livres ni ses échantillons ; si elle entretient le jardin, elle reçoit des remontrances parce qu'elle abîme ses précieux myxomycètes. Cependant, elle finit par cerner le caractère un peu puéril de son mari, apprend à le contrôler habilement et devient un soutien pour lui.

© J-C Valmalette

Propriété où résida Kumagusu durant ses années à Tanabe. Elle comprend une maison d'habitation, une maison pour l'étude et un entrepôt pour les spécimens et les outils au rez-de-chaussée et les ouvrages au second étage. Il y découvrit une nouvelle espèce de myxomycète.

La famille de Kumagusu, alors âgé de qurante-huit ans, dans le jardin de sa propriété à Tanabe (en partant de la gauche : la domestique, sa femme, Matsue, son fils, Kumaya et Kumagusu. En bas : sa fille, Fumie. Source: Minakata Kumagusu Archives.

L'année suivant leur mariage voit la naissance d'un fils, Kumaya, et quatre ans plus tard naît une fille, Fumie. Kumagusu est un père aimant qui s'occupe beaucoup de ses enfants. Pour sa famille, il refuse même une invitation alléchante du professeur Swingle du ministère américain de l'Agriculture, et passe le reste de sa vie à Tanabe. La maison de Nakayashikimachi, la dernière où a vécu la famille, est entourée d'arbres pour les recherches de Kumagusu et le jardin abrite un chien, un chat et une tortue, ainsi que des poissons-chats japonais, des grenouilles et même des scorpions d'agrément. Grâce à cet environnement, Kumagusu découvre sur un plaqueminier de son jardin un myxomycète inconnu dont il envoie un échantillon à Gulielma Lister en Grande-Bretagne, et qui s'avère être une nouvelle espèce. Ce myxomycète, baptisé *Minakatella longifila* (« le long fil de Minakata »), est si rare qu'il donne naissance à une nouvelle famille, les *minakatella*. Aujourd'hui encore, la végétation est luxuriante dans l'ancienne résidence Minakata de Tanabe, à côté de laquelle se dressent maintenant les Archives Minakata Kumagusu ; les deux bâtiments sont ouverts à la visite.

Kumagusu travaillant dans sa maison de Tanabe. Source: Minakata Kumagusu Archives.

Après son mariage, Kumagusu continue à voyager pour collecter des échantillons. Il embauche un bûcheron pour lui servir de guide et de porteur et dort dans les collines ou à l'auberge, il lui arrive parfois de ne pas rentrer pendant plus d'un mois. Un jour de grande chaleur, Kumagusu descend de la montagne nu comme un ver, un maillet dans une main et un filet dans l'autre. Son porteur, un homme imposant qui a fait la guerre de Russie, court sur ses talons, lui aussi à demi-nu. Pris par la pente, incapables de stopper leur course, ils dévalent du haut de la colline en poussant des cris perçants, comme des bêtes. Une vingtaine de paysannes paisiblement occupées à repiquer des plants de riz, qui se trouvent par malheur sur leur chemin, prennent la fuite en hurlant : « Des *tengyan* (*tengu*) ! », et des enfants qui jouent aux alentours défaillent, paralysés de terreur.

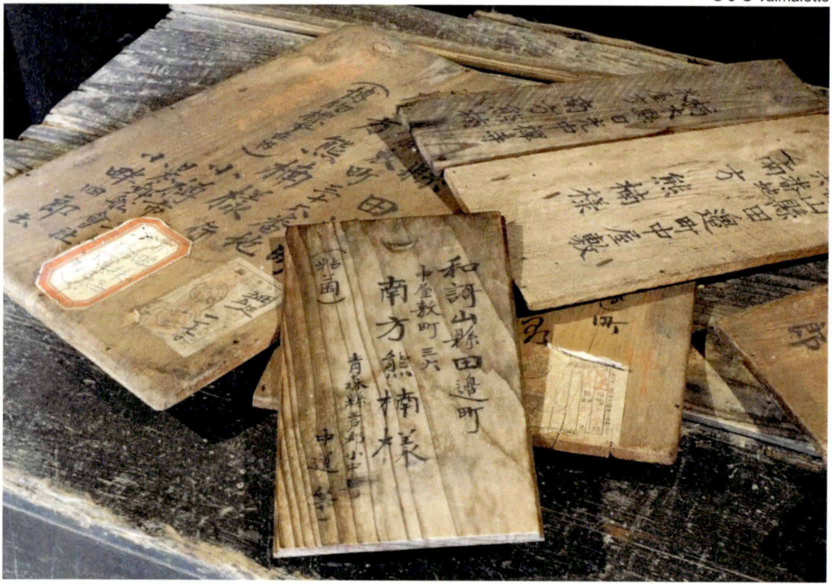

Couvercles des boîtes dans lesquelles étaient expédiés les échantillons pour Kumagusu avec la mention : « De la part de M. Nakamichi (Aomori) pour M. Minakata Kumagusu (Tanabe), échantillons à analyser pour vérifier s'il s'agit d'une nouvelle espèce de myxomycète ».

À cette époque, en parallèle de ses recherches botaniques, Kumagusu contribue toujours plus activement à un large éventail de publications japonaises et étrangères : une quarantaine de journaux, magazines et revues scientifiques. Par exemple, la série « Réflexions sur les douze branches terrestres », dans laquelle il présente les traditions populaires liées aux animaux du zodiaque chinois, paraît pendant une dizaine d'années dans la célèbre revue littéraire *Taiyô*. Il publie aussi des articles sur les traditions de la région de Kishû dans la revue scientifique *Kyôdo kenkyû* et son article

« L'Entremetteur » pour le magazine mensuel *Fuji*, dans lequel il évoque les relations incestueuses en Orient et en Occident, lui vaut une amende de cent yens pour outrage aux bonnes mœurs.

Il continue de publier à l'étranger aussi, principalement dans *Notes and Queries* et *Nature*. Par ailleurs, à la demande du docteur de Nissl, de l'ambassade des Pays-Bas, il écrit également pour la revue néerlandaise *Vragen en Mededeeligen*. Ses contributions d'une grande érudition, dans des domaines variés et au ton humoristique, commencent à être appréciées au Japon et sa renommée gagne le pays entier. Conséquence de ce succès, le nom de Kumagusu apparaît en quatrième position de la première division de l'Est, avec entre autres ceux de Tsuyoshi Inukai (1855-1932, premier ministre de 1931 à 1932), et Maresuki Nogi (1849-1912, général de l'armée impériale), dans le « Classement des contemporains excentriques » de la revue *Shin-kôron*, inspiré du tableau de classement *bankuze* des lutteurs de sumô.

Par ailleurs, grâce à un effet de synergie entre le dynamisme de sa production écrite et la notoriété qu'elle lui apporte, son cercle de relations s'élargit et le nombre de ses soutiens et sympathisants croît. Seiga Môri, fondateur du journal *Muron Shinpô*, et le journaliste Teijirô Saika ou encore le « trio des myxomycètes » formé de ses disciples Shirô Koaze, Shigeru Uematsu et Daizaburô Hiranuma, le soutiennent tant sur le plan psychologique que matériel. Enfin, la fréquentation de personnalités comme le folkloriste Kunio Yanagita ou le journaliste Gaikotsu Miyatake contribue à asseoir sa réputation.

Pour Kumagusu, la quarantaine est donc une décennie heureuse et fructueuse. Cependant, il existe une ombre tableau : l'entrée en vigueur en 1906 (an 39 de l'ère Meiji) de l'ordonnance sur le regroupement des sanctuaires. L'objectif est d'abandonner les divinités locales au bénéfice du shintô d'État et de consacrer à l'agriculture les terrains des sanctuaires supprimés. Les intérêts en jeu sont immenses : les arbres plus que centenaires des sanctuaires, dont les imposants camphriers, protégés depuis les temps anciens, sont vendus pour en faire du bois de première qualité. Leur valeur suscite la cupidité de certains fonctionnaires et négociants en bois malintentionnés qui les monnaient pour leur propre compte. Cette triste politique nationale s'accélère en 1908, avec l'arrivée de Tôsuke Hirata au ministère de l'Intérieur. En trois ans, environ 50 000 des quelque 190 000 sanctuaires existants avant l'entrée en vigueur de l'ordonnance ont disparu, en même temps qu'un nombre considérable d'arbres abattus sans pitié, parmi lesquels de nombreux camphriers.

C'est Kumagusu qui, le premier, s'insurge contre cette politique. Depuis des générations, l'abattage de ces arbres considérés comme des divinités était tabou. De ce fait, les bois entourant les sanctuaires constituaient un véritable réservoir biologique, ainsi qu'un environnement de travail essentiel pour Kumagusu. Par ailleurs, celui-ci s'inquiète des nombreuses conséquences négatives de la déforestation. Le déboisement des montagnes réduit la capacité des sols à absorber l'eau, d'où des inondations, et la disparition des forêts s'accompagne d'une diminution du nombre d'oiseaux et d'une augmentation de celui des insectes nuisibles pour l'agriculture : tout cela, Kumagusu le prévoit. Enfin, il redoute l'impact négatif du regroupement des sanctuaires sur la psychologie des habitants, leur vie quotidienne et leurs relations communautaires, mais aussi sur les us et coutumes, les traditions et la culture.

Le mouvement d'opposition au regroupement des sanctuaires lancé par Kumagusu débute en 1909, avec la publication dans le journal local, le *Muron Shinpô*, d'une tribune contre la mise en vente du parc Ôhamadaiba de Tanabe. Par la suite, Kumagusu critique à de nombreuses reprises, toujours dans les colonnes du *Muron Shinpô*, la politique de regroupement des sanctuaires. C'est dans ce contexte qu'il apprend la disparition programmée du sanctuaire Ôyama auquel est rattachée sa famille depuis des générations ; il s'enflamme et finit par faire le coup de poing. En août 1910, informé de la participation de Kazuo Tamura, un fonctionnaire favorable au regroupement des sanctuaires, au séminaire d'été de sylviculture organisé par la préfecture de Wakayama au collège de Tanabe, Kumagusu se rend sur place, ivre, et provoque un esclandre. Il rapporte lui-même l'événement dans ces termes : « J'ai envoyé voltiger comme une grenouille le commissaire qui tentait de s'interposer. » Il semblerait, en réalité, qu'il ait été aisément maîtrisé par les gardiens et expulsé de la salle. Cependant, des fonctionnaires malveillants qui lui tiennent rancune de son opposition mettent adroitement à profit cet accrochage pour le faire emprisonner au commissariat pour violation de domicile. Mais la fougue de Kumagusu, qui se consacre corps et âme à son engagement, a déjà gagné les habitants de Tanabe. Ses amis et de nombreuses personnes de son entourage, des artisans, pêcheurs et agriculteurs locaux ainsi que des activistes et même des artistes de sa connaissance, réagissent en protestant vivement auprès du commissaire et des officiels. Parmi eux figure le jeune Morihei Ueshiba. Grâce à leur intervention, au bout du compte, Kumagusu est innocenté et libéré à l'issue de plus de deux semaines de détention.

On raconte que, après son transfert à la maison d'arrêt, il reçoit la visite de Seiga Môri, qui lui apporte un microscope. Normalement, les visites sont interdites en maison d'arrêt, mais à la différence du commissariat, ici, tout le monde est favorable à Kumagusu, depuis le procureur jusqu'aux gardiens. De ce fait, tous semblent fermer les yeux lorsqu'il reçoit des visites. « Il fait frais en prison, et si je m'assoupis en lisant, eh bien je dors, c'est vraiment le paradis sur Terre », rapporte Kumagusu avec décontraction. Le plus surprenant est encore qu'il découvre dans la cour de l'établissement une nouvelle espèce de myxomycète, *Stemonitis fusca*. Sans doute est-il le seul chercheur au monde à avoir fait en prison une découverte dans le domaine de la biologie. À sa sortie, dit-on, il brandit fièrement devant les personnes venues l'accueillir le mouchoir en papier dans lequel il conservait son échantillon.

« Attraperai-je une puce ou le Ciel ? Jouons le tout pour le tout »

« Attraperai-je une puce ou le Ciel ? Jouons le tout pour le tout », se dit Kumagusu lorsqu'il entame, en utilisant des bactéries, ses travaux sur les méthodes de fixation de l'azote dans l'air, proches des recherches actuelles sur la biomasse. Son idée, originale, est d'abord de trouver une bactérie particulière qui fixe l'azote, puis de la faire proliférer grâce à une algue terrestre, la *palmoglea*, que l'on trouve partout à Wakayama. Cela revient à utiliser un procédé enzymatique, que l'on qualifierait aujourd'hui de « biotechnologie », à la place des méthodes employées par l'industrie chimique qui requièrent des conditions de pression et de température coûteuses et polluantes. La réussite de ce projet apporterait la richesse au Japon, veut-il croire, et il s'attelle aux expérimentations. C'est un thème de recherche éminemment ambitieux et passionnant, porteur de pistes pour répondre aux problèmes environnementaux et énergétiques actuels.

Kumagusu consacre vaillamment plus de cinq années à ses recherches aux méthodes de fixation de l'azote dans l'air, mais ses travaux n'aboutissent pas, en partie à cause des obstacles posés par un voisinage hostile. Néanmoins, cette période n'est pas toute noire pour autant. Dogi Hôryû, avec lequel il correspond depuis son époque londonienne, est nommé supérieur du mont Kôya, où il invite Kumagusu. Ravi, celui-ci entraîne Shirô Koaze et d'autres disciples à gravir le mont Kôya pour y collecter des échantillons. Ces retrouvailles interviennent vingt-sept ans après leur dernière rencontre à Londres. Ému, Kumagusu écrit un premier vers sur une feuille de papier déployée sur les tatamis : « *Le mont Kôya avant l'aube* », puis un deuxième : « I am ever dreaming fondly », composant ainsi le premier poème nippo-occidental du monde pour Hôryû. Kumagusu et ses amis, logés au temple Ichijô-in sur les conseils de Hôryû, passent une dizaine de jours au mont Kôya, où ils joignent l'utile à l'agréable et récoltent des *fungi* avant de rentrer à Tanabe.

Lorsqu'ils découvrent une plante ou un animal rare, les habitants de Tanabe se font une joie de l'apporter à Kumagusu pour qu'il l'examine ; lui aussi se réjouit de leurs visites impromptues. Un pêcheur lui a même apporté une créature particulièrement étonnante : une chose mesurant une soixantaine de centimètres, tout en longueur, recouverte de belles rayures horizontales rouges et blanches, avec des boules translucides sur la queue. Kumagusu détermine qu'il s'agit en fait d'un simple serpent marin, appelé *uga* à Tanabe ; les boules translucides sont des anatifes, un crustacé proche des balanes. Néanmoins, il est extrêmement rare que des anatifes se fixent sur la queue d'un serpent marin : c'est un spectacle exceptionnel. Les pêcheurs ont pour habitude, lorsqu'ils trouvent un *uga*, de lui couper la queue pour l'offrir à la divinité protectrice de leur bateau. Kumagusu conserve dans de l'alcool ce précieux serpent marin à la queue parée de coquillages, un porte-bonheur qu'il gardera soigneusement tout le restant de sa vie.

Au cours de ces années, Kumagusu se consacre aussi à la création de l'Institut de recherche botanique Minakata, dont la direction doit lui revenir. Le docteur en agriculture Chôzaburô Tanaka, qui a toujours soutenu les recherches de Kumagusu, se trouve à l'origine de cette initiative. Le document fondateur de l'établissement, rédigé par Tanaka pour l'occasion, rassemble une impressionnante galerie de soutiens. Outre Takashi Hara (1856-1921, premier ministre de 1918 à 1921) figurent le marquis

Yorimichi Tokugawa, le supérieur du temple Kongôbu-ji au mont Kôya, Hôryû Dogi, le marquis Shigenobu Ôkuma (1838-1922, lui aussi premier ministre en 1898, puis de 1914 à 1916), le gouverneur de la préfecture de Wakayama Shinzô Ohara, le député Kunisuke Okazaki, le membre de la Chambre des pairs et directeur de l'école Keio Gijuku Eikichi Kamata, le baron Eitarô Miura (1887-1964, considéré comme le père des études séricicoles au Japon), le gouverneur civil de Taiwan Hiroshi Shimomura, le président-directeur général du grand quotidien *Ôsaka Mainichi Shimbun* Hikoichi Motoyama ou encore le directeur des sondages du *Tôkyô Asahi Shimbun* Hirotarô Sugiyama. Dans ce document, Tanaka insiste sur l'importance de promouvoir et soutenir la recherche scientifique, présente les travaux auxquels Kumagusu s'adonne au point d'en oublier de se nourrir et de dormir et vante son érudition et sa créativité. En 1922, Kumagusu se rend à Tokyo pour rassembler des fonds. C'est la première fois en plus de trente ans, depuis son départ pour les États-Unis, qu'il y remet les pieds. Au cours de ce séjour d'environ cinq mois, il rencontre des personnalités politiques de premier plan comme le chef du gouvernement, Korekiyo Takahashi, qui est aussi l'un de ses anciens professeurs respectés, et le ministre des Affaires étrangères Kôsai Uchida, un ami des années britanniques. Il retrouve également ses camarades d'Ann Arbor. Parmi eux se trouve le banquier Eijirô Ono, qui s'engage à faire un don en faveur de l'institution. Ono, homme d'un grand sérieux, avait paraît-il enjoint à ses enfants, en clin d'œil à son ami, de ne surtout pas devenir un anticonformiste comme Kumagusu ; il est amusant de noter qu'on trouve parmi ses petits-enfants une autre anticonformiste, l'artiste Yoko Ono, épouse de John Lennon.

De retour à Wakayama, Kumagusu continue à collecter des fonds ; il envoie au directeur-adjoint de l'agence d'Ôsaka de Nippon Yusen, Yoshio Yabuki, qui s'intéresse à la botanique, un curriculum vitae écrit sur un rouleau de plus de sept mètres de long, pour obtenir sa coopération.

La recherche de financements avance bien dans un premier temps, mais à cause de la trahison de Tsunegusu, le cadet de Kumagusu, qui s'était engagé à verser une somme importante, les objectifs ne sont pas atteints et, hélas, l'Institut de recherche botanique ne voit pas le jour.

Cueilli par la fleur violette

Le début de l'ère Shôwa (1926-1989), qui correspond aux dernières années de Kumagusu, est assombri par l'approche de la guerre. Lui-même connaît moins de joies, mise à part une surprise qui sera le plus grand honneur de son existence. En 1929 (an 4 de l'ère Shôwa), il est approché par le ministère des Affaires impériales pour donner une conférence devant l'empereur Shôwa à l'occasion d'un voyage que prépare celui-ci dans la région du Nanki, dans la province de Kii. Le souverain, qui est aussi biologiste, s'intéresse fortement aux myxomycètes et il semble que le véritable objectif de son voyage dans le Nanki soit, en réalité, de rencontrer Kumagusu et de visiter l'île de Kashima, riche en myxomycètes. Au mois de mars, le docteur Hirotarô Hattori, professeur à l'université Gakushûin et conseiller de l'empereur, gagne discrètement Tanabe, où il rend une visite impromptue à Kumagusu pour lui parler en personne de cette question. Le mois suivant, Hattori envoie une missive et un télégramme de confirmation : le voyage de l'empereur et sa rencontre avec Kumagusu commencent à prendre forme. À l'époque, l'empereur est pour les Japonais un être d'essence divine ; c'est peut-être ainsi que le considère Kumagusu. Qu'un chercheur indépendant, sans diplôme ni titre, donne une conférence devant l'empereur est plus qu'exceptionnel et Kumagusu se réjouit d'avoir « vécu assez longtemps pour voir cela ».

Kumagusu et sa femme après l'exposé présenté à l'empereur Showa (1929): Source: Minakata Kumagusu Archives.

Le 1er juin 1929, jour de la visite du souverain, il tombe dès le matin une pluie fine comme un brouillard. Kumagusu revêt sa vieille redingote râpée, souvenir de ses années passées à l'étranger qu'il a fait rapiécer dans la nuit ; il coiffe son chapeau melon aux couleurs fanées. Posté sur la jetée d'Ôhama en compagnie de nombreux amis, il contemple le *Nagato*, la forteresse flottante battant pavillon aux armes de l'empereur stationnée au large. Peu après 13 heures, il part en chaloupe pour l'île de Kashima, qu'il fait visiter à l'empereur. Sur place, les deux hommes cherchent sous la bruine ces myxomycètes rares autrefois récoltés par Kumagusu, mais sans succès à cause de la pluie qui a tout lavé. Néanmoins, la conférence donnée ensuite par Kumagusu à bord du *Nagato* est un franc succès. L'empereur invite Kumagusu, au garde-à-vous devant lui, à s'asseoir pour soulager ses jambes, ce qui l'émeut profondément. Kumagusu fait un exposé sur la répartition des plantes et des *fungi* dans la préfecture de Wakayama, et on rapporte que l'empereur rit par moments. Les vingt-cinq minutes allouées à la conférence s'écoulent en un clin d'œil et, lorsque le chambellan signifie la fin de l'entretien, l'empereur demande à Kumagusu de poursuivre et montre un vif intérêt pour l'*uga* couvert de coquillages qu'il a apporté. La prolongation d'une conférence privée est pour l'empereur tout à fait exceptionnelle. De plus, le souverain et son entourage sont ébahis par le cadeau offert par Kumagusu : des échantillons de myxomycètes emballés dans du papier journal et disposés dans une grande boîte à caramels. Les cadeaux à l'empereur sont habituellement présentés dans de riches boîtes en bois de paulownia – c'est encore le cas de nos jours –, mais pour le chercheur qu'était Kumagusu, une boîte à caramels était bien mieux adaptée à la conservation des échantillons qu'un coffret en paulownia.

Kumagusu, personnage de manga [Mizuki Shigeru]. À droite : Kumagusu offre à l'empereur des échantillons emballés dans une boite de caramels.

Au plus fort de son action contre le regroupement des sanctuaires, Kumagusu s'est particulièrement attaché à la protection de l'île de Kashima. Composée de deux îlots flottant sur la baie de Tanabe, cette île d'une superficie d'environ trois hectares est une zone sacrée, protégée depuis les temps anciens et entièrement recouverte d'une riche forêt primaire. En 1902, lorsqu'il y pénètre pour la première fois, Kumagusu constate qu'il s'agit d'un véritable réservoir d'espèces végétales rares, un endroit précieux où il découvrira, à l'occasion de ses visites ultérieures, de nouvelles espèces de myxomycètes. Mais en 1909, le sanctuaire de Kashima est désaffecté et l'année suivante, il est envisagé d'abattre toutes les forêts de l'île. Ce projet est abandonné grâce à la forte opposition des pêcheurs, mais ensuite, le village auquel est rattachée l'île décide de vendre le bois des arbrisseaux pour financer la construction d'une école primaire. Kumagusu s'étonne de ce projet municipal ; il rend immédiatement visite au maire, lui explique que les arbrisseaux sont précisément cruciaux pour l'écosystème des végétaux et obtient l'abandon de cette idée. Pour éviter l'adoption de projets aussi absurdes à l'avenir, il se consacre à la protection de Kashima. Dans ce contexte, la visite de l'empereur Shôwa sur place confère un nouveau souffle à son action. Désormais, plus personne ne tente de détruire la nature de cette île devenue un lieu sacré lié à l'empereur. Porté par son enthousiasme, un an après sa conférence privée, Kumagusu fait ériger à Kashima une imposante stèle sur laquelle est gravé un poème de sa composition : « *Souffle, vent du large, mais prends soin de la moindre branche / Cette forêt est bien-aimée de notre empereur* ». Par la suite, grâce à l'action de Kumagusu et de ses sympathisants, Kashima sera classée site historique, pittoresque et naturel par le ministère de l'Éducation.

Après son soixante-dixième anniversaire, Kumagusu commence à ressentir les effets de l'âge et son vieillissement s'accélère avec la disparition, les uns après les autres, de ses amis proches. Plus de dix années se sont écoulées depuis sa rencontre avec l'empereur. Kumagusu, qui a vu le jour dans un Japon qui s'ouvrait au monde après deux siècles d'isolement, assiste à l'intensification de l'expansionnisme japonais. En décembre 1941 (an 16 de l'ère Shôwa), l'attaque sur Pearl Harbor vient d'être déclenchée. Il contracte une sclérose rénale doublée d'une jaunisse et s'éteint paisiblement le 28 du même mois. « Ma pensée est infinie mais la vie a une fin » : Kumagusu disparaît à l'âge de soixante-quatorze ans en prononçant ces mots : « Au plafond, je vois s'épanouir les fleurs violettes ». D'après Fumie, qui a soigné son père en ces ultimes instants, ces fleurs violettes, fruits d'une hallucination, étaient certainement du lilas de Perse (*melia azedarach*), une superbe plante qu'il aimait particulièrement.

Après la mort de Kumagusu, son immense collection d'échantillons et de livres est scrupuleusement conservée sur place par son épouse Matsue et sa fille Fumie. Kumagusu, sentant la mort approcher, avait déclaré qu'il serait « satisfait si, au vu des échantillons et des documents entreposés ici, quelqu'un se souvenait qu'il y avait eu à Tanabe un homme qui s'était consacré à tout cela. » Son souhait a été exaucé : aujourd'hui encore, on peut voir aux Archives Minakata Kumagusu, construites en 2006 à côté de sa maison, plusieurs dizaines de milliers de précieux documents et effets lui ayant appartenu.

Après-guerre, l'empereur Shôwa aurait confié d'un ton amusé à Keizô Shibuzawa, alors ministre des Finances : « Minakata était un homme surprenant. Quand je suis allé à Kashima, il m'a offert des échantillons rares. Normalement, les cadeaux m'arrivent dans un somptueux coffret en bois de paulownia, mais lui, il avait apporté le sien dans une boîte à caramels. Mais ce n'était pas grave. » En mai 1962 (an 37 de l'ère Shôwa), l'empereur en visite à Shirahama dans le Nanki a évoqué dans un poème sa rencontre avec Kumagusu, trente-trois années plus tôt : « *Kashima sous un voile de pluie / Me rappelle Kumagusu Minakata né au pays de Kii* ». L'empereur

Shôwa a écrit plusieurs milliers de poèmes, mais celui dédié à Kumagusu est, semble-t-il, le seul dans lequel apparaît un nom de personne : ce fait surprenant laisse imaginer que l'empereur tenait Kumagusu en haute estime. Il lisait en effet régulièrement *Nature* depuis qu'il était jeune et le nom de Kumagusu, qui apparaissait fréquemment dans ses pages, avait éveillé son intérêt ; il semble avoir éprouvé un profond respect pour lui bien avant leur conférence privée. Par ailleurs, l'empereur Shôwa aurait à plusieurs reprises parlé en bien de Kumagusu à ses proches. De ce fait, aujourd'hui encore, des membres de la famille impériale se rendent de temps à autre au Musée Minakata Kumagusu qui, malgré sa taille modeste, est équipé d'un salon qui lui est réservé.

La dernière phrase de l'ouvrage de Jirô Kôsaka, *Le Géant prisonnier, la vie de Kumagusu Minakata*, témoigne du lien fort entre l'empereur Shôwa et Kumagusu : « Le monument qui porte le poème de l'empereur, érigé au sommet du mont Bansho à Shirayama, et la stèle sur laquelle est gravé celui de Kumagusu commémorant la venue de l'empereur à Kashima, qui s'étend à ses pieds, se dressent aujourd'hui encore dans le scintillement des courants marins et la brise, comme si l'empereur et Kumagusu, liés par la science, poursuivaient leur discussion. »

OBSERVATION ET INTUITION

Du *kusunoki* guérisseur à la fleur violette : une vie de biologiste

L'ombre embaumante du *kusunoki* du sanctuaire Fujishiro est apaisante pour le très jeune Kumagusu, probablement en vertu des propriétés antivirales ou immunostimulantes des molécules que diffuse cet arbre : de protecteur, le *kusunoki* devient guérisseur. La vie de Kumagusu sera désormais une quête permanente des mystères du monde vivant qui l'entoure, jusqu'à ce qu'il tourne son dernier regard vers le plafond où fleurissent des fleurs violettes.

Il écrit : « Je pourrais acheter un microscope et passer toute une vie à y observer l'univers infini compris dans l'univers, lui-même compris dans l'univers, jusqu'à l'univers qui englobe tous les autres, je ne m'en lasserais pas encore. » Le microscope est son meilleur partenaire de travail.

Kumagusu (à droite) et deux assistants collectent des échantillons dans les montagnes de la péninsule de Kii. Source: Minakata Kumagusu Archives.

Son enfance n'est que collecte d'échantillons, consultation et transcription d'encyclopédies chinoises qui font une large place notamment aux effets des plantes médicinales. Il poursuit activement sa collection et constitue des herbiers partout où il se trouve, dans la péninsule de Kii, en particulier dans les espaces enveloppant les sanctuaires shintô et où la biodiversité est préservée par le caractère sacré de la nature qui entoure ces lieux, dans les parcs de Tokyo, aux États-Unis, notamment en Floride, et dans les Caraïbes. Le nombre d'échantillons amassés est considérable : cryptogames, fongi, myxomycètes, champignons, algues, poissons, insectes... Certains ont été collectés par lui-même, d'autres lui ont été envoyés de tout le Japon avec des demandes d'identification. Il en a aussi expédié à des biologistes en Europe ou au États-Unis, mais bon nombre d'entre eux sont aujourd'hui conservés aux Archives Minakata.

© J-C Valmalette

Tanabe, Archives Minakata Kumagusu. Source: Minakata Kumagusu Archives.

Kumagusu évoque dans les termes suivants les plaisirs de la recherche : « L'univers est infini, mais pas l'esprit de l'homme. Cet esprit fini trouve dans l'univers ce qui peut le réjouir, à sa mesure. Nous tirons notre plaisir d'un morceau de l'univers. C'est, je crois, ce que l'on appelle l'intelligence. »

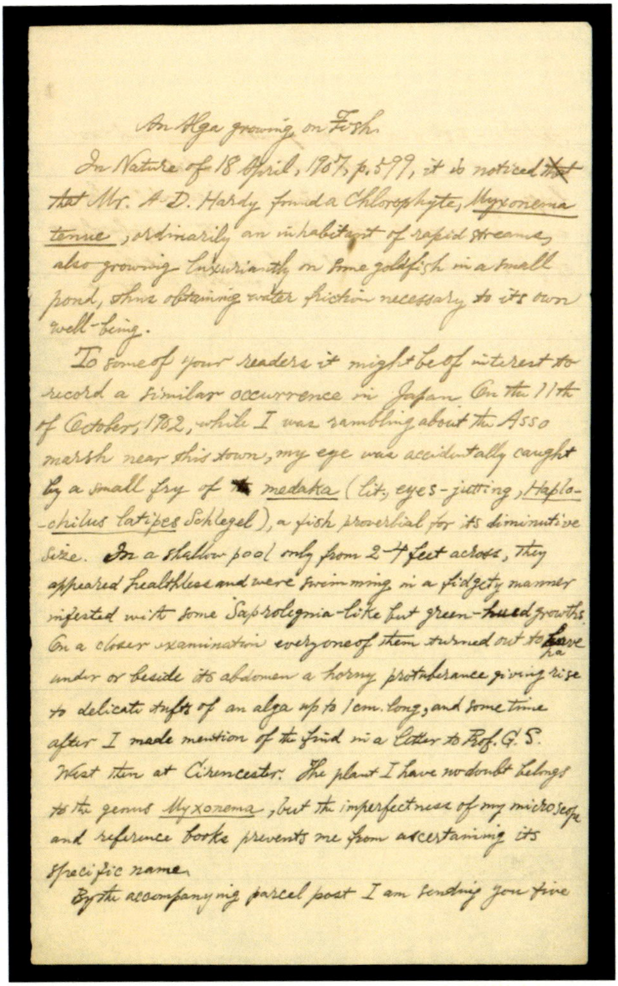

An Alga growing on Fish.

In Nature of 18 April, 1907, p. 599, it is noticed that Mr. A. D. Hardy found a Chlorophyte, Myxonema tenue, ordinarily an inhabitant of rapid streams, also growing luxuriantly on some goldfish in a small pond, thus obtaining water friction necessary to its own well-being.

To some of your readers it might be of interest to record a similar occurrence in Japan. On the 11th of October, 1902, while I was rambling about the Asso marsh near this town, my eye was accidentally caught by a small fry of medaka (lit, eyes-jutting, Haplochilus latipes Schlegel), a fish proverbial for its diminutive size. In a shallow pool only from 2-4 feet across, they appeared healthless and were swimming in a fidgety manner infested with some Saprolegnia-like but green-hued growths. On a closer examination everyone of them turned out to have under or beside its abdomen a horny protuberance giving rise to delicate tufts of an alga up to 1 cm. long, and some time after I made mention of the find in a letter to Prof. G. S. West then at Cirencester. The plant I have no doubt belongs to the genus Myxonema, but the imperfectness of my microscope and reference books prevents me from ascertaining its specific name.

By the accompanying parcel post I am sending you five

Manuscrit d'un article décrivant la symbiose entre une algue et un poison, publié dans la revue Nature *en 1908 sous le titre « An Alga growing on a Fish ». Source: Minakata Kumagusu Archives.*

Il a abondamment contribué à la revue *Nature* : cinquante articles au total dont une large part est consacrée à l'étude d'objets biologiques. En cette fin du XIXe siècle et au début du siècle suivant, cette revue est bien sûr une source de connaissances apportées par les contributions des auteurs ; elle est davantage, pourtant : un puissant moyen d'échange et de confrontation entre les membres de la communauté scientifique disséminés à travers le monde. La participation de Kumagusu en témoigne : en avril 1907 paraît une étude de A.D. Hardy portant sur une algue, *myxonema tenue*, qui se développe de façon abondante sur les poissons rouges vivant dans les étangs. En novembre de la même année, Kumagusu fait remarquer qu'il existe quelque chose de semblable au Japon et raconte comment, lors d'une randonnée dans les marais, non loin de la ville d'Asso, son regard est tombé sur un petit poisson, un *medaka*, qui semblait avoir des difficulté à nager dans le marécage peu profond. En regardant de plus près, il s'aperçut que le corps de l'animal était recouvert de protubérances constituées d'algues pouvant atteindre un centimètre de longueur. Il dit être convaincu qu'il s'agit d'une *myxonema* mais qu'il ne peut l'identifier avec certitude étant donné la mauvaise qualité de son microscope et le manque d'ouvrages à sa disposition à Tanabe. Il envoie donc dans un colis joint, cinq exemplaires de ce petit poisson recouvert d'algue ainsi que quelques préparations sur des lames de microscope dans l'espoir qu'un biologiste puisse « gentiment » les identifier.

Kinoko, *champignon collecté par Kumagusu. Source: Minakata Kumagusu Museum.*

Un article intitulé *The Earliest Mention of Hydrodictyon* apporte en 1904 un commentaire très court sur l'algue verte *Hydrodictyon utriculatum* dont il retrouve les premières traces dans une encyclopédie chinoise du IXe siècle. Elle y est décrite dans un bassin de l'empereur Wu-ti (dynastie Han, 140-87 av. J.-C.). Cette algue est aussi appelée *Water-net* en raison de sa forme en filet dense hexagonal qui peut s'étendre sur plusieurs dizaines de centimètres.

En 1910, Kumagusu adresse à l'éditeur ainsi qu'aux lecteurs de la revue *Nature* une note sous le titre *Singular Mammal called Orocoma.* Il leur demande si l'existence d'un prétendu mammifère, l'*orocoma*, dont il a trouvé des traces dans le récit d'un père jésuite demeurant à Buenos Aires daté de 1729, a effectivement existé dans la mesure où il n'a retrouvé nulle part ailleurs trace de ce mammifère, visiblement issu de l'imagination de ce prêtre.

Dans la livraison de 1903 (*Distribution of Pithophora*), il signale la présence de l'algue *Pithophora oedogonia* dans une rizière très ancienne, non loin de Tanabe, qu'il considère comme une espèce endémique au Japon.

Parmi tous les organismes qu'il étudie, les myxomycètes sont sans aucun doute ceux qui le fascinent le plus. Il en découvre de nombreuses espèces ; l'une, qu'il trouve dans le jardin de sa maison de Tanabe, recevra le nom de *Minakatella longifila Lister*. Selon Tsurumi Kazuko, Kumagusu est attiré par la métamorphose incessante des myxomycètes qui illustre pour lui la transgression par la nature des catégories analytiques généralement admises.

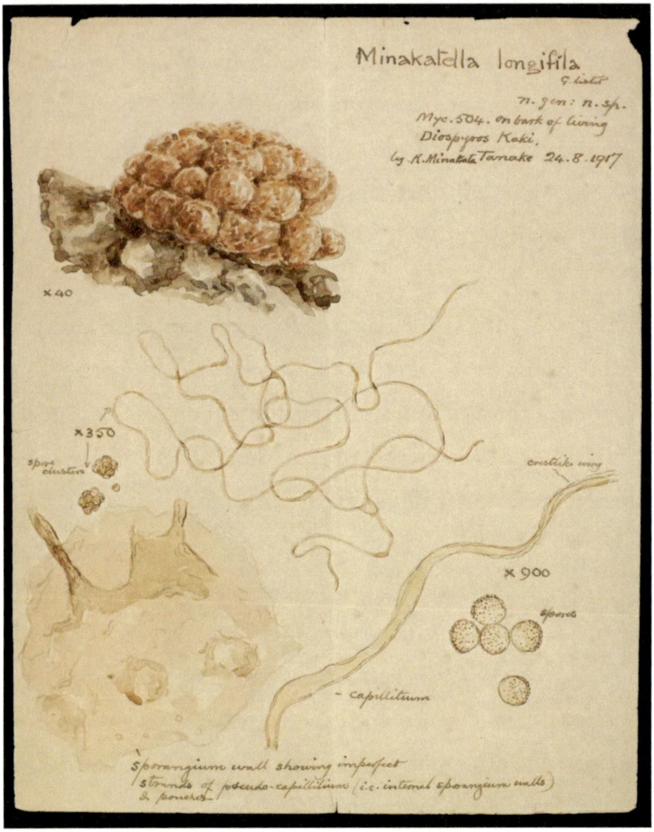

Minakatella Longifila *Nom donné par Gulielma Lister à cette nouvelle espèce de myxomycète en hommage à Kumagusu qui l'a découverte sur un plaqueminier de son jardin à Tanabe en 1917 (Peinture de G. Lister). Source: Minakata Kumagusu Archives.*

La notion de classement a été le fondement même des sciences naturelles occidentales ; elle a permis leur formidable essor. L'approche orientale, à l'inverse, reposait sur la conception de chaque organisme à la fois comme un tout et inscrit au sein d'une interrelation avec son environnement ; en témoignent les nombreuses pharmacopées. On sait aujourd'hui que la notion même de classement, en particulier en biologie, devient difficile tant les systèmes apparaissent complexes et semblent échapper aux frontières auxquelles les esprits occidentaux voudraient les contraindre. Il devient alors nécessaire de créer progressivement autant de cases que d'organismes sous peine de s'exposer à sa propre contradiction. À titre d'illustration, considérons l'une des distinctions les plus évidentes entre les plantes et les animaux. Ces derniers sont incapables de capter l'énergie lumineuse et sont donc tributaires des premières pour recevoir l'ATP, le carburant de toute cellule vivante. Et pourtant, des travaux récents semblent montrer qu'un insecte au moins, le puceron du pois, possède le gène lui permettant de synthétiser le carotène, qu'il utilise ensuite dans certaines conditions pour produire son ATP grâce à la lumière, lorsque la ressource alimentaire se raréfie.

Les myxomycètes

Ces (mycétozoaires) ont fasciné Kumagusu. Malgré la racine *myc-* qui désigne les champignons, ce ne sont ni des moisissures ni des champignons, ni même des bactéries. D'abord parce que leurs spores libèrent des cellules amiboïdes (des myxamibes) ; ensuite parce que les zygotes ne se scindent pas : seule la division nucléaire se répète pour former une grosse amibe (le plasmode) dotée d'une multitude de noyaux. En biologie, on distingue généralement cinq règnes : animal, végétal, fongique, protiste et bactérien. Bien qu'ils forment des spores comme les *fungi*, les myxomycètes sont des organismes unicellulaires, d'où leur appartenance au règne protiste. Cependant, du point de vue phylogénétique, les myxomycètes constituent une catégorie à part entière, au même titre que les animaux ou les plantes. Ils tirent leur nom de leur caractère visqueux quand ils croissent (*myxo-* signifie « gélatineux, gluant »). Enfin, en japonais, on les appelle également *hokori-kabi* (« moisissure-poussière ») parce que leurs spores se dispersent comme de la poussière.

Aujourd'hui, on connaît 700 espèces de myxomycètes appartenant à 60 familles, dont environ 10 % sont présents dans le monde entier ; au Japon, quelque 350 espèces ont été répertoriées. On trouve des myxomycètes tout au long de l'année, mais ils sont semble-t-il plus nombreux depuis la saison des pluies jusqu'au début de l'automne, sur les troncs d'arbre pourris et sous les feuilles mortes, après la pluie. Le cycle de vie des myxomycètes débute sous la forme de spores, qui, après avoir germé, se divisent, se multiplient puis fusionnent pour former un plasmode visqueux.

C'est ainsi le seul organisme connu dont la croissance se produit à partir d'un regroupement de cellules indépendantes et non par leur division. Cette croissance est régulée par un gène appelé *smlA*. On se reportera sur cette question à l'ouvrage de Nicole Le Douarin, *Les cellules souches, porteuses d'immortalité*, Odile Jacob, 2007. Les cellules communiquent entre elles au moyen de la propagation d'un signal chimique appelé chimiotactique. Les recherches en cours sur ce processus biochimique revêtent une très grande importance pour la compréhension des mécanismes de migration des cellules à l'intérieur d'autres organismes.

Le plasmode, qui possède des caractères animaux, se déplace par mouvements amiboïdes à la vitesse de plusieurs centimètres par heure en se nourrissant de bactéries et de moisissures, et continue à croître sous la forme d'un filet. Parvenu à maturité, il quitte son lieu d'origine à la recherche d'un environnement adapté à la formation des spores. Ensuite, le plasmode (l'amibe), qui a délaissé son aspect de filet pour une forme plus ramassée, se transforme en une seule nuit en sporophore (un champignon) et libère ses spores ; c'est le point de départ d'un nouveau cycle de vie des myxomycètes.

Les travaux de recherche les plus en pointe sur ces organismes montrent que le plasmode des myxomycètes, qui possèdent des caractéristiques animales, se nourrit en se déplaçant. Le plasmode est-il intelligent ? Comment peut-il être doué d'intelligence alors qu'il ne possède pas de cerveau ? Nakagaki Toshiyuki apporte la réponse suivante à ces questions : même en l'absence d'une « existence particulière » comme le cerveau qui émet des instructions, un simple « phénomène de structuration autonome » entre éléments de même nature permet de générer une « intelligence ». La découverte par M. Nakagaki, aujourd'hui professeur à l'Institut de recherche en sciences électroniques de l'Université de Hokkaido, de cette intelligence des myxomycètes « capables de sortir d'un labyrinthe » a été couronnée d'un prix igNobel en 2008.

De tels phénomènes de structuration autonome sont nombreux dans la nature et, au bout du compte, on peut imaginer qu'il se passe la même chose dans notre cerveau. Le cerveau n'est qu'un amas de cellules nerveuses aux propriétés similaires ; il n'y a pas à l'intérieur une existence particulière qui serait aux commandes. On estime aujourd'hui que le fonctionnement du cerveau est étroitement lié aux phénomènes de structuration autonome. Etudiés dans le domaine des recherches actuelles sur les cellules souches, les myxomycètes pourraient constituer une précieuse indication pour comprendre le mécanisme des « frontières de la vie », l'émergence du vivant dans le monde tangible.

Kumagusu semblait déjà envisager sous l'angle des manipulations et améliorations génétiques les « mutations » qui interviennent lorsqu'on mélange les plasmodes de myxomycètes de types différents. Il faut lui reconnaître une extraordinaire intuition scientifique.

Encore un mot sur les myxomycètes. Aujourd'hui, les films d'animation japonais ont acquis une notoriété mondiale, certains sont même élevés au rang d'art ou de culture à part entière. L'un des réalisateurs emblématiques de ce genre est sans aucun doute Hayao Miyazaki. Dans ses œuvres, nombreux sont les personnages visqueux et gluants inspirés du plasmode des myxomycètes. C'est par exemple le cas de Nago dans *Princesse Mononoké* ou du Sans-visage du *Voyage de Chihiro*, lorsqu'il s'énerve.

Ces plasmodes ont inspiré à Kumagusu une sorte de théorie de la vie : « Les plasmodes qui apparaissent à l'homme comme des glaires sans intérêt sont au contraire des organismes pleins de vitalité, et les beaux sporophores qui semblent vivants à première vue sont en réalité comme morts. De la même façon, le dualisme de la lumière et de l'obscurité, de notre monde et de l'enfer, sont des concepts arbitrairement établis par l'homme, mais la nature véritable de l'existence se trouve ailleurs, à un niveau où les deux sont inséparables. » La pensée de Kumagusu, qui dépasse ce dualisme, ne serait-elle pas à l'origine des personnages visqueux de Miyazaki ? C'est l'avis du critique de cinéma Kanô Seiji, spécialiste de l'œuvre du réalisateur.

Kumagusu voit dans le statut intermédiaire et ambigu des myxomycètes, entre la plante et l'animal, une sorte de monstre vrai, un *bakemono*. Plus généralement, ce sont les domaines-frontières qui l'intéressent. Il en va de même pour son étude des coutumes, du folklore qu'il met en relation avec l'environnement, avec le souci constant d'établir une relation entre les choses matérielles et immatérielles. Cette représentation est bien évidement imprégnée de l'*ukiyo* (terme désignant le « monde flottant » qui, au début de l'ère Edo, a désigné la gravure sur bois plus communément appelée « estampe japonaise ») et peut être considérée comme l'un des fondements de l'imaginaire japonais. Elle repose sur la notion bouddhiste de l'impermanence où tout est mouvement et incessante métamorphose.

Kumagusu consacre ainsi plusieurs articles aux myxomycètes et plus particulièrement aux quatre-vingt-six espèces qu'il a recensées dans l'archipel (« Colours of Plasmodia of some Mycetozoa », *Nature*, 1910. Il fait également connaître à la communauté scientifique internationale de très nombreux texte chinois inédits, dont l'un datant du IXe siècle évoquant des « abeilles » (ou des « guêpes ») vivant sur les *canarium pimela*, résineux de la famille des Burséracées originaire des régions tropicales que l'on utilise dans la fabrication de l'encens et dont le fruit comestible (en anglais : *Chinese Black Olive*) fournit une huile aux qualités nutritives remarquables. Le texte indique que ces « abeilles » semblent avoir saisi les feuilles de l'arbre avec leurs pattes d'une manière telle que ces feuilles sont devenues une part d'elles-mêmes. Il précise qu'elles sont utilisées à cette époque comme philtres et que, pour les recueillir, les habitants abattent les arbres et attendent le dessèchement des feuilles pour pouvoir les collecter. Il ajoute qu'il s'agit là probablement du texte le plus ancien faisant mention des phasmes. Tout comme celui consacré aux croyances orientales relatives aux abeilles et aux guêpes en lien avec le rituel des Bugonia, attesté dans des textes anciens de la Méditerranée, et reposant sur une croyance selon laquelle il y avait génération spontanée d'abeilles au sein des carcasses de grands mammifères à l'instar de l'Énigme de Samson (*Livre des Juges*), cet article illustre la volonté de Kumagusu de lier sciences naturelles et traditions.

Un encyclopédiste entre Orient et Occident

Le parcours de Kumagusu de l'Orient en direction de l'Occident puis de l'Occident vers l'Orient est singulier. Les exemples d'Occidentaux partis à la découverte des terres inconnues et à la conquête des océans sont innombrables. Nous pourrions faire des hypothèses sur le cheminement personnel de Kumagusu qui conduit son parcours, mais il est plus aisé de s'arrêter sur les sujets qui ont retenu son attention. En effet, les récits de voyageurs extrême-orientaux explorant les terres d'Occident sont rares et ceux d'individus au parcours solitaire le sont davantage encore.

Sa première publication dans la revue *Nature* suivie d'un fort retentissement s'intitule « Les Constellations de l'Extrême-Orient » (*Nature*, vol. 48, n° 1249, p. 541-543, 1893). Cet article répond aux deux dernières des cinq questions sur les constellations posées par un certain M. A. B. dans le courrier des lecteurs du numéro du 17 août de *Nature*. Il s'agit d'une interrogation : « D'autres peuples que les Assyriens et les Grecs possèdent-ils leurs propres constellations ? » et d'une proposition : « Les différences et similitudes entre de telles constellations ne pourraient-elles servir à identifier les relations de proximité entre divers peuples ? » Dans son article, Kumagusu commence par présenter les constellations chinoises, radicalement différentes des constellations grecques organisées autour des héros de la mythologie et des animaux. Le système chinois, sur la base du cycle lunaire, divise la voûte céleste en vingt-huit maisons et intègre dans les constellations l'empereur, des édifices de la capitale, les relations familiales et même des concepts moraux. Kumagusu présente ensuite les constellations indiennes, qui découpent aussi la voûte céleste en vingt-huit parties, et développe son argumentation à travers la comparaison entre constellations chinoises et indiennes. Par exemple, la division en vingt-huit quartiers dans les deux cas est surprenante, mais Kumagusu montre que les constellations chinoises et indiennes des temps anciens se sont développées de façon indépendante. De plus, il souligne que, malgré leur développement autonome, une comparaison attentive de ces systèmes de constellations montre un certain nombre de ressemblances. Enfin, sur la base de ces considérations, il termine ainsi son article :

« En conclusion, j'aurais tendance à dire que la particularité, dans les cas où elle existe, peut sans nul doute être d'une grande valeur pour les étudiants en sociologie, en ce qu'elle pourrait les aider dans une certaine mesure à réaliser diverses découvertes importantes. [...] D'un autre côté, pour ce qui est de l'avantage de l'utiliser pour établir une affinité raciale, je dois émettre des réserves car, alors qu'il ne manque pas d'exemples de si remarquables analogies chez des peuples aussi hétérogènes que les Chinois et les Indiens, le sujet est résolument l'un de ces acquis sociaux d'une nature hautement transmissible, ses caractéristiques actuelles étant davantage le résultat de liens entre nations que d'affinités raciales.

Kumagusu Minakata, 15 Blithfield Street, Kensington, 31 août. »

La particularité des articles écrits par Kumagusu en anglais est de débattre d'un point précis avec simplicité, de toujours présenter un titre clair et un texte soigneusement rédigé, qui traite du sujet avec concision. La précision de l'expression et la structure logique n'ont rien à envier aux contributions scientifiques d'aujourd'hui. Le contraste est frappant avec ses longs articles et textes en japonais, émaillés de digressions et ardus ; leur compréhension demande parfois un certain effort. L'un des grands objectifs des articles en anglais de Kumagusu est de montrer que « l'Orient aussi a une tradition de pensée scientifique », à une époque où l'influence des sciences occidentales est prépondérante, comme le souligne Matsui Ryûgo, l'un des chercheurs sur Kumagusu faisant aujourd'hui autorité. Plus tard, la vision académique de Kumagusu dépassera le cadre de la simple présentation de la pensée scientifique et de la culture orientales pour adopter un point de vue plus universel, englobant jusqu'aux sciences occidentales, et dont les bases ont sans aucun doute été jetées avec la rédaction de ces articles scientifiques à Londres.

Kumagusu consacre plusieurs articles à la confrontation entre croyances occidentales et croyances orientales comme l'exemple du rituel des Bugonia décrit plus haut, mais sa contribution la plus représentative a pour titre « Le Juif errant » (*The Wandering Jew*). L'histoire du Juif errant est celle du cordonnier juif Ahaswerus qui, pour avoir refusé froidement d'aider le Christ en route vers le Golgotha, est condamné à l'errance éternelle sur Terre. Cette légende, dont l'existence est déjà attestée au Moyen Âge, se répand au XIXe siècle dans toute l'Europe, à la faveur de la montée de l'antisémitisme. De nombreux poèmes traitent de la désolation d'être condamné à errer éternellement sans pouvoir mourir et, en France, le roman-feuilleton d'Eugène Sue *Le Juif errant* rencontre un énorme succès. Kumagusu va montrer dans son article intitulé « Le Juif errant » la force des similitudes de cette histoire avec le mythe bouddhiste de Pindola Bharadvaja que l'on retrouve au Japon sous le nom de *Binzuru*. Ce personnage est banni du nirvâna par Bouddha pour avoir utilisé ses pouvoirs magiques ; condamné à ne pas connaître la mort, il est destiné à l'errance éternelle sur Terre, habillé de façon misérable et doté de pouvoirs surnaturels. Kumagusu compare en détail ces deux légendes, examinant leurs points communs et leurs divergences. Ajoutons que dans cet article, dans lequel il se réfère à des histoires chinoises similaires, Kumagusu conclut à une « dissémination » du mythe, qu'il corrigera plus tard en « développement autonome » avant de revenir à l'idée de « dissémination ». Quoi qu'il en soit, grâce aux récits et légendes d'une religion encore quasiment inconnue en Europe à l'époque, il a sans doute voulu émettre l'idée d'une mythologie à la fois commune et nécessaire à l'humanité.

Depuis Tanabe, il fait publier en mars 1907 une requête ironique dans *Notes and Queries* sur la manière dont l'*Encyclopedia Britannica* traite de l'islam au Japon à l'entrée *Sunnites and Shiites* ; il cite l'encyclopédie « [...] Le Japon est rangé au nombre des pays dans lesquels la religion de Mahomet est plus ou moins répandue. [...] On estime à une trentaine de millions le nombre de mahométans vivant au Japon, en Chine et dans les îles voisines », et il ajoute : « Je souhaite être informé de tout avis ou de toute observation faisant autorité et susceptible de constituer un fondement raisonnable pour de telles affirmations. »

En 1914 il lance la requête suivante dans *Notes and Queries* au sujet du noircissement des dents : « [selon un texte publié à Hanovre en 1847], les grandes dames russes peignent leurs joues en rouge vif et autrefois elles coloraient fréquemment leurs dents en noir, est-ce que l'un de vos lecteurs peut me dire quelle préparation était employée pour le noircissement des dents ? Autrefois, les femmes japonaises avaient également l'habitude de peindre leurs joues et de noircir leurs dents. Ce premier usage ancien a disparu au cours du XVIIIe siècle, alors que le deuxième se rencontre encore occasionnellement dans les campagnes. »

Il publie peu après un article intitulé « Avocat moderne du druidisme » dans lequel il écrit : « Je me souviens une fois avoir lu un écrivain moderne en Grande-Bretagne ou en Irlande ayant subi l'anathème public en s'étant fait l'avocat de la religion des anciens druides ; mais maintenant j'ai totalement oublié son nom aussi bien que le titre du livre contenant son explication. Je serais heureux d'avoir une information sur eux. »

C'est probablement sa lecture du fameux conte anglais *Dick Whittington et son chat* qui révèle le mieux son exceptionnelle connaissance encyclopédique qui transcende les frontières entre Orient et Occident. L'histoire est celle d'un jeune garçon pauvre dont le chat débarrasse un navire des rats qui gâtaient sa cargaison. Le propriétaire du navire est un riche marchand qui, par gratitude, va donner en retour sa fortune et sa fille au jeune homme, lequel sera ensuite anobli par le roi. Ce conte est connu en Europe, en Russie et en Perse dès le XIIIe siècle, mais Kumagusu en trouve la trace dans une traduction chinoise du *Mūlasarvāstivāda* (dont l'original date du VIIe siècle), texte de l'une des plus vieilles écoles bouddhistes. Cependant, dans cet ouvrage ancien, le sauveur qui enrichit le jeune Indien est une souris. Pour éclaircir ce point, et en s'appuyant sur le fait que le chat est détesté dans l'hindouisme, le zoroastrisme et le bouddhisme, Kumagusu s'intéresse aux diverses valeurs attribuées aux animaux. Le bouddhisme a pour particularité de préférer le serpent, la fourmi, la grenouille ou la souris au chat qui a eu le malheur de se réjouir de la mort de Bouddha.

Choboroku et la souri par Kumagusu. Source: Minakata Kumagusu Museum. © J-C Valmalette

Kumagusu et les chats

Kumagusu adorait les chats, il en élevait déjà un avant son mariage. À l'étranger, il recueillait des chats errants ; même dans les temps les plus difficiles, il en avait toujours un pour lui tenir compagnie. Les chats avaient beau changer, ils portaient tous le même nom, Choboroku. À Londres, alors qu'il peinait à se nourrir, Kumagusu mastiquait d'abord les morceaux de viande pour en tirer la partie nutritive et donnait le reste à manger à son chat. En hiver, il lui arrivait de dormir avec l'animal, en guise de chaufferette. Après son mariage, Choboroku, bien nourri, grossit ; sa mission était de protéger les précieux myxomycètes contre les limaces.

Dans son article intitulé « Discovery of Japan » (*Nature*, 1903), Kumagusu s'interroge sur l'idée selon laquelle Marco Polo aurait été le premier à mentionner l'existence du Japon en Occident. Il s'appuie sur l'ouvrage de Jean-Baptiste Tavernier *Les six voyages* (1676) dans lequel l'auteur évoque un lieu nommé *Jabadi* par les géographes anciens et qui pourrait provenir de l'ancienne désignation *Yamato*, ou plutôt de sa transcription chinoise, *Yamadai* ou *Jabatai*. Il évoque ensuite la traduction française d'un texte, *Les voyages de deux Arabes du IXe siècle*, où il est question d'une île près de la Chine, dont les habitants paient un impôt à ce pays en échange de la paix. Il met ce passage en relation avec le texte *Lun Hang* du philosophe Wang Chung (Ier siècle ap. J.-C.), qui décrit la Chine de Ching-Wang (dynastie Chau, vers 1100 av. J.-C.) à l'époque où elle jouit d'une paix durable dont bénéficient les peuples voisins comme ceux du Laos ou du Japon. Kumagusu cite enfin les *Second Annals of Japan* qui évoquent le passage de voyageurs arabes, parmi lesquels plusieurs femmes, qui durant les VIIIe et IXe siècles ont visité le Japon ou s'y sont installés. Cette Chine, très prospère, a vu se croiser des populations issues de toute l'Asie. Pour illustrer ce fait, Kumagusu rapporte l'anecdote selon laquelle, durant un banquet donné à l'occasion du nouvel an (en 753 ap. J.-C.), l'ambassadeur du Japon dispute la place d'honneur à son homologue arabe ; l'ambassadeur japonais finit par l'emporter. Déjà à cette période, Japonais et Perses entretenaient des relations. Kumagusu relate ensuite d'autres épisodes qui se sont déroulés à partir de 1407, soit plus d'un siècle avant l'arrivée des Portugais, dans lesquels il est curieusement déjà question de *namban*, ou *barbares du Sud,* terme qui sera employé pour désigner les Européens, « hommes blancs », « au long nez » et « aux manières rustres », arrivant en grand nombre dans les ports du Japon à partir de 1543 et jusqu'au XVIIe siècle. Qui sont ces *namban* présents au Japon près d'un siècle et demi avant les « premiers » Européens ? L'article se poursuit par une mise en relation des conceptions philosophiques, morales et religieuses de l'Orient et de l'Occident, en particulier du bouddhisme et du christianisme. Il insiste sur l'attraction qu'exerçait la Chine ancienne : elle offrait au Japon l'opportunité d'entretenir d'importantes relations avec les peuples situés au-delà de l'Empire du Milieu plusieurs siècles avant la constitution des empires européens.

Dans une série d'articles intitulés « Remakable Sounds » publiés dans *Nature*, Kumagusu rapproche les croyances européennes anciennes qui entourent les bruits de la nature, comme le hurlement du vent ou le craquement de la glace en Europe septentrionale, et les légendes inspirées par le souffle des volcans ou des sources chaudes au Japon. Il évoque aussi les *dônari* (« sons du temples »), que l'on entend autour du village de Kurotori durant les beaux jours d'automne, juste avant que le temps ne tourne à l'orage, et qui figurent parmi « les sept merveilles de la province d'Echigo ».

Kumagusu écrit une multitude de notes ou d'articles, souvent en réponse à d'autres articles, dont le seul lien apparent semble être la mise en relation de l'Orient avec l'Occident (« La trépanation chez les peuples anciens »). Dans « Witty Boy » (« Le garçon plein d'esprit »), il fait un parallèle entre un conte chinois et une plaisanterie italienne de l'époque médiévale et démontre que, malgré leur absence d'influence mutuelle, ces deux récits présentent une finalité commune. Dans « Beaver and Python » (« Le castor et le python »), la légende occidentale rapporte que le castor traqué par le chasseur préfère s'automutiler pour échapper à ce dernier, tout comme le fait le python de la légende chinoise qui, recherché pour le liquide contenu dans sa glande, est capable de se vider afin de fuir la convoitise du chasseur.

Dans « Moon and crabs » (« La Lune et les crabes »), Kumagusu se demande si, en Europe, la taille des crabes dépend des phases de la Lune comme en Inde ou au Japon. Dans ces pays, en effet, on raconte que, lors de la pleine lune, les crabes, effrayés par leur ombre, se terrent sous des pierres et renoncent ainsi à leur nourriture. Il s'étonne de ce que, dans les textes chinois anciens, l'inverse soit rapporté : les crabes, les coquillages, les tortues seraient plus gras lors de la pleine lune.

Pièce de travail dans la propriété de Kumagusu à Tanabe.

Dans « On Augury from Combat of Shellfish » (« Sur l'augure du combat de crustacés ») le destin des guerriers japonais, chinois ou cambodgiens se lit dans le fond des bassins où se déroulent les combats entre crustacés. Kumagusu interroge les lecteurs sur d'éventuelles pratiques similaires dans d'autres parties du monde. Il apporte une réponse dans un article intitulé « Shell-fish » qui relate des méthodes de divination répandues en Allemagne et en Russie chez les jeunes filles qui déploient des efforts pour tenter de prédire le sort de leur mariage dans le mouvement des coquillages.

Dans « Maize », il s'intéresse aux mentions qui sont faites du maïs dans les textes anciens à travers le monde et les confusions possibles avec certaines variétés de sorgho d'Asie.

« Flying cups » met en regard un texte de Marco Polo décrivant un tour de magie qui se pratiquait à la cour impériale chinoise et le récit de cette même scène par Jakushô, moine bouddhiste japonais du XIe siècle ; ayant été invité à s'y essayer, il échoua.

« Footprints of Gods » évoque les légendes associées à travers les époques aux empreintes de pieds sur tous les continents, des bords de la Vienne au temps de Clovis jusqu'aux îles Samoa, du Mexique ancien aux sculptures de l'Âge de Bronze trouvées en Suède. Les Japonais reconnaîtraient sans difficulté les esprits du folklore lithuanien (« Lithuanian Folklore : Legless Spirits ») : ils y sont représentés sans jambes, tout comme leurs fantômes. Selon la légende indienne Nâgârdjuna, les êtres spirituels ne laissent aucune empreinte alors que les hommes, même ceux qui, par magie, tentent de devenir invisibles, sont trahis par leurs empreintes.

Dans sa note « Breaking the glass at Jewish Weddings », Kumagusu rapproche la tradition juive, qui veut que le jeune marié brise un verre pour rappeler la destruction du temple de Jérusalem, et le bris du *suribachi* (mortier d'usage quotidien servant à la préparation du *miso*) accompagné de cris de joie, qui achève la cérémonie du mariage, dans sa province de Kii et la province voisine d'Izumi, lorsque les jeunes mariés se sont retirés dans la chambre nuptiale.

« Life Star Folklore » propose un rapprochement étrange : durant les trois jours précédant la mort de saint Thomas d'Aquin, une étoile brillante était visible au-dessus de son abbaye ; elle disparut à l'instant de sa mort. Les Chinois sont convaincus que la disparition d'une étoile ou la chute d'une météorite sont toujours associées à la mort d'un homme illustre.

Kumagusu accordait une grande importance au folklore comparatif : la liste de ses contributions est longue ; citer leurs titres montre la curiosité de leur auteur. « Les vicissitudes du langage », « Les serpents buvant du lait », « Le fils désobéissant », « L'origine du diabolo », « Les superstitions liées à l'éternuement », « Le mort vivant », « Les machines volantes de l'Extrême-Orient », « L'enfant dit son destin », « La favorite enviée », « L'homme aux yeux bandés : variante japonaise », « La tortue et le tonnerre », « Méthodes pour réveiller un dormeur », « La figure de Bouddha dans l'œil et le cou », « L'utilisation des animaux dans la guerre », « Les moustaches du tigre », « Superstitions des maisons et des jardins », « La perversité du vieil homme », « La bière, le cheval et l'aubergine », « Une parabole de l'éternité », « La corde de sable », « Les plantes qui prospèrent mieux lorsqu'elles sont volées », « L'emprunt japonais des mots européens », « Un paysan et un théâtre », « Un prix pour le plus fainéant »,... mais parfois, les contributions de Kumagusu se résument à une phrase ou une question. Un exemple : « Est-ce que l'un des lecteurs pourrait m'indiquer où le cardan a été conçu pour la première fois ? »

Sa lutte contre le regroupement des sanctuaires est emblématique de sa volonté de préserver traditions, légendes et mythes, cet héritage de l'histoire populaire que les historiens peuvent être tentés d'effacer ou de transformer pour faire émerger de nouveaux mythes.

Le regard de Kumagusu sur l'Occident est celui d'un folkloriste, d'un ethnologue qui explore les similitudes des pratiques pour tenter de mettre en évidence leur présence universelle. Ainsi, Kumagusu invite le lecteur occidental à déplacer le point de son observation et s'immerger dans l'histoire des peuples devenus « modernes ». Cette quête semble aller à contre-courant des mouvements qui participent à la modernisation du pays et bouleversent son organisation politique et sociale tels l'introduction des technologies et la mise en œuvre de modèles économiques. Dans sa démarche, Kumagusu considère l'Occident non dans son expression la plus contemporaine, mais, au moment où les élites japonaises subissent la fascination de ce qui a fondé sa puissance, il en propose une analyse diachronique. À ceux qui ont pour ambition de copier l'Occident, il adresse un message clair : le Japon est semblable à l'Occident et réciproquement. Ce qui les différencie, ce n'est pas le processus de transformation de leur société mais la rapidité de ce processus qui permet de figer plus ou moins durablement l'ancrage dans le passé. Paradoxalement, la transformation lente de l'Occident a fait disparaître ce qui, au Japon, a résisté à une mutation brutale.

L'observateur occidental identifie toutes sortes de « contradictions ». Mais la lecture de ces transformations ne peut se faire en-dehors du milieu naturel où elles se sont produites. Cette constatation s'applique particulièrement au Japon qui, dans son essence même, intègre le surnaturel.

Dans son ouvrage « Civilization and Monsters : Spirits of Modernity in Meiji Japan » (Duke University Press, 1999), l'historien Gerald Figal estime que les fantômes, les monstres et les mystères de toutes sortes jouent un rôle fondamental dans la construction de la modernité du Japon Meiji. Le terme « modernisation » évoque une sorte de siècle des Lumières, des images de progrès, de technologies avancées dans une région qui en ressentait la nécessité. Le même auteur affirme que «... ces images sont si convaincantes que l'on se pose rarement la question des prétendus avantages que la modernisation entraîne. Ainsi, la restauration Meiji est perçue comme un impressionnant bond en avant [...] de sorte que le Japon occupe une place respectable parmi les nations industrialisées de l'Occident [...] par la création d'institutions politiques fortes, centralisées, et assimilant avidement les dernières avancées de la technologie industrielle ou militaire. Mais peu d'attention est accordée à l'angoisse collective, ou traumatisme que ces transformations ont pu engendrer dans la population en général. »

La question de la modernité est centrale chez Kumagusu. Il cherche à l'étendre au-delà du champ occidental, à l'articuler entre rationalité et croyance. La question de l'écologie illustre bien ce paradigme. D'un côté, le sanctuaire shintô, lieu de croyance, protège les communautés qui s'y regroupent à de nombreuses occasions. Les essences distillées par les camphriers millénaires, les contes et légendes qui s'y racontent, la préservation de la biodiversité, contribuent à tisser des liens entre les individus : d'irrationnelle, la croyance y devient rationnelle. De l'autre, les décisions rationnelles visant le regroupement de ces sanctuaires selon un schéma calqué sur celui des villages, des communes et des préfectures, entraînent la disparition des pratiques villageoises, le changement des comportements, la disparition des camphriers et de l'écosystème, l'invasion d'insectes « nuisibles » ; elles conduisent Kumagusu à considérer cette tentative de rationalisation de l'organisation sociale et sacrée comme totalement « irrationnelle ».

L'émergence d'une pensée écologique en Orient

Le gouvernement japonais lance en 1906 un vaste programme sur six ans visant à renforcer son emprise sur les localités et à structurer le territoire rural alors composé d'une multitude de communautés organisées autour de sanctuaires et de divinités enracinées dans la mémoire millénaire. Les habitants s'y regroupent fréquemment lors des nombreuses célébrations qui rythment les saisons. Le shintoïsme des origines peut être considéré comme une religion de la forêt : plus qu'abri des divinités, les *kami*, elle est elle-même divinité.

© J-C Valmalette

Hongū-taisha, grand sanctuaire shintô de Kumano.

Ces sanctuaires qui s'égrènent tout le long de l'archipel sont autant d'espaces de transition, localisés non au centre mais aux abords des villages, des hameaux ; ils sont lieux de passage entre la platitude des domaines cultivés et les premières pentes recouvertes de forêts primaires, entre l'habitat des hommes et celui des divinités, entre le profane et le sacré. Ainsi, le village n'est pas organisé *autour* mais à l'intérieur du sacré et ses habitants s'en trouvent enveloppés. Le petit sanctuaire, modeste construction de bois, a besoin d'être protégé de la foudre et des insectes. C'est le camphrier millénaire qui s'en charge, non seulement grâce à sa hauteur et sa capacité à se régénérer perpétuellement à partir de la souche après chaque attaque de la foudre mais aussi par les substances volatiles qu'il sécrète et qui invitent les insectes à accorder un léger sursis au bois du sanctuaire avant d'entamer sa décomposition. En retour, les villageois qui protègent le sanctuaire soignent le *kusunoki* et la forêt qui l'entoure. Cette symbiose est un pacte entre l'homme et son environnement, entre l'écologie et le sacré. Il suffit de suivre les pas du jeune garçon dans *Mon voisin Totoro* (du réalisateur Hayao Miyazaki) pour découvrir avec lui que les entrailles du *kusunoki* géant, ce « maître de la forêt qui fait germer les graines », sont le passage vers cet imaginaire bien réel dans l'esprit des Japonais. Les découvertes récentes de la biologie expriment dans un autre langage cette réalité du pouvoir caché des racines bienfaisantes qui abritent cette diversité microbienne indispensable au redéploiement de la vie.

Hongū-taisha, grand sanctuaire shintô de Kumano

Kusonoki *millénaire sur le chemin de Kumano.* © J-C Valmalette

Kumagusu assiste au bouleversement profond de cet équilibre subtil. Dès les premières années de l'ère Meiji, le pouvoir impérial souhaite renforcer son autorité : une première ordonnance (*Shisei-choson-sei*, 1888) vise à moderniser le pays en le dotant d'un système administratif efficace. Elle ordonne le regroupement des villages et des villes en unités administratives plus importantes et déclasse les plus petits. Parallèlement, le gouvernement Meiji extrait le shintoïsme du bouddhisme et tente de le promouvoir comme religion d'État. Ainsi, une deuxième ordonnance (*Jinja-goshi-sei*, 1906) a pour but la modernisation morale et spirituelle de la nation japonaise. Elle stipule qu'il ne doit plus y avoir qu'un sanctuaire par unité administrative, à quelques rares exceptions près. La transformation qui s'opère est profonde, le culte primitif alors tombé en désuétude, excepté dans les zones rurales, va servir de substrat à l'émergence d'une « religion de l'empereur », forme de tropisme par lequel se modernise et s'industrialise le Japon jusqu'à la formation d'un empire, à l'instar des puissances occidentales. Le shintoïsme passe d'une religion de villageois et des montagnes à une religion centralisée avec la création de sanctuaires d'État (*kansha*) où sont déposées les offrandes impériales et les sanctuaires du peuple (*minsha*) classés en trois catégories selon leur importance. Les desservants, qui bénéficiaient d'une charge héréditaire et d'avantages fonciers, deviennent des fonctionnaires au service du culte de la nation (*kokka no soshi*) incarnée par l'empereur. Les nouvelles structures administratives tracent des frontières qui dessinent à leur tour le schéma d'organisation locale des sanctuaires. Cette transformation implique le regroupement des sanctuaires existants et la disparition de dizaines de milliers de sanctuaires répartis à travers le territoire. Dans la seule préfecture de Wakayama, le nombre des sanctuaires diminue brutalement de 3 721 en 1906 à moins de 600 cinq ans plus tard.

© J-C Valmalette

Regroupement de sanctuaires shintô d'Inami, village situé dans la province de Wakayama d'où est originaire Satoshi Ohara, co-auteur du présent ouvrage. Chaque sanctuaire était auparavant situé en bordure de son hameau et placé sous la protection de kusunoki *millénaires. Aujourd'hui encore, à l'occasion des nombreuses fêtes qui rythment le calendrier shintô, les habitants se retrouvent par communautés autour de ces sanctuaires dont la taille varie en fonction de l'importance des villages.*

Les communautés se mobilisent différemment contre ce programme selon qu'elles espèrent pouvoir continuer de célébrer leurs divinités sur les mêmes lieux ou que cette possibilité leur sera refusée. C'est le cas par exemple de la communauté de Takahashi qui se rassemble sur le mont Iyo Kumano. Dans certains cas, l'opposition est virulente, les villageois revendiquent leur indépendance vis-à-vis des sanctuaires qui leur sont imposés : ils tiennent leurs cérémonies en-dehors, refusent de participer aux célébrations officielles, reconstruisent leurs sanctuaires et parfois même adoptent de nouvelles divinités.

Dans la préfecture de Wakayama, durement frappée par la diminution des sanctuaires de « rang villageois » et « sans rang », Kumagusu s'inquiète de ce que les arbres immenses entourant les anciens temples soient abattus pour être vendus comme bois précieux. Il redoute que la modification de la structure de ces lieux millénaires ne perturbe les oiseaux, ne modifie leur répartition et n'ait pour conséquence l'augmentation du nombre d'insectes et la nécessité pour les paysans d'utiliser des insecticides qui, rejetés dans la mer, nuiraient aux poissons ainsi qu'à ceux qui les mangent. Peu de temps auparavant, Shôzô Tanaka avait, en 1902, secoué l'opinion publique à la suite de l'affaire de la contamination du Watarase, fleuve de la région très peuplée du Kantô, provoquée par la mine de cuivre d'Ashio et qui est considérée par certains historiens comme l'un des deux événements les plus importants de l'histoire intérieure du Japon de l'ère Meiji avec la tentative d'assassinat de l'Empereur en 1911. Tanaka, devenu député à la Diète impériale, s'est également soulevé contre le gigantesque programme de prévention des inondations mené par le gouvernement Meiji dans la plaine du Kantô. Pour donner un ordre d'idée, durant la seule année 1911, plus de deux cents millions de mètres cubes de terre ont été déplacés pour ce chantier, soit bien davantage que pour le canal de Panama.

Quoi qu'il en soit, il semble que Kumagusu ait été le premier à employer au Japon le terme d'« écologie ».

Lancée dans le *Muron Shinpô*, son action finit par s'étendre à tout le pays. Il est convié à développer ses arguments dans de grands quotidiens comme le *Tôkyô Asahi* et l'Ôsaka Mainichi ; il intervient aussi auprès d'hommes politiques et de savants pour obtenir leur soutien.

Kunio Yanagita

Considéré comme le fondateur de l'ethnologie japonaise, Yanagita a usé de son influence pour faire connaître les revendications de Kumagusu dans la lutte qu'engage celui-ci contre la politique du gouvernement Meiji sur les sanctuaires shintô. Ses travaux sur l'origine d'une identité japonaise ont par la suite été utilisés pour soutenir le courant nationaliste, mais Kumagusu a violemment dénoncé l'absence de fondement scientifique de cette théorie.

En tant qu'ethnologue, il s'est inspiré des nombreux travaux de Kumagusu sur l'étude des contes et coutumes du Japon ancien. Il a sollicité son aide pour localiser le « peuple des montagnes » (*sanka*) qu'il considère comme le peuple japonais originel, ainsi que le prouve le discours qu'il a prononcé lors de la cérémonie d'intronisation de l'empereur Taishô en 1915: « En regardant vers les pentes du mont Nyakoji, j'ai vu quelques nuages de fumée s'élever dans la forêt de pins. Ah, les sanka parlent ! ». Il situe cette origine dans la région des montagnes de Kishû, non loin de l'endroit où s'est retiré Kumagusu. Mais celui-ci ne répond pas à la requête. Bien au contraire, il attaque Yanagita, lui reprochant sa méthode ethnographique qu'il qualifie de pseudo-scientifique et « positiviste » (lettre du 23 décembre 1916). Yanagita finit par abandonner cette idée du peuple des montagnes ; il transfère alors sur Okinawa sa volonté d'attribuer une origine monogénétique au peuple japonais : la migration aurait suivi la route de la mer et emporté la culture du riz. Les recherches ultérieures ont mis en lumière des origines multiples faisant intervenir également des peuples mongols.

Yanagita est l'un de ceux que son ardeur passionnée touche. Il finance sur ses deniers l'impression d'un pamphlet de Kumagusu résumant les graves conséquences de la déforestation sur l'écosystème, qu'il distribue aux personnalités influentes de divers secteurs sous le titre « Deux écrits de Minakata ».

Par ailleurs, grâce à la coopération de Keijirô Nakamura, élu de la Diète impériale, Kumagusu s'efforce de faire valoir son opinion auprès des instances nationales. Son action ébranle peu à peu l'État. Le nouveau ministre de l'Intérieur, Hirata Tosuke, en charge de ce programme, est sensible aux arguments de Kumagusu et, en 1912 (an 45 de l'ère Meiji et an 1 de l'ère Taishô), la Diète impériale commence à étudier la question de l'opposition au regroupement des sanctuaires, avant de finir par voter en 1918 (an 7 de l'ère Taishô) la suppression de l'ordonnance. Trop tard : le sanctuaire Ôyama lié à la famille Minakata a hélas été victime du regroupement. Le combat de Kumagusu n'est donc pas couronné d'une victoire totale. Cependant, son opposition à la politique nationale, d'abord solitaire, a réussi à mobiliser l'opinion publique et il est parvenu à protéger l'environnement, ce qui fait de lui l'un des pionniers des mouvements de protection de la nature au Japon. Cependant, la réflexion de Kumagusu reste davantage en marge des courants dominants plutôt que dans leur opposition.

Les nombreux *kusunoki* millénaires que l'on trouve encore aujourd'hui dans l'archipel doivent leur survie « miraculeuse » à la présence des petits sanctuaires contre la disparition desquels Kumagusu a lutté. Son action n'est pas motivée par des raisons religieuses ou écologiques au sens que nous prêtons à ce mot en Occident, elle s'inscrit profondément dans la relation symbiotique qui lie l'écologie au sacré. Cette prise de position préfigure l'écologie moderne, à la fois culturelle, quand elle vise à maintenir les coutumes locales, et naturelle, lorsqu'elle se propose de préserver les espèces.

Kumagusu est aujourd'hui considéré comme le précurseur de l'éthique environnementale au Japon. En conduisant une opposition parfois violente à la réorganisation des sanctuaires shintô, il a agi en pionnier de la préservation de l'environnement dans un but indissociable de protection de la nature et de ce qu'on appelle la « communauté sociale ». Il souligne ainsi le fait que la stabilité de la communauté implique le maintien des relations mutuelles entre les êtres humains et les choses naturelles. Cette conception d'une « communauté écologique » au sens d'un organisme vivant qui s'inscrit dans une circulation de choses naturelles sera développée ensuite par Aldo Leopold (1887-1948) dans sa fameuse « éthique de la terre ». Ainsi, selon Kumagusu, la terre maintient l'ordre et la stabilité tels que l'on peut les observer dans la chaîne alimentaire. Dès la fin du XIXe siècle, la pensée de Kumagusu préfigure la transition d'une protection de l'environnement « anthropocentrique » à une conception « biocentrique ».

Tout comme John Muir, mais beaucoup moins connu en Occident, Kumagusu peut être considéré comme un proto-environnementaliste :

en ce début de XXe siècle, suivant une réflexion holistique, il entrevoit l'idée d'une universalité et pose les fondements d'une pensée écologique. Aujourd'hui, l'anthropologue Sophie Houdart considère que cette pensée va bien au-delà d'une simple « protection de la nature pour la nature » : elle consiste en une véritable « écologie sociale », voire en une « écologie spirituelle ».

Près d'un siècle après ces mouvements de protestation contre le regroupement des sanctuaires shintô, devait se tenir à Nagoya, en 2005, la première Exposition universelle « non moderne » du nouveau millénaire, selon l'anthropologue Bruno Latour, sur le thème « Au-delà du développement : à la redécouverte de la sagesse de la nature ». Le projet, dans sa phase initiale, était animé par une réflexion théorique entre anthropologues, historiens d'arts, et philosophes par le biais de la revue *Coucou no chi* (« La divinité et l'esprit des arbres ») créée pour l'occasion. Dans son article intitulé « Un chaos savamment organisé », Sophie Houdart a ainsi résumé la démarche : « Comment donne-t-on corps à une utopie ? La préparation de l'Exposition universelle qui s'est tenue au Japon, dans la banlieue de Nagoya, en 2005, a été l'occasion de suivre le lent travail, à la fois conceptuel et matériel, au moyen duquel émerge une forme inédite de relations entre l'homme et la nature. Donnant la « redécouverte de la sagesse de la nature » comme nouveau métronome universel, les concepteurs de l'Expo 2005 et les architectes appelés à œuvrer au projet devaient entre autres sortir leur proposition de l'étau local dans lequel elle avait vu le jour, pour la porter à une autre échelle en la transformant en véritable alternative de développement pour les sociétés technicisées. »

© J-C Valmalette

© J-C Valmalette

Péninsule de Kii, chemin de Kumano. Gauche : diversité de la forêt primaire. Droite : « forêt industrielle » de sugi *(cryptomères) plantés à partir de la période Showa pour faire face à la croissance économique du Japon. Ces deux photos ont été prises depuis le même point en se tournant de 180°.*

Kumagusu entretenait lui-même une relation intime avec la nature, notamment avec la forêt. Voilà pourquoi il est devenu un pilier de la pensée écologique. Nakazawa, qui participe à la réflexion sur ces sujets aux côtés de penseurs français, dont Claude Lévi-Strauss et Michel Serres, estime que dès l'origine, sa pensée évite le piège de la contradiction à laquelle va se heurter l'écologie moderne par ses clivages entre nature et culture, naturel et artificiel, sensibilité et raison. Kumagusu est un encyclopédiste qui œuvre de manière indiscernable comme biologiste, folkloriste, philosophe ; ces appréhensions multiples le conduisent à concevoir une « écologie sociale ». Il annonce le structuralisme écologique d'un autre grand penseur solitaire, l'anthropologue français Claude Lévi-Strauss. Sophie Houdart conclut ainsi : « [...] là où le parcours de Minakata liait si radicalement la sagesse de la nature aux forêts japonaises, le structuralisme écologique l'en dégage - plus précisément, il ne suspend pas la spécificité culturelle, mais la comprend, l'englobe. On n'a donc rien perdu, on a gagné au passage un peu d'universalité (un peu de l'esprit cher à Levi-Strauss). »

Les années 1970 ont été, dans l'histoire de l'Archipel, la décennie la plus marquée par la pollution industrielle. Une usine de la société Shin-Nippon Chisso Hiryô avait rejeté pendant trente-six ans des effluents de méthylmercure à haute concentration dans la baie de Minamata, dans le Kyûshû, qui ont couvert de boues les fonds marins et contaminé poissons et coquillages. La maladie de Minamata, une affection du système nerveux central causée par la consommation de ces produits de la mer, a frappé plusieurs dizaines de milliers de personnes. Cependant, dans le contexte de forte croissance économique de l'époque, l'État a fermé les yeux sur cette pollution. L'une des personnes à avoir donné l'alerte a été la sociologue Kazuko Tsurumi, spécialiste en sociologie comparée et en relations internationales, elle-même fortement influencée par la pensée de Kumagusu. Elle a aussi fait connaître la portée des travaux de Kumagusu, et sa pensée pionnière dans son ensemble. Elle avait souligné son « goût pour la droiture », l'un des fondements de cet esprit libre : loin d'obéir aveuglément à l'autorité, il a toujours préféré s'appuyer sur son savoir et son expérience pour aborder chacune des questions qui se posaient à lui.

Aujourd'hui, le Japon est confronté à l'immense catastrophe industrielle provoquée par l'accident nucléaire de Fukushima survenu le 11 mars 2011. Dans ce contexte où beaucoup de Japonais se sentent membres d'une « communauté écologique », la vie et l'œuvre de Kumagusu, qui puise dans les traditions ancestrales du Japon, résonne encore plus fortement.

Le mandala de Minakata : la science moderne face à l'Orient

Derrière la vie d'un homme d'exception se dissimule une quête dont le sens n'émerge souvent que dans les dernières années de sa vie. Gerald Figal, qui a exploré le rôle de Kumagusu dans la modernisation du Japon à travers les sciences sociales et la psychologie, résume l'objectif de celui-ci en ces termes : « Ce qui semble motiver l'activité intellectuelle de Minakata sont les lacunes, plutôt que la plénitude des sciences dans leur traitement des phénomènes naturels et humains. »

Le chemin de Kumagusu débute dans l'enseignement bouddhiste Shingon, erre dans les forêts et collines de Tanabe, parcourt les mers et les océans pour revenir aux montagnes sacrées de son enfance. Déjà très jeune, il tourne le dos aux institutions et aux faveurs qu'elles procurent, s'affranchit de l'étiquette, construit et organise son savoir selon une méthodologie qui lui est propre. Durant les dernières années de sa vie, au cœur des bouleversements des années 30, Kumagusu se consacre à cette quête ultime de la connaissance, de la méthodologie scientifique indissociable selon lui de la démarche spirituelle. Il renoue ainsi avec les premières sources de savoir également sources de spiritualité telles qu'on en retrouve les traces dès la fin de la préhistoire. Si d'un côté, dans l'Inde ou la Chine ancienne ou bien dans l'Europe du Moyen Âge, il n'y a pas de spiritualité sans savoir, Kumagusu va proposer un nouveau paradigme suivant lequel il n'y a pas de savoir sans spiritualité. Le contre-pied est surprenant en cette période d'avant-guerre où le monde espère, plus qu'à n'importe quelle époque, en une science omnipotente par la technologie et la puissance économique et politique qu'elle engendre. Le savoir encyclopédique de Kumagusu oscille entre Orient et Occident, entre passé et présent.

Il est généralement admis que l'élaboration de connaissances scientifiques consiste en une nouvelle combinaison d'idées ou leur association d'une manière inhabituelle. Or, ce processus peut être considéré depuis plusieurs points de vue selon la représentation que l'on se fait de la « logique ». Il est influencé pour une part plus ou moins grande par l'environnement dans lequel se construit un individu. Ainsi les scientifiques de ce début de XXe siècle se trouvent confrontés à la difficulté que l'on rencontre à mettre du sens là où il y a du hasard. En effet, les religions judéo-chrétiennes perçoivent un monde réglé de façon déterministe par un « horloger divin ». La pensée bouddhiste insiste sur la beauté, l'harmonie et l'unité de l'univers ; les choses n'y ont pas d'existence par elles-mêmes mais seulement une vacuité ; il en résulte que l'observateur détermine la nature du réel qu'il observe. Pour illustrer cette différence, il suffit d'observer un jeune étudiant occidental qui peine à concevoir que la lumière soit à la fois « onde électromagnétique » (au sens de la mécanique classique), et « grain de lumière » ou « photon » (au sens de la mécanique quantique). L'étudiant oriental n'y verra pas de contradiction dans la mesure où c'est à l'observateur qu'il revient de déterminer la nature du réel.

L'environnement de Kumagusu est donc très différent de celui des scientifiques occidentaux de cette époque ou même des scientifiques japonais de cette période de modernisation du Japon : eux, ou leurs maîtres, ont été formés lors d'un passage dans les grandes universités britanniques, américaines, allemandes. Il est d'ailleurs intéressant de noter qu'à cette période, les scientifiques japonais de retour dans leur pays se divisent sur les limites de ce qui doit être « emprunté » au modèle occidental et de ce qui doit revêtir un caractère spécifiquement « japonais » dans le fonctionnement de l'éducation.

Il peut paraître surprenant que les sciences soient fortement imprégnées des représentations culturelles, et parfois même religieuses de ceux qui les élaborent. Ainsi, depuis l'organisation du savoir jusqu'à la démarche scientifique qui y conduit, les savants occidentaux sont les héritiers naturels de la philosophie aristotélicienne. Pour eux, définir consiste à distinguer dans un ensemble plus vaste, à souligner les différences. Un exemple est donné par la grande place qu'ils ont accordée à la classification systématique des espèces ou à la description d'un organisme par les sous-systèmes qui le composent. On serait tenté de dire « à l'inverse », mais, en réalité, c'est « autrement », les savants orientaux ont recherché les interactions entre des objets sans limites précises et en évolution constante dans leur milieu. Ils considéraient chaque organisme comme un tout en interrelation avec un environnement en perpétuelle transformation. Cependant, les concepts, une fois élaborés dans leur milieu d'origine, mais en réalité souvent en relation avec d'autres milieux, se retrouvent dépourvus de ces représentations culturelles et de leurs valeurs morales pour atteindre un caractère universel. Ils sont alors prêts pour être de nouveau intégrés dans un processus culturel. Ces différences ont profondément marqué Kumagusu tout au long de son parcours entre Orient et Occident.

Kumagusu écrit dans sa correspondance avec Dogi Hôryû : « La science d'aujourd'hui résout (c'est du moins ce à quoi on s'attend) les mystères de la causalité. Elle recouvre précisément ce que le bouddhisme appelle *in* (因), mais pas ce qu'il appelle *en* (縁). Je me dois de m'interroger sur cette question. *En* est ce qui émerge de l'entrelacement d'une série de causes à effet avec une autre. Afin de saisir l'image du monde dans sa totalité, on devrait comprendre à la fois la cause et l'effet (*in*) ainsi que leur interrelation (*en*). » On peut résumer ainsi l'idée de Kumagusu : la science d'aujourd'hui comprend les causes et les effets, mais pas le rapport entre elles ; l'étude de ces rapports est notre mission.

Pour tenter de comprendre ce qu'il veut dire, revenons à la signification du mot *innen* (因縁). On peut le traduire par « chaîne de causalité », il est construit à partir de deux *kanji* dont le premier signifie « causalité » ou « parce que » dans un sens proche d'une prédiction déterministe, un lien quasi-mécanique entre un ensemble d'événements. Selon Kumagusu, la science, jusqu'à son époque, s'est intéressée exclusivement à cet aspect du lien entre un ensemble de causes et des effets qui s'ensuivent. Il veut interroger le scientifique qu'il est sur le sens à donner au deuxième caractère 縁. Celui-ci se retrouve par exemple dans le mot *ennichi* (縁日) qui signifie « jour en relation ». Il caractérise les jours de l'année qui sont en relation avec les divinités shintô et bouddhistes et qui font l'objet d'offrandes aux *kami* et à Bouddha. Ce caractère est également présent dans le mot *engi* (縁起) dont le sens bouddhique « production conditionnelle » exprime le concept de conditionnalité, de dépendance et de réciprocité ou enfin dans le mot *engawa* (縁側) qui désigne la coursive qui met en relation les pièces des maisons traditionnelles japonaises.

Naturaliste, botaniste, folkloriste, traducteur, activiste politique, activiste environnemental, selon le philosophe Alan Little : « [Kumagusu] offre une curieuse série de parallélismes avec des motifs de développements non-linéaires et un réseau de relations établies dans son champ d'études qui a été son premier centre d'intérêt : la mycologie. »

La nature même des sciences modernes réside dans la description des liens de cause à effet (*in*). Mais Kumagusu est convaincu que cela ne suffit pas à décrire des systèmes dont l'évolution semble liée au hasard. En s'appuyant sur la vision du bouddhisme Mahayana (*innen*), il propose, pour ce faire, d'introduire la notion de relation mutuelle qui peut se produire entre deux liens de causalité pour perturber leurs évolutions respectives. Au travers de sa correspondance avec Hôryû Dogi, on voit s'affirmer la quête d'une nouvelle méthodologie scientifique. Il égrène des tentatives de diagrammes complexes qu'il trace au pinceau sans parvenir à une « réponse » satisfaisante. En 1978, Tsurumi Kazuko, qui travaille alors à son premier ouvrage sur Kumagusu, se voit proposer le terme de « mandala de Minakata » par Nakamura Hajime, grand érudit bouddhiste et philosophe frappé par la ressemblance de ces figures tracées par Kumagusu avec le mandala bouddhiste.

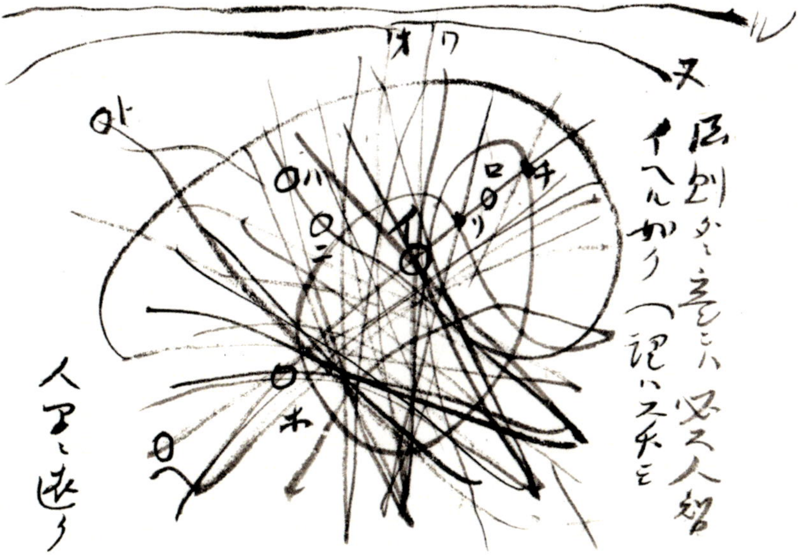

Le mandala de Kumagusu. Source: Minakata Kumagusu Archives.

Sa théorie repose sur l'existence possible d'une relation mutuelle (*en*) entre plusieurs liens de causalité. Dans ce cas, l'évolution de l'un ou plusieurs des systèmes peut se faire d'une manière différente de celle induite par les liens de causalité (*in*) pris isolément. Kumagusu interprète donc le hasard comme le résultat de cette interaction mutuelle entre liens de causalité. Il propose en réalité une réinterprétation du mandala du bouddhisme Shingon qui représente le bouddha Dainichi Nyorai (« Grand Soleil ») au centre de toute relation.

Pour essayer de comprendre l'idée développée par Kumagusu dans son mandala, il faut se replacer dans le contexte de la physique de cette fin de siècle qui débat de la nature de l'atome et ne connaît d'autre mécanique que la mécanique newtonienne. Il faudra encore quatre ans avant que Thomson ne réalise dans son laboratoire de Cambridge les preuves du concept d'électron, et dix-huit avant que Rutherford, élève de Thomson, ne parvienne à montrer l'existence du noyau. La mécanique quantique, quant à elle, n'apparaît réellement qu'à partir de 1925. Le principe de causalité dans son sens déterministe domine la science à la période à laquelle écrit Kumagusu, mais il décide de remettre en question ce déterminisme ou « démon de Laplace », suivant lequel la connaissance totale d'un système à un instant donné permettrait d'en connaître l'évolution si les mêmes causes produisent les mêmes effets.

La conception occidentale s'est construite depuis Aristote avec la conviction, tout d'abord, que les lois qui régissent le ciel sont différentes de celles qui valent sur Terre, mais, à la fin du XVIIe siècle, Newton découvre que ce sont les mêmes lois qui s'appliquent sur Terre et dans tout l'Univers. Au cours du siècle suivant, plusieurs savants, dont Maxwell, parviennent à l'unification des lois qui régissent les phénomènes électriques, magnétiques et optiques. Au XXe siècle, Einstein unifie l'espace et le temps et aujourd'hui, on tente par une « théorie du tout » d'unifier les quatre interactions fondamentales. Mais parallèlement à cette unification des lois apparaît la nécessité de faire intervenir une part croissante du hasard ou de la probabilité. C'est d'abord le cas avec la théorie cinétique des gaz introduite notamment par Bernouilli à la fin du XVIIIe siècle puis formalisée par Boltzman au cours du XIXe siècle. La notion de probabilité se généralise au début du XXe siècle avec l'introduction de ce qu'on appelle la « fonction d'onde », outil nécessaire pour représenter l'état quantique d'un système (ou amplitude de probabilité). La fameuse expérience des fentes d'Young, rassemblant la double nature corpusculaire et ondulatoire de l'électron, en est l'illustration la plus connue.

À partir de la seconde moitié du XXe siècle, émerge le concept d'intelligence artificielle qui repose lui aussi sur une logique devenue « logique floue », puis c'est au tour de la biologie de connaître une évolution de nature similaire. À ses débuts, la génétique se concevait comme le décryptage d'un code informatique dans lequel tout le développement d'un organisme aurait été contenu, comme résultant d'un lien de causalité « déterministe ». Mais avec la découverte récente d'importantes régions non-codantes du génome (que l'on appelle parfois à tort « ADN poubelle »), on a commencé à comprendre que la fonction biologique de ces régions, a priori non spécifiques, résiderait dans leur sensibilité à l'environnement par le biais de réactions chimiques simples, de manière difficilement prévisible. Cependant, ces théories récentes sont l'objet de beaucoup de controverses.

On pourrait également citer le système immunitaire dont on sait aujourd'hui qu'il repose sur deux types de processus. Un premier, que l'on pourrait qualifier d'inné, est capable de réagir rapidement à une agression extérieure pour laquelle il a été programmé. Un deuxième, plus lent à se mettre en action, plus subtil, aussi, résulte d'une adaptation du système immunitaire à son environnement au cours de la vie de l'individu et des générations qui l'ont précédé. Enfin, les découvertes récentes en neurosciences sont peut-être sur le point d'illustrer ce double caractère du principe de causalité qui est au cœur du mandala de Kumagusu : plusieurs équipes de chercheurs se penchent aujourd'hui, notamment grâce aux techniques d'imagerie du cerveau, sur le processus de créativité qui permet l'apparition soudaine d'une idée. On peut tenter d'expliquer de façon très schématique ce processus comme résultant de l'interaction de deux zones distinctes du cerveau dont les structures neuronales sont très différentes : la première, située dans le cortex cérébral gauche, constituée de dendrites courtes, densément interconnectées, où le flux est très rapide, rendant possibles les déductions logiques ou ce qu'on appelle l'« intelligence » ; une deuxième zone se situe dans le lobe temporal droit, le gyrus temporal supérieur ; les connections y sont moins denses, mais les dendrites, beaucoup plus longues, facilitent la circulation de l'information, plus lentement mais sur des distances plus grandes, permettant ainsi la mise en relation de zones très éloignées. C'est précisément de cette zone, dont l'activité semble aléatoire, qu'émergent les ondes gamma lors d'un flash créatif. La plupart du temps, ces deux zones sont assez peu en relation, notamment en raison de l'activité d'une troisième zone, le cortex visuel, qui perturbe la communication entre les deux premières zones. Pour que les ondes gamma issues de la zone « créatrice » atteignent la zone où sont possibles les déductions logiques, l'activité du cortex visuel doit se mettre en veille pour que soit interprétable le flash créatif.

Cette structure du cerveau rappelle étrangement les entrelacs du mandala de Kumagusu, longues courbes singulières venant parfois à la rencontre de lignes courtes fortement connectées. Le cerveau, réalité physique du mandala de notre pensée ?

Il est intéressant de noter que Kumagusu souffrait de crises d'épilepsie généralisée tonico-clonique avec une impression de « déjà vu ». En 1998, une équipe scientifique du département de psychiatrie de l'Université de Kyoto, travaillant sur le sujet de l'activité créative et du génie, s'est intéressée au cas de Kumagusu. Ses membres ont réalisé une imagerie par résonance magnétique post-mortem qui révèle une atrophie de l'hippocampe droit caractéristique d'une épilepsie du lobe temporal. Ils la relient au comportement de Kumagusu.

On voit apparaître, au travers de ces quelques exemples tirés de la science contemporaine, des similitudes frappantes entre le raisonnement scientifique et le principe de causalité *innen* qui a occupé le centre de la réflexion philosophique de Kumagusu il y a un siècle. Force est de constater que la science contemporaine a effectivement connu un changement de paradigme : à la composante « déterministe » liée à l'ordre est venue s'ajouter une composante « probabiliste » liée au désordre, qui contient la nécessaire interaction du lien de causalité avec son environnement. Tension entre ordre et désordre, c'est ainsi que le Prix Nobel de physique Muray Gell-Mann dans son ouvrage L*e quark et le jaguar : voyage au cœur du simple et du complexe* définit la complexité. Bien avant lui, et de manière poétique, les *haïku* décrivaient déjà le monde comme un équilibre entre *fueki* (« stabilité »), sorte de lois immuables, prévisibles, déterministes, et *ryûkô* (« fugacité »), qui traduit l'éphémère, l'imprévisible. Charles Baudelaire n'écrivait-il pas que « la modernité, c'est le transitoire, le fugitif, le contingent, la moitié de l'art, dont l'autre moitié est l'éternel et l'immuable » ? D'une autre manière, dans le jardin japonais, cette même tension s'exprime dans la juxtaposition de formes et de texture. Les lignes tendues des murs qui l'entourent ou les sillons marqués dans le sable soulignent l'entrelacs de rochers, de mousses, ou d'arbustes, et invitent le témoin d'un instant à ressentir le fragile équilibre du monde.

*

*   *

Uni à la terre, à la pierre, à l'arbre de la forêt, absorbé par les éléments de l'univers, Kumagusu Minakata se souvient-il de sa vie passée ? Elle est achevée ; elle est devenue rêve. Sur son linceul s'est déposée une pluie de violettes. Laissons, pour terminer cet ouvrage, la fumée de l'encens porter jusqu'à l'autel qui garde sa mémoire ce court poème de son ancien camarade Natsume Sôseki :

Je voudrais renaître
Mais le pourrai-je jamais
Simple violette

Kumagusu dans les montagnes de la péninsule de Kii durant l'hiver. Source: Minakata Kumagusu Archives.

BIBLIOGRAPHIE

Pour la rédaction de cette bibliographie, nous nous sommes appuyés sur de nombreux documents de la plume (ou plutôt du pinceau) de Kumagusu Minakata ou se rapportant à lui, et notamment aux ouvrages suivants :

ADACHI Isao. Globally Pioneering Ecologist: Kumagusu Minakata (1867-1941) Thought of Diversity from Buddhist World. Japan Spotlight, 2011.

ALLARD Aurélien. « La Réorganisation des sanctuaires au Japon de l'époque Meiji à l'époque Taisho-Osugi jinja : dernier sanctuaire de l'ancien village de Takahashi ». *Cipango*, 2010, 17, p. 298-300.

BLACKER Carmen. "Minakata Kumagusu: A neglected Japanese Genius". *Folklore,* 1983, vol. 94:ii.

FIGAL Gerald. Civilization and Monsters: Spirits of Modernity in Meiji Japan. Durham, NC : Duke, University Press, 1999. (Asia-Pacific: Culture, Politics, and Society.) HOUDART Sophie. « Un chaos savamment ordonné : l'élaboration conceptuelle de l'Exposition internationale japonaise en 2005 ». *Ethnographies japonaises*, 2006, vol. 30.

IIKURA Shôhei, MATSUI Ryûgo, TAMURA Yoshiya, NAKANISHI Sumi. Réflexions sur les articles scientifiques en anglais de Kumagusu Minakata dans la revue *Nature [Minakata Kumagusu eibun ronkô : Nature-shi hen].* Tokyo : Shueisha, 2005.)

KAYASHIMA Nobuko. Le Développement de l'éducation au cours de l'ère Meiji (1867 – 1912) : modernisation et montée du nationalisme au Japon. Paris : Unesco, 1989. (Cahiers de I'IIPE, 78).

KOSAKA Jirô. Le Géant entravé : la vie de Kumagusu Minakata [*Shibarareta kyojin – Minakata Kumagusu no shôgai*]. Tokyo : Shinchosha, 1987.

LITTLE Frederick Alan. Lost in Translation: Non-Linear Literary, Cultural, Temporal, Political, and Cosmological Transformations : the Anglo-Japanese Productions of Minakata Kumagusu. PhD Thesis, 2012.

LUTUM Peter, KUNIO Yanagita. Die Japanischen Volkskundler Minakata Kumagusu. Lit Verlag, 2003.

MATSUI Ryûgo. "*Mandala as a Synthetic Theory of Modern Sciences. On Minakata Kumagusu's Philosophy in His Letters to Dogi Horyu*"国際文化研究, 2007, 11, pp.29 - 41, 龍谷大学国際文化学会

MATSUMOTO Jun, IZAWA Masana. Les myxomycètes : l'énigme d'une étonnante force vitale *[Nenkin – odorokubeki seimeiryoku no nazo]*. Tokyo : Seibundo Shinkosha, 2007.

MIZUKI Shigeru. NEKO-GUSU Minakata Kumagusu no Shogai (manga).

SADAMICHI Kato. "The Three Ecologies in Minakata Kumagusu's environmental movement" *Organization & Environment*, 1999, vol. 12, n°1, p. 85-98.

TSURUMI Kazuko. Minakata Kumagusu. Tokyo : Kodansha, 1981.

TSURUMI Kazuko. Minakata-Mandala A paradigm Change for the Future. Tokyo : Sophia University, 1995. (Research papers / Institute of International Relations; Ser. A. UNESCO Forum: Tokyo Symposium "Science and Culture: A Common Path for the Future," September 10-14, 1995.

Index des personnes

Akiyama *(Saneyuki).* Camarade de Kumagusu qui fréquenta avec lui l'école préparatoire de Tokyo ; il devint vice-amiral.

Calkins *(William).* Avocat de Chicago, ancien colonel de l'Union durant la Guerre de Sécession et grand spécialiste de fongus et de lichens.

Dairoku *(Kikuchi).* Mathématicien japonais qui étudia à Cambridge. Il fonda la prestigieuse université de Tokyo avant de devenir ministre de l'Éducation.

Dickins *(Frederick Victor).* Directeur de l'Université de Londres, spécialiste de littérature et d'art japonais, avocat et ancien militaire en poste à Yokohama.

Dogi *(Hôryû).* Moine de l'école bouddhiste Shingon en charge du monastère du mont Kôya. Représentant du bouddhisme japonais au Parlement mondial des religions à Chicago. Kumagusu le rencontra la première fois à Londres. Tous deux ont ensuite échangé une correspondance abondante avant de se rencontrer à nouveau dans la péninsule de Kii.

Douglas *(Sir Robert Kennaway).* Conservateur en charge du tout nouveau Department of Oriental Printed Books and Manuscript du British Museum.

Edwards *(Henry John).* Doyen de l'université de Cambridge.

Franks *(Sir Augustus Wollaston)*. Grand collectionneur, figure du British Museum et membre de l'aristocratie britannique.

Gesner *(Conrad).* Naturaliste suisse de la Renaissance à qui Kumagusu vouait une admiration sans limite.

Haga *(Yaichi).* Camarade de Kumagusu à l'école préparatoire de Tokyo, il devint professeur de littérature japonaise à l'Université de Tokyo.

Honda *(Kôtarô).* Camarade de Kumagusu à l'école préparatoire de Tokyo, il devint professeur à l'Université du Tohoku et premier directeur de l'Institut de recherche sur les métaux.

Jiang Shengzong. Chinois originaire de Canton qui tint l'épicerie à Jacksonville (Floride) où travailla et logea Kumagusu.

Kanchû. Vieillard affable, supérieur du temple Enju-in où Kumagusu trouva refuge de retour au Japon.

Kataoka *(Masayuki, dit le Prince).* Antiquaire japonais vivant à Londres et marié à une riche anglaise.

Koaze *(Shirô).* Directeur de l'agence de Kobe de la célèbre compagnie maritime Nippon Yusen.

Kropotkine *(Piotr Alekseïevitch).* Scientifique et penseur russe qui a élaboré la théorie du communisme libertaire et figure comme l'un des fondateurs du mouvement anarchiste.

Masaoka *(Shiki)*. Grand maître japonais du haïku (camarade de Kumagusu à l'école préparatoire de Tokyo)

Minakata *(Tsunegusu)*. Frère cadet de Kumagusu.

Minakata *(Yahei)*. Père de Kumagusu.

Mishima *(Katsura)*. Etudiant japonais qui fréquente la Michigan State School of Agriculture à Lansing en même temps que Kumagusu. C'est un bagarreur invétéré qui se livre avec Kumagusu et d'autres étudiants japonais à des affrontements qui tournent mal. Il deviendra ensuite le responsable des cérémonies officielles du Ministère impérial.

Mitsuda *(Takijirô)*. Membre d'une troupe de cirque que Kumagusu rencontra à Londres et qui lui donna l'occasion de rencontrer Masayuki Kataoka.

Morrison *(Arthur)*. Auteur de romans policiers à succès.

Murata *(Genzô)*. Étudiant japonais de la Michigan State School of Agriculture à Lansing avec lequel Kumagusu se trouve impliqué, en état d'ébriété, dans plusieurs bagarres aux côtés d'autres étudiants japonais.

Mulken *(Rowland J.)*. Nationaliste irlandais, membre du Restoration Party, ami de Sun Yat-sen, qui fit office de garde lorsque celui-ci vivait à Londres. Il prit part aux côtés de Sun Yat-sen à la seconde insurrection à Huizhou.

***Nylander*.** Botaniste qui identifia la nouvelle espèce de lichen trouvée par Kumagusu à Cuba.

Ono *(Eijirô).* Camarade de Kumagusu lorsqu'il séjournait à Ann Arbor (Michigan). Il devint banquier et s'engagea à soutenir le projet de Kumagusu de fonder un institut de recherche en botanique. C'est le grand père de l'artiste Yoko Ono.

Osten-Sacken *(baron Carl Robert)*. Grand entomologiste du XIXe siècle, membre de la noblesse russe, il fut également diplomate.

Satow *(Sir Ernest).* Diplomate britannique qui fut en poste au Japon durant plus d'un quart de siècle entre 1862 et 1883, puis de 1895 à 1900.

Sōseki *(Natsume).* Romancier (camarade de Kumagusu à l'école préparatoire de Tokyo).

***Sun Yat-sen*.** Voir encart p. 56.

Tadayasu *(Yoshikawa).* L'un des principaux initiateurs de la politique *wakon yosai* (« Esprit japonais, talent occidental »).

Tajima *(Tan, né Hamaguchi).* Voir encart page 48.

Takahashi *(Kinichi)***.** Courtier en estampes à Londres et personnage interlope, allergique au travail et grand buveur.

Takesaburô *(Kitahaba)*. Médecin et ami de Kumagusu à qui il écrivit depuis Cuba.

Tamura *(Matsue)*. Épouse de Kumagusu.

Thompson. Employé du British Museum avec lequel Kumagusu eut des démêlés jusqu'à son fameux coup de poing qui entraîna son exclusion du British Museum.

Tokugawa Yorimichi. 15ème Tokugawa de la branche de Kishû. Kumagusu fit sa connaissance à Londres.

Toriyama *(Hiraku)*. Intellectuel et professeur au collège de Wakayama que fréquenta Kumagusu. Célèbre auteur de la Warship March (hymne de la Marine impériale et de l'actuelle force maritime d'autodéfense japonaise).

Ueshiba *(Morihei)*. Fondateur de l'aïkido.

Volkhovsky *(Feliks)*. Dissident révolutionnaire russe échappé d'un camp de Sibérie, il organise le soutien de l'opinion occidentale au mouvement révolutionnaire russe, notamment auprès des partis socialistes britannique, allemand et français.

Yamada *(Bimyô)*. Camarade de Kumagusu qui fréquenta avec lui l'école préparatoire de Tokyo ; il devint un écrivain et poète.

Yanagita (*Kunio*). L'un des plus grands ethnologues japonais, considéré aujourd'hui comme le fondateur de l'éthologie au Japon.

Annexe I : Publications dans *Notes and Queries*

The Invention of the Gimbal (1899) s9-III (75): 427.

A Witty Boy (1899) s9-III (75): 426.

Walrus (1899) s9-III (78): 487.

Chinese Medicine (1899) s9-IV (79): 10-11.

Beaver and Python (1899) s9-IV (80): 24.

Reference Wanted (1899) s9-IV (81): 54.

Swin-Shell (1899) s9-IV (82): 68-69.

The Wanderng Jew (1899) s9-IV (85): 121-124, (1899) s9-IV (87): 166, (1900) s9-V (122): 333-334.

Maize (1899) s9-IV (92): 276.

Flying Cups (1900) s9-V (113): 145-146.

Pictures Composed of Handwriting (1900) s9-VI (138): 131, (1903) s9-XII (296): 172.

Footprints of Gods, &c. (1900) s9-VI (140): 163-165, (1900) s9-VI (143): 223-226, (1900) s9-VI (148): 322-324, (1903) s9-XI (280): 375, (1904) s10-II (30): 65.

Japanese Monkeys (1903) s9-XI (283): 430-432, (1903) s9-XI (287): 517, (1904) s10-I (17): 334.

Owl (1903) s9-XI (285): 467.

Single Tooth (1903) s9-XI (286): 488, (1907) s10-VII (168): 205-206.

Magic Ring (1903) s9-XI (286): 490-491.

Folklore or Botany (1903) s9-XI (287): 514-515.

Legend of Serpent's Feet (1903) s9-XII (293): 112-113.

Story of ungrateful Son (1903) s9-XII (293): 116.

Anthropoid Ape (1903) s9-XII (296): 169.

Palo de Cobra (1903) s9-XII (302): 288.

A Flea in the Ear (1904) s10-I (2): 34.

Red Rag to a Bull (1904) s10-I (4): 77.

Vicissitudes of Language (1904) s10-I (4): 74.

Hobgoblin's Claw (1904) s10-I (5): 93.

Water of Jealousy (1904) s10-I (8): 147.

Chinese Ghosts (1904) s10-I (9): 176-177.

Breaking Glass at Jewish Weddings (1904) s10-I (10): 195.

Mangosteen Markings (1904) s10-I (11): 212.

Ghost's Markets (1904) s10-I (11): 206.

A Japanese Master of Lies (1904) s10-I (25): 485-486.

Stealing no Crime (1904) s10-II (52): 509.

Wooing Staff (1904) s10-II (52): 504.

The Envied Favourite (1904) s10-II (52): 505-506.

Mohammedamism in Japan (1907) s10-VII (166): 167.

Lunar Halo and Rain (1907) s10-VII (167): 193.

Sindbad the Sailor: Monkeys and Cocoa-Nuts (1907) s10-VII (171): 271-272.

Bat Bear away (1907) s10-VIII (184): 15.

Arrow-Breaking: Its Moral Lessons (1907) s10-VIII (185): 25.

Life-Star Folklore (1907) s10-VIII (185): 34-35.

Maru (1907) s10-VIII (190): 131-133, (1907) s10-VIII (202): 376.

Moon and Crabs (1907) s10-VIII (193): 186.

Red Rag and Antelope (1907) s10-VIII (194): 205.

Goat's Blood and Diamonds (1907) s10-VIII (197): 270-271.

Lithuanian Folklore: Legless Spirits (1908) s10-IX (211): 34-35.

Seaweed Needing Rain (1908) s10-IX (219): 194.

Bees and Lucky Days (1908) s10-X (250): 285-286.

Tiger Folklore and Pope (1908) s10-X (253): 358.

Guernsey Lily (1908) s10-X (254): 368.

The Disobedient Son (1908) s10-X (256): 408.
Born with Teeth (1908) s10-X (258): 453-454.
Dead Animals Exposed on Trees and Walls (1908) s10-X (258): 457-458, (1909) s10-XI (282): 413-414.
Snakes Drinking Milk (1909) s10-XI (269): 15-158.
Names Terrible to Children (1909) s10-XI (279): 35-357.
Flying Machines of the Far East (1909) s10-XI (283): 425-426, (1909) s10-XII (306): 374.
The Storm Ship (1909) s10-XI (286): 488-489.
Sneezing Superstition (1909) s10-XII (292): 97-98.
Virgin Mary's nut (1909) s10-XII (297): 187-188.
Chinese Proverb in Burtons 'Anatomy' (1909) s10-XII (301): 277-278.
The Living Dead (1909) s10-XII (306): 366.
St. Gratian's Nut (1910) s11-I (1): 10.
Fly Painted on a Shield : Japanese Variant (1910) s11-I (14): 266.
Child Telling its own Fate (1910) s11-I (16): 305-306.
The Neglected Old Father: Chinese Parallel (1910) s11-II (34): 145-146.
Marriage Relationships (1910) s11-II (52): 506; (1911) s11-III (75): 433.
Corpse Bleeding in Presence of the Murderer (1911) s11-III (73): 398.
The Blindfolded Man: Japanese Variant (1911) s11-III (75): 424-425; (1912) s11-V (106): 6-7.
Horses' Ghosts (1911) s11-IV (85): 127.
Twins and second Sight (1911) s11-IV (86): 156.
Spider Stories (1911) s11-IV (102): 477-478.
Whittington and his Cats: Eastern Variants (1911) s11-IV (104): 503-504.
Whittington and his Cats (1912) s11-V (121): 313-314 ; (1912) s11-VI (143): 236.
Pausanias (1912) s11-V (128): 448.
Snake Oison (1912) s11-VI (144): 254-255.

Legends of Flying (1912) s11-VI (146): 291-293.

Human Souls interchanged (1912) s11-VI (153): 430.

Earth-eating (1912) s11-VI (157): 514; (1913) s11-VII (162): 98; (1913) s11-VII (173): 318.

Botany (1913) s11-VII (161): 72.

Scolopendra cetacea (1913) s11-VII (175): 347-348; (1913) s11-VIII (189): 116-117, (1920) s12-VII (129): 267.

Extraordinary Fountains in Ireland, Brittany, and Sicily (1913) s11-VII (181): (475.

Double Flowers in Japan (1913) s11-VII (182): 490-491, (1920) s12-VI (114): 310, (1921) s12-IX (177): 189.

Onions planted with Roses (1913) s11-VII (183): 516.

Extractiong Snakes from Holes (1913) s11-VIII (188): 85.

"Agonda» and «Akoda» (1913) s11-VIII (191): 147.

A slip in «The Encyclopaedia Britannica» (1913) s11-VIII (193): 187.

Crab, the pretended Astrologer (1913) s11-VIII (196): 243-244.

Botanical Press and Entomological (1913) s11-VIII (197): 270.

Cathertal Bell stolen (1913) s11-VIII (198): 290-291.

Divination by Twitching (1913) s11-VIII (204): 417.

Mica (1913) s11-VIII (206): 453.

Dido's Purchase of Land (1914) s11-IX (212): 47-48; (1914) s11-IX (227): 353-354; (1914) s11-IX (233): 474; (1914) s11-X (257): 430; (1915) s11-XII (293): 109.

Turtle and Thunder (1914) s11-IX(223): 268; (1914) s11-IX(226): 336.

Weather Prognostications (1914) s11-IX (226): 327-328; (1914) s11-IX (235): 513.

Chinese Proverb in Burton's 'Anatomy' (1914) s11-IX (226): 326.

Octopus Venus's ear, and Whelk (1914) s11-IX (231): 434; (1914) s11-X (239): 72.

Feast of Shells (1914) s11-IX (232): 455-456.

Modern Advocate of Druidism (1914) s11-X (256): 408.

The Original of 'Aladdin' (1914) s11-X (256): 414.

The Purchasing of Dreams (1914) s11-X (257): 421-422.

Medicinal Mummies (1914) s11-X (259): 476; (1915) s11-XI (284): 438.

Tooth-blackening (1914) s11-X (259): 467.

Dreams and Literature (1915) s11-XI (281): 385-386.

Hair used in Magic (1915) s11-XII (292): 84-85.

"Sympathies» and «Antipathies» of Plants (1915) s11-XII (292): 88-89.

Theological Disputations by means of Signs (1915) s11-XII (293): 96-97; (1915) s11-XII (307): 387.

Easter Hare (1915) s11-XII (294): 124-125.

Phosphorescent birds (1915) s11-XII (299): 213-215.

Dragon's lamp (1915) s11-XII (300): 240.

Poilu (1915) s11-XII (301): 266-267.

The virtues of onions (1915) s11-XII (306): 367-368.

Methods of waking a sleeper (1915) s11-XII (310): 440.

Folk-lore: the danger of crossing (1916) s12-I(12): 238.

The figure of Buddha in the eye and neck (1916) s12-I (13): 245-246.

Cat Folklore (1916) s12-I (13): 251-252.

Phosphorescent Spiders (1916) s12-I (14): 267.

Horse Washed with Rice (1916) s12-I (15): 289.

Employment of Wild Animals in Warfare (1916) s12-I (16): 311-312.

Cuckoo in Folklore (1916) s12-I (17): 338.

The Dragon-fly (1916) s12-I (17): 328.

Tiger's Whiskers (1916) s12-I (18): 355.

Stories of the Swarming and Ascension of Fishes (1916) s12-I (21): 404-405.

Folklore: Red Hair (1916) s12-II (45): 379.

House and Garden Superstitions (1916) s12-II (47): 419.

Employment of Wild Beasts in Warfare (1916) s12-II (49): 454-455.

The Sight of Savages (1917) s12-III (66): 259.

Fire Putting out Fire (1917) s12-III (70): 372.

Cutting off the Hair as a Preservative Against Headache (1917) s12-III (74): 484-485, (1919) s12-V(92): 138.

Submarines: Ironclads (1918) s12-IV (79): 112-113.

Medical Men Assassinated (1918) s12-IV (87): 339.

Boys Born in May (1919) s12-V (88): 25.

Kimono (1919) s12-V (90): 80.

Submarines (1919) s12-V (92): 131.

The Ant-Bear and the Tortoise (1919) s12-V (92): 125.

Grain-Seeds Lent by Churches (1920) s12-VI (100): 13.

Birds Poisoning Captive Young (1920) s12-VI (101): 48.

Bats: Hair (1920) s12-VI (112): 280.

Monkey's Wine (1920) s12-VI (113): 295, (1920) s12-VII (126): 216.

Magpie in Augury (1920) s12-VI (114): 310.

Folklore: The Dangers of Crossing (1920) s12-VI (115): 343.

Wild Boar in Heraldry (1920) s12-VII (122): 138.

Wine Bibber (1920) s12-VII (126): 211.

Peacocks' Feather (1920) s12-VII (129): 277, (1920) s12-VII (139): 477, (1921) s12-VIII (143): 37.

The Ice-Worm (1920) s12-VII (137): 430-431.

Fair Maids of Foscott (1920) s12-VII (138): 448.

Folklore of the Elder (1921) s12-VIII (142): 18.

A Proverb about Eating Cherries (1921) s12-VIII (151): 190.

Raining in the Sunshine (1921) s12-VIII (157): 307.

Corsican War-Dogs: Island of Fowls (1921) s12-VIII (161): 392.

Crucifixion of Dogs (1921) s12-VIII (161): 390.
The Centipede (1921) s12-VIII (162): 411.
Old Man's Perversity (1921) s12-VIII (163): 42-430.
Wolf (1921) s12-VIII (164): 447-448.
War Portents (1921) s12-IX (174): 139.
Burnt in his Boats (1921) s12-IX (176): 177.
Rice (1921) s12-IX (176): 177.
Latin Proverb: «We are in the same boat» (1921) s12-IX (182): 298.
Gleaning by the Poor (1921) s12-IX (188): 412.
Hero and Leander: A Japanese Variant (1921) s12-IX (189): 425-426.
The Beer, the Horse and the Aubergine (1922) s12-X (210): 308.
An Asiatic Orpheus (1922) s12-XI (245): 513-515, (1922) s12-XI (246): 533-535.
Children Carried off by Eagles (1923) s12-XII (253): 136-137, (1923) s13-I (23): 455.
The Eagle Stone (1923) s13-I (3): 52-54, (1923) s13-I (4): 74-75, (1923) s13-I (5): 92-93, (1923) s13-I (6): 111-113, (1923) s13-I (8): 153-155.
A Parable of Eternity (1923) s13-I (4): 75, (1923) s13-I(17): 336.
The Eagle Stone «Barrenwort» (1923) s13-I (16): 312.
Rope of Sand (1923) s13-I (23): 454-455.
Stigmata (1923) s13-I (26): 513.
Plant-Symbolism in Japan (1924) 146 (28): 34-35.
Drums of Human Skin (1924) CXLVI (jan23): 139-140, (1924) CXLVII (dec27): 468.
Bell and Serpent Poem (1924) CXLVI (mar29): 232-234.
Silent as a Fish (1924) CXLVI (apr12): 272-273.
The Judges of Sodom (1924) CXLVI (apr19): 286.
Brereton, Cheshire: Saint-Maurice, Burgundy (1924) CXLVI (apr26): 311-312.

Ganesa: Elephant and Mouse (1924) CXLVI (may24): 380-381, (1924) CXLVII (aug23): 143.

Artificial Eyes (1924) CXLVI (may24): 380.

Martuccio's Device in Archery (1924) CXLVI (may31): 395-396.

The peasant's Clever Daughter (1924) CXLVI (jun07): 414.

The Legend of Gerbert's Escape (1924) CXLVI (jun28): 463-464.

Forced and Counterfeit Tears (1924) CXLVI (jun28): 467.

The Cranes of Ibycus (1924) CXLVII (jul05): 6.

The Story of the Split-Mouthed Schoolmaster (1924) CXLVII (jul12): 24-25.

The Cock as Discoverer of the Drowned (1924) CXLVII (jul26): 61-62.

Lizard with two Tails (1924) CXLVII (aug02): 80.

Stories of Giant Crabs (1924) CXLVII (sep06): 169-170, (1924) CXLVII (sep13): 186-187.

Animal folklore (1924) CXLVII (oct04): 249.

Legal Trials of Animals (1924) CXLVII (nov22): 375.

The Horse and the Buffalo (1924) CXLVII (dec13): 426.

"Man in the Moon» : «Rabbit in the Moon» (1926) 150 (24): 428-429.

The Ladybird (1926) CLI (aug21): 138-139.

Folklore: Plants that Thrive Best when Stolen (1926) CLI (oct09): 260.

Spiders and Spiders' Web as Medicine (1927) CLII (feb19): 140.

Popular Fallacies: Bibliography (1927) CLII (feb19): 140.

Remedy Worse than the Disease (1927) CLII (apr23): 300.

The Hart and the Serpent (1927) CLII (may28): 386.

Hair Suddenly Turned White (1927) CLIII (nov05): 338.

The Blind Men and the Elephant (1928) CLIV (feb25): 139.

Japanese Heraldry (1928) CLIV (mar24): 212.

Finger-Metal (1928) CLIV (mar24): 209.

A Jewish Tradition (1928) CLIV (may05): 319.

Mysterious Figures (1928) CLIV (may12): 336-337.

Folklore: The Tigress Crossing a River with her Whelps (1928) CLIV (may12): 333, (1928) CLV (aug04): 85.

Urchin-Fish as Shop-Sign (1928) CLV (jul21): 47.

The Fox and the Ice (1928) CLV (jul21): 43.

Rain-Making (1928) CLV (nov03): 316.

Folklore of Snow (1928) CLV (nov03): 316.

Observations of Phosphorescence (1929) 156 (14): 247.

Filtering Stone (1929) 156 (17): 296

Folklore of Silver (1929) 156 (17): 303.

Horses and Wolves (1929) CLVII (jul20): 47.

Japanese Borrowing of European Words (1929) CLVII (oct19): 284.

Medicine for Habitual Theft (1929) CLVII (oct19): 281.

Cows as Guides (1930) 158 (13): 225.

Disarmed Spiny Plants (1930) 158 (20): 352-353.

Extraordinary Memory (1930) 158 (21): 367.

A Countryman and a Theater (1930) 158 (22): 383.

Folklore of Bells: The Bell of Aragon (1930) 158 (22): 388.

A Prize for the Laziest (1930) 158 (24): 427.

Cattle in Hades (1930) CLIX (aug09): 105.

Japan in 1627 (1931) CLXI (sep05): 177.

Annexe II : publications dans la revue *Nature*

The Constellations of the Far East (1893) 48, 541.

Early Chinese Observations on Colour Adaptations (1893) 48, 567.

Some Oriental Beliefs about Bees and Wasps (1894) 50, 30.

The Earliest Mention of Dictyophora (1894) 50, 54.

An Intelligence of the Frog (1894) 50, 79.

On Chinese Beliefs about the North (1894) 51, 32.

Chinese Beliefs about Caves (1894) 51, 57.

The Antiquity of the "Finger-Print" Method (1894) 51, 199-200 ; (1896) 53, 317-318.

"Finger-Print" Method (1895) 51, 274.

Chinese Theories of the Origin of Amber (1895) 51, 294.

Hesper and Phosphor (1895) 51, 417.

The Invention of the Net (1895) 52, 197.

The Story of the "Wandering Jew" (1895) 53, 78.

Remarkable Sounds (1896) 53, 317, (1896) 53, 414 ; (1896) 53, 605, (1896) 54, 78.

The Mandrake (1895) 51, 608, (1896) 54, 343-344 ; (1898) 57, 412.

Marriage of the Dead (1897) 55, 224-225.

On Augury from Combat of Shell-fish (1897) 56, 30-31 ; (1898) 57, 342.

The Centipede-Whale (1897) 56, 445-445 ; (1898) 58, 570-571.

Acquired Immunity from Insect Stings (1897) 56, 589.

Oat Smut as an Artist's Pigment (1898) 57, 437.

Notes on the Bugonia-Superstitions - The Occurrence of Eristalis Tenax in India (1898) 58, 101-103.

The Invention of the Gimbal (1898) 59, 150.

Plague in China (1899) 59, 370.

The Natural Prey of the Lion (1899) 59, 585.

Walrus (1899) 60, 150.

Indian Corn (1900) 61, 392, (1900) 61, 515.

Crab Ravages in China (1900) 61, 491.

Illogicality concerning Ghosts (1900) 61, 564.

Artificial Deformations of Heads, and some Customs connected with Polyandry (1900) 62, 437.

Distribution of Pithophora (1903) 67, 586.

The Discovery of Japan (1903) 67, 610.

Distribution of Calostoma (1903) 68, 296.

The Earliest Mention of Hydrodictyon (1904) 70, 396.

Early Chinese Description of the Leaf-Insects (1907) 77, 173.

Polypus Vinegar—Sea-blubber Arrack (1908) 79, 8.

An Alga Growing on Fish (1908) 79, 99.

Baskets used in Repelling Demons (1909) 80, 369.

Colours of Plasmodia of some Mycetozoa (1910) 83, 489, (1912) 90, 220.

A Singular Mammal called "Orocoma" (1910) 84, 40.

Trepanning among Ancient Peoples (1914) 92, 555-556.

Remerciements

Nous exprimons nos plus sincères remerciements aux *Minakata Kumagusu Archives* (Tanabe) [illustrations des deux intérieurs de couverture et des pp. 12, 26-27, 46, 59, 75-78, 88, 95-97, 100, 112, 133, 138], au *Minakata Kumagusu Museum* (Shirahama) [illustrations pp. 22, 38, 58, 98, 109] ainsi qu'au *British Museum* (Londres) [illustrations pp. 54, 60] pour avoir mis à la disposition des auteurs les documents d'archives et les objets utilisés pour l'illustration de ce livre. Sans ces informations précieuses, cet ouvrage n'aurait pas été possible.

Nous tenons également à remercier le Service commun de documentation de l'université de Toulon pour son aide dans les recherches bibliographiques ainsi que la société *Astron Fiamm* pour avoir conçu et mis à disposition un éclairage innovant (de type OLED) utilisé à titre expérimental pour les prises de vue en intérieur des objets et documents servant à l'illustration de cet ouvrage.

Enfin, un grand merci à Johann Chaigne Valmalette pour son aide et son travail créatif sur les retouches photos.

Les publications d'AnimaViva multilingüe

Golden Nihon Collection
dirigée par Jacques KERIGUY

IKKYÛ. L'impertinence au service de la foi
Sôshô YAMADA, 2012
livre imprimé ISBN 978-99920-1-966-5 (bilingue français/japonais)

2e Édition 2015
livre imprimé ISBN 978-99920-68-18-2 (bilingue français/japonais)
Epub: ISBN: 978-99920-68-19-9
Mobi: ISBN: 978-99920-68-20-5
(En préparation: versions française seule, japonaise seule)

Penser le nucléaire. Autopsie d'une illusion
Hiroaki KOIDÉ, 2015
Postfaces Jean-Jacques DELFOUR/René de CECCATTY
livre imprimé français ISBN 978-99920-68-06-9
Epub: ISBN: 978-99920-68-16-8
Mobi: ISBN: 978-99920-68-17-5
(anglais 2015 : *Rethinking nuclear energy, autopsie of an illusion*)

L'Étrange voyage de Confucius au Japon
Olivier ANSART, 2015
livre imprimé français ISBN: 978-99920-68-07-6
Epub: ISBN: 978-99920-68-08-3
Mobi: ISBN: 978-99920-68-09-0
(anglais 2015 : *The strange travel of Confucius to Japan*)

MINAKATA Kumagusu. L'émergence d'une pensée écologique entre Orient et Occident
Satoshi OHARA / Jean-Christophe VALMALETTE, 2015
livre imprimé français ISBN 978-99920-68-21-2
Epub: ISBN: 978-99920-68-22-9
Mobi: ISBN: 978-99920-68-23-6
(anglais en préparation)

En préparation :
Gidayû TAKEMOTO. Bunraku, voix de la poupée
Akiko ÔTA, 2016
livre imprimé, e-books (français)

Golden Tagore Collection

publiée sous le Memorandum of Understanding (MoU) entre Visva-Bharati University, Santiniketan (Inde) et AnimaViva multilingüe, Principauté d'Andorra

The Original Gitanjali by Rabindranath Tagore

Rabindranath TAGORE / Udaya Narayan SINGH (narration, analysis, translation), 2014

ISBN 978-99920-68-05-2 (livre imprimé, 2015)
ISBN 978-99920-68-25-0 (ePub) ; ISBN 978-99920-68-04-5 (mobiKindle)
(anglais, espagnol, catalan, français)

En préparation :

Beyond Language: Towards Silence
Tagore's Journey into Art & Poetry

Udaya Narayana SINGH, 2016
livre imprimé, e-books, (anglais, français, espagnol, catalan)

Collection Essais

Ecriture et Plasticité de Pensée

Marc-Williams DEBONO, 2013
Préface Michel CAZENAVE
ISBN 978-99920-68-19-9 (ePub) ; ISBN 978-99920-68-28-1 (mobiKindle)
ISSN 2311- 3936
livre imprimé 2015 (français) ISBN 978-99920-68-36-6

En préparation :

L'essence de l'amour selon Søren KIERKEGAARD

Francesc TORRALBA, 2016
livre imprimé, e-books, (français, anglais, espagnol, catalan)

DALAI LAMA et Carl Friedrich von WEIZSÄCKER
Where Spirituality & Science meet

DALAI LAMA, Carl Friedrich von WEIZSÄCKER, 2016
livre imprimé, e-books, (français, anglais, tibétain)

Collection Poésie

Eloge de l'impossible

Angel IYÉ, 2015
livre imprimé français ISBN: 978-99920-68-24-3
Epub: ISBN: 978-99920-68-25-0
Mobi: ISBN: 978-99920-68-26-7

livre imprimé catalan ISBN: 978-99920-68-27-4
Epub: ISBN: 978-99920-68-28-1
Mobi: ISBN: 978-99920-68-29-8

livre imprimé bilingue français/catalan ISBN: 978-99920-68-30-4
Epub: ISBN: 978-99920-68-31-1
Mobi: ISBN: 978-99920-68-32-8

Collection Accents
dirigée par Heinz WISMANN

En préparation :

Avant la philosophie
Arnaud VILLANI, 2016
livre imprimé, e-books, (français)

Penser le design
Jean Philippe TESTEFORT, 2016
livre imprimé, e-books, (français)

L'éthique de l'éthique
Heinz WISMANN, 2016
livre imprimé, e-books, (français, anglais, allemand)

Devant la mort
Lise HADDAD, 2016
livre imprimé, e-books, (français)

Golden Gibran Collection

En préparation :

Le Prophète
Kahlil GIBRAN, 2016
livre imprimé, e-books, (français, anglais, espagnol, catalan, arabe)